When Crazy's Coming...
The Midlife Misadventures of a Midlife Diva

By t l thomas

Cover Photography: www.Canstock.com, 2014
canstockphoto9263981 (Cover)
canstockphoto9263977 (Back)

Cover Design: Coulton Thomas, Coultonthomasdesign.com

Brainy B Publishinghouse
bbpco., an indie publishing house
www.brainybpublishinghouse.com
Produced in the United States of America
ISBN-10:
0983959919
ISBN-13:
978-0-9839599-1-5

Acknowledgments and Thank You

**To Marquetta for prying the pages from my fingers
when I was hesitant to let them go**

and

**To Coulton for listening when all I could
Jabber about was "the book, the book, the book"
Thanks for believing!**

When Crazy's Coming, The Midlife Misadventures of a Midlife Diva

By t l thomas

Prologue

"One is not born, but rather becomes, a woman."
Simone de Beauvoir

And So It Begins…

Geez! Sometimes I just cannot believe people! Especially the women in my life. Late, late and late! All three of them! My best friend, Sonni and my sister, Niecee. Even my mother, Mama Jett, is late!

Groaning, I slumped back against the hard metal chair in the noisy gymnasium, my fingers tugging in vain at the hem of the crinkly crunchy linen skirt that I wore, trying to smooth the wrinkles away. Who on earth thought making every summer outfit out of linen was a good idea anyway? I folded my arms across my chest, annoyed.

Well, now that I think about it, Niecee may be the only one of the three who has a valid excuse for her tardiness; after all, she is coming in from Chicago to witness her only nephew's graduation from high school. Heck, make that her only sister's only child, so yes, this is kind of a big deal. Well, I guess that if I considered this, I would have to cut Mama Jett some slack for her lack of timeliness as well; her tardiness was to be expected since her task for the occasion was to pick Niecee up from the airport.

"Go on ahead, Mikki and save us some seats," Mama Jett had urged me in the smoky alto voice I've always envied. "I'll be right behind you when your sister touches down."

So, ever the obedient daughter, even at the ripe "old age" of forty-five, I do what I am told and here I sit — alone — in a wrinkled outfit that looked as if I'd slept overnight at the gymnasium, watching the throng of people attempting to squeeze through the set of double doors at the back of the auditorium. Not a familiar face among them.

Dereon's school had arranged to hold their graduation ceremony in the large auditorium of a religious organization and though the place was spacious, there still did not seem to be enough room. Unfortunately, some of these individuals would find themselves in the overflow rooms set up for just this occasion.

People milled about, some chatting, some just standing looking for others in their group. Some clutched huge cameras; expensive pieces of equipment hanging from their necks, looking like paparazzi preparing to photograph the Queen of England rather than a high school graduation.

I pursed my lips together as I studied one woman in particular, deep in conversation with another attendee while the line of people stacked up behind them. I don't know why some people had the annoying habit of standing around blocking the doorway, making it difficult for others coming in. How does a person justify stopping right smack in the middle of the flow of traffic to carry on a full conversation with someone else while people stack up behind her, the human logjam, waiting to get in?

Hopefully the jam will have cleared before the rest of my group arrived but really who on earth knew if they would arrive before the program started! With the way airport security was these days, it is a miracle anyone gets anywhere on time anymore! The Transportation Security Administration is working overtime to combat terrorism of all forms, investigating reports of tennis shoe bombs, underwear bombs and the like. What would they try next? Scope mouthwash? Chocolate chip cookies? God, I hope not; I really like chocolate chip cookies. I like chocolate anything, actually. I frowned, rubbing a hand across my brow. In spite of the chill in the gym, I still managed to have intermittent periods of sweating and freezing.

At any rate, this makes for very long wait times, you can no longer park up front to unload so airport security forces you to drag your luggage around for what seems like a half mile across the parking lot to the terminal as you try to keep up with your purse, carryon, boarding pass, identification and whatever else you might have. You are still expected to have all of this stuff readily available and accessible to prove you are who you say you are to whichever random authority asks. Sure, no problem, I'll just hold onto all of that in my third hand… I mean, come on!

Oh, right, then they wand you and wand you again and search your luggage. I hate that part; I especially hate the thought of some strange person pawing through my personal belongings, leaving a postcard in my luggage as some bizarre kind of introduction, "Hello! This luggage was checked by Employee Number Whoever" while you hope and pray that Employee Number Whoever wasn't some kind of weirdo that gets off on handling women's undergarments.

And as if things are not bad enough, should the items in your carryon bag not meet their stringent requirements for instant visibility, the person at the boarding gate may have to send you out of the line to collect some of those little airport approved plastic bags, which they happen to have for a fee, in which to place your carry-on objects.

And since you are already good and ticked off, they will wand you again for good measure and if you are lucky and clear all of these hurdles, they will finally motion for you to proceed — barefoot no less — through the huge beeping monstrosity that could probably tell everyone what you had for breakfast that morning. Snuck in that extra half of bagel? Forget about it, woman, no secrets here! Everybody's going to know!

No chance of sneaking anything on board a plane from one of those shops at the airport, even if you wanted to. Authorities will chase you down shouting, "Stop! Drop that package of gum, woman!"

Hey, don't get me wrong, believe me, I can appreciate everything these fine men and women are doing to keep me safe. I am just saying that it is no wonder that my sister is late.

Niecee Robbinson, the busy Public Relations Executive. Always wheeling and dealing, working long days and most nights. Much too busy to have kids of her own, so she lives vicariously through me.

I chuckled out loud at that one. If that is what you could call it, living through me. Ha! Niecee seems to have all the fun. She proclaims herself to be the best aunt on the planet, and Dereon agrees if for no other reason than she gives the best gifts imaginable. Yes, Niecee spoils her nephew beyond reason. This is fine, actually. While I pay for room and board, food, and clothes and oh, I don't know, just for everything in general, Aunt Niecee gets to look like the Patron Saint of Dereon simply because she sends him the PlayStations and the Xboxes and whichever video games are "in" at the time.

The UPS guy probably thinks that I am running some sort of racket from my home because of the numerous packages that constantly arrive via delivery, each containing a cool hat or jersey from wherever she is traveling this month. Or special deliveries of the newest pair of Nike tennis shoes, jerseys, or hooded sweatshirts straight from Niketown or any other store on Chicago's Michigan Avenue Magnificent Mile. For a child who had only the standard-issued two feet we were all born with, Dereon has more tennis shoes than I even knew existed, all for the most part, courtesy of Aunt Niecee.

"Let me spoil him, Mikki," Niecee would whine whenever I halfheartedly protested about Dereon's lack of storage space due to all the gifts and things that she gives him. "He's all that I have, Mikki."

Well, he is as long as you did not count the little furry "child" Niecee kept in her purse, Miss Lucy the Pomeranian or some kind of fluffy nippy thing, all cinnamon colored fur with attitude to spare. Probably acts all nippy to make up for her lack of stature, I suppose. There is something about the little tyrant-in-a-bag that just does not sit right with me.

I have to admit, I was glad that Miss Lucy was not coming along for this particular trip. I don't think that she likes me much, and it does not grieve me one bit to say that I know how she feels. I am not keen on the little pint-sized dictator either. That dog just looks crazy. There is something about those little marble eyes when she is fixing them on me, I can only imagine what she is thinking. She is probably wishing it were me inside the little purse instead of her.

Oh, Lucy, Lucy, Lucy! Apparently, Niecee did not want to interrupt Lucy's routine, so she decided to leave her in Chicago - at a dog hotel, no less. Have you ever heard of such craziness?

This little dog might weigh all of five pounds — maybe — if she were sopping wet, and she had to stay behind at a dog hotel? A fancy boarding spot where her every need, whatever a five pound dog could need anyway, was met complete with social time and all the amenities of home. What in the world "social time" means for a purse-sized dog is anybody's guess. I need to remember to ask Niecee if she would like to adopt me, if for no other reason than I would be able to stay behind in a "sister hotel" when she is dashing around the country and have all of my needs taken care of. I could use a break.

No, I shook my head at nothing in particular, sighing deeply. I think that it is me who is living vicariously through Niecee. Niecee always lived her life by the book, always playing it smart, playing it safe. By all accounts, I was always the hellion of the family, refusing to toe the line, more willing to go my own way no matter where that would take me. Not Niecee. She had always followed "the plan," and was always the best at everything, life, school. You grow up, get the college degree or two, and get the high-powered job. Then, once you find Mr. As Successful As You Are, maybe you can settle down and have a kid or two. People loved her, respected her.

Well, she got most of it right, anyway. All except for the Mr. Successful part, having discovered the hard way that once you accomplished all of these things — the successful career, the perks, the big expense account, and the corner office overlooking downtown Chicago - it was difficult to find a Mr. Successful who is just as successful as you are. Or, perhaps the correct thing to say is it is difficult to find the Mr. Successful who is comfortable enough and secure enough with himself — and you — to accept you for your own successes.

I pressed my lips together, turning slightly in my seat to get a better look at the crowd pushing through the door. I groaned audibly, irritated as I felt. I draped my jacket across the chairs next to me, my brown worn handbag occupying the chair on the other side of me.

Niecee's so called "problem" baffled me. I still have no idea why this would be a problem for anyone. You would think that life would be fantastic if your wife was earning as much, if not more than you were. Just think of the things that you two could accomplish together. The places that you could go, the things that you could see and do together.

No, the crazy thing was that some men, or at least the men that Niecee seemed to meet, still held on to the old school attitude that the man should be the breadwinner taking care of "his woman" and all of his little responsibilities. If unable to do this, he is doomed to feel insecure about himself and his manhood, resenting the earning power of his wife. That's crazy, right?

So, Niecee remains single and keeps herself busy. Very busy. Mr. Successful would just have to wait. As a partner in one of the largest Public Relations firms in Chicago, it was all that Niecee could do to be available for Miss Lucy.

In a world where one's image is truly everything, instead of raising children and spouses, Niecee spends her time "raising" her high-powered clients, managing the reputations of athletes, politicians, high power corporate executives and the like, ushering both the client and their egos through whatever fiasco they got themselves into and trust me, there seemed to be plenty. Enough "managing" to keep her jetting around more than anyone else I knew.

In lieu of the spouse, the child, the quaint little house in the suburbs with a backyard and a swing set, Niecee has an ultra chic, ultra modern "apartment" in a high-rise building in downtown Chicago, her castle in the sky, that rivals my own humble condo square foot by square foot. She had Miss Lucy, the temperamental Pomeranian. And Dereon.

I have to admit that I am a little in awe of my big sister. Not in a scared to death kind of way you find with a lot of sister relationships where the big sister tortures the little sister just because she's being bratty. But awed in a kind of "you're so cool," kind of way. Always the smart one, Niecee would never have made the missteps I had made.

Me? I am the baby of the family, the spoiled younger sister who was hardheaded and determined to have things my own way. Who cared about the consequences? The younger Mikki had skipped through life taking silly, stupid chances with an "act now, and think later" attitude.

I sighed, rolling my neck to relieve the tension bunching my shoulders together underneath the fabric of my blouse. Lately I found myself wishing that I had paid more attention to my life. Like my big sister, I attended college. Twice, if you include returning to earn a Master's Degree. While Niecee was pursued by top companies, I "landed" in a good job. Nothing to sneeze at, I have good benefits and an expense account, but if one would compare me to Niecee, I could have done better.

Barely out of college, I had a child out of wedlock changing my life and my plans forever. I've never regretted having Dereon, not for one-second. I may have, however, regretted my choice in Dereon's father. God bless him anyway, he just was not father material. Heck, he had barely been boyfriend material, but at that particular stage of my life, I thought that he was what I needed.

As a non-event in Dereon's life, he just disappeared. Well, maybe disappeared is the wrong word, he was not kidnapped by aliens or terrorists or held for ransom or anything. He is not a member of the Secret Service or a spy or anything like that. I am sure that he is somewhere out there; by his choice he is just not involved in his son's life. As he so carefully, so unwaveringly explained it to me, he was just "not ready to be a father," at least not to my baby. He did not want to be a dad, not then, not ever. And with that, he was gone.

So... I work...and work to provide for my only child. I am employed by the Great Big Greeting Company or GBGC as I lovingly call it, a family owned conglomerate with its worldwide headquarters in Kansas City. I don't think that there is anything that this company is not dabbling in; greeting cards, gifts, gift-wrap, stores dedicated to GBGC cards, stuffed animals and the like that can move, sing, and do everything but cook your dinner. Oh yes, and there are collectible Christmas ornaments, and magazines, there is even a cable television channel bearing the company's name and logo.

Not as aggressive at climbing the corporate ladder as Niecee, I moved up in my company, earning my stripes in the Emerging Markets Division as a Marketing Executive, a sort of pulse taker functioning as the eyes and ears of the company, deciphering the purchasing habits of our consumers and their changing needs by analyzing market conditions.

Blah, blah, blah, I know, sometimes it sounds like major boring stuff but honestly, GBGC is an awesome company to work for, the company owners pride themselves for their ability to connect people with one another via the greeting cards and gifts it produces that give them a voice for their feelings.

Don't know how to say you're sorry? Buy a GBGC greeting card. Don't know what you are apologizing about; buy a thinking of you card from GBGC. Want to apologize for being a selfish jerk and standing your girlfriend up for the third time this week? I am sure that GBGC has a card for that, although I am certain that the individuals in our Creative Division would word it far more eloquently than I ever could.

I slumped against my seat, my mind racing ahead as I stared at nothing for a long second. I wonder what type of card GBGC would have produced for a day like today. Today I was losing my baby.

Baby! I laughed, blowing out a noisy breath, the action ruffling the bangs curling at my brow. Dereon hadn't been a baby for a long time, the little prince in a kingdom of Queens. Gone was the little boy with the deep dimples and the bright eyes who would ask what seemed like twenty questions in a row without taking a breath. A little round face with deep dark eyes that glittered like twin jewels and dark ringlets of hair; that child always had the most amazing hair, even if had to say so myself. Wistfully, I reached up to sweep my own tangle of curls away from my face.

Now standing in that little boy's place at a solid six feet six inches tall stood a tall, lanky, very handsome young man with a mustache. A mustache! Oh…my…goodness! How I had panicked when that mustache showed up! It seemed as if all of the girls had shown up right afterward! I felt the increasingly familiar tightness grip my throat again as I blinked back the tears that seemed to have been on standby for most of the day. Damn! This was killing me!

Help me GBGC! What kind of card do you give to a woman whose baby is being wrenched from her arms? I chuckled. God, Mikki, how you go on! I had to laugh at myself. It had to happen; the little prince would one day graduate from high school and leave the nest for college — and life without Mom. Without Mom …

I looked around studying the faces in the ocean of parents, trying to determine if any of the other parents felt the strange anxiety that I felt. Probably not. This group seemed more than ready to chuck their fledglings from the nest — the sooner, the better.

Dereon had elected to come to the ceremony with one of his friends, so I really had no idea where he was at this moment. I probably wouldn't see him until all of this was over, which was probably for the best. I am certain that Dereon would not want to be embarrassed by a sobbing, blubbering mother. I shook off the thought, forcing my lips into a weak smile as my stomach clenched, and my breath seemed to catch in my chest. Keep it together, Mikki, I cautioned myself.

The sight of a crazy woman sitting all alone crying might actually touch off a wildfire of pandemonium in the auditorium, the resulting casualties too numerous to consider. Women would come to my rescue, "Oh honey, are you ok?" Bystanders would stand by awkwardly, wondering if there was anything that could be done to help the hysterical woman I would evolve into. "Are you hurt? Can I help you?"

Then I would have to explain how I was scared to death that I was losing my baby. My eighteen-year-old baby. Great! Get the white jacket and the rubber room prepped! Mothers would hide the eyes of their children, rushing them away so that they could not see the strange lady acting crazy. Yes, it is better that he decided to come with his friends. I could not be trusted to keep it together.

I turned around again for what seemed like the hundredth time to check the entrance. The auditorium was large, the noise of multiple conversations dissolving into one dull roar, frequently punctured by a laugh or two. Where was my family?

Niecee had an excuse, as did Mama Jett. But Sonni ... I had no idea why Sonni was late! That girl lives right here in Kansas City, probably closer than anyone else but that child is always late. Never for work, mind you, but outside of work, her punctuality could use a lot of work!

Sonni, my best friend, was probably as close to me as my own sister and truly lived on "Sonni time". Apparently this girl would be late even if she lived across the street from the auditorium, seeming to treat being late as if it were a sport! The only thing Sonni will not be late for is her own funeral and that is only because she will not be driving. Or dressing herself. Or applying her makeup for that matter.

For Sonja Denise, everything had to be just so, after all, she had an image to maintain. Tiny and beautiful, brutally beautiful, I would say with sharp defined features, large dark almond shaped eyes and skin as smooth and as clear as sweet dark honey and a spiky pixie haircut that always looked like a fashionable case of bed head. A total fashionista, Sonni was always immaculately dressed from head to toe. Her hair and nails would be done, her makeup would be perfect and she would breeze into the room with a "hey, I'm here" and everyone would notice her.

Even if she wore a workout suit, it was never just a workout suit. And, there would always be the perfect handbag, usually some big name brand designer or another, that would accentuate the entire outfit. Her shoes would match the workout suit — although, I swear the girl never worked out but somehow managed to maintain her petite five foot four slender figure with minimum effort. Lucky thing! At an even five feet seven inches tall, I had to monitor everything that I ate, drank, or even breathed for that matter, I seemed to be a carb magnet.

At "thirty-nine and holding" as she was always quick to say, Sonni was every bit the diva. But no matter how many thirty-ninth birthday parties Sonni celebrated, the cruel truth was that she and I were only a week apart at the ripe "old age" of forty-five. Somehow, Sonni's effervescence seemed to keep her younger in spirit and much younger looking than our forty-five years of age. Sonni insisted on living her life as an adventurer. There was nothing that she would not try at least once. If she really liked it, as she always said, she would try it twice. She was sharp, successful and fiercely loyal to the core.

Passion was what Sonni had and what, secretly, what I wanted as well. Whatever it was, it seemed to burst from her every pore and spilling over into every part of her life. She was passionate about living, about life and everything; if you do not love it do not waste time with it.

This is not to say that Sonni is foolish, not by any stretch of the imagination. As a very successful Certified Financial Planner ... oh, pardon me, a successful "Wealth Advisor" for a large Certified Planning and Advisory firm in Kansas City, Sonni is no doubt one of the most strategic people that I have ever met. With a mind like a steel trap and a sharp wit, Sonni seems to know every variable and every detail of a situation, and I have to give it to her, the girl knows how to make money and her clients love her for that.

Great at making money, horrible at being punctual. I made yet another mental note to myself, this time to give all of these women a good talking to — once they arrived that is. I sat up straight, stretching my spine a bit as I shifted on my hard metal chair, adjusting my belongings again across the chairs, making sure to save enough seats for all of us.

A heavy set woman walking past gave me a dirty look as she eyed the chairs on either side of me then looked back at me. I gave the woman the look right back. Please! You do not even want to go there with me, sister. Not today. I am not even the one for that! I am already stressed out, and believe me, you will not win.

The woman frowned, doubling what was already a double chin. Whatever! Look at me crazy if you want to, just as long as you keep it moving. If you wanted this seat, you should have gotten here earlier, like me, to get the primo seats. I shook my head, frowning slightly. With a huff and a wag of her double chin, the woman moved on, obviously, she didn't want to pursue the issue. Smart woman...

I felt my brow rise as I studied the attire of the people filing into the auditorium, simply in awe of how some people come dressed to these types of events. I myself had attempted to put forth my best effort; after all, this was probably our last big hurrah before I send Dereon out into the world of college bound children so I wanted to look nice. Above all, I did not want to embarrass

Dereon; I seemed to do that way too often already as parents of teenagers usually do.

Some of the attendees showed up for program looking as if they'd just dashed in from a 5K run or maybe a side trip to the grocery store, not bothering with the finer details of preparation such as showering or brushing their hair, like, oh, I need some lettuce, some green beans, some milk and oh, I might as well stop by little Tommy's graduation since I'm already out running errands. Poor Tommy, his graduation was an afterthought and his friends and family decided to come as they were. Let's hope that his loved ones at least remembered to pick up a congratulatory gift during their outing at the grocery store.

I rubbed absently at the goose bumps on my arms, wishing I could pull on the jacket that was serving as a seat saver. An older gentleman in a short sleeve blue polo shirt tottered across my field of vision, the fabric of his shirt stretched so tightly on the surface of his enormous belly that the "miracle" fabric seemed to scream for mercy.

Polo man seemed oblivious to the fact that he had a brown stain on the underside of his vast belly…what was that? A spot of…. No, I think that maybe it was a splatter of gravy or something, perhaps a remnant of a celebration breakfast or lunch.

The gravy was positioned just so under the flap of said belly, far enough out of sight to avoid detection. As the man walked, the stains seemed to wave and gyrate with each heavy pulsing footstep. Thump, thump, thump, each heavy thud caused the mound of his belly to bounce and sway hypnotically. Honestly, I think I'm beginning to feel a little seasick…

I marveled as I continued to stare at the spot floating rhythmically against the man's immense belly. I must be tired! Strangely, the spot begins to look like Mickey Mouse, a little brown Mickey Mouse hanging on to the side of a blue mountain. No, maybe Mickey was hanging ten on a big blue wave. Or maybe Mickey was in a life and death struggle, trapped under an immense swimming pool cover.

Sweet mercy, I must be tired! Now I am hallucinating! Help me, somebody please help! Mickey is crying, perched precariously on the huge swell of the blue wave of the man's belly. Hanging on for dear life, Mickey is crying, crying for help, crying for something. Poor Mickey, someone really should end the poor little gravy mouse's battle with the big blue wave.

I know how you feel Mickey; I sympathized with the little gravy mouse, I feel that same wave towering over me. Stretched too tight beyond comprehension. Trapped, drowning and helpless. Going under fast. After today, after all of the pomp and circumstance and all of the congratulations and all of the hat tossing and slapping each other on the back, after all of the high fives and after all of the pictures are taken, after all of the parties and so forth, my number one job, the raising of Dereon Robbinson, for all intents and purposes, will be over. And secretly, I am afraid.

I know, someone find a shrink quickly. I have not fallen on my head or anything, nor have I lost my mind. But listen, even though I know that this is around the time when I should start doing the happy dance, I'm scared senseless! With the wrap up of Dereon's final year of high school, my "mortality" seemed to smack me right between the eyes. The "hard work" — the "raising" of Dereon Robbinson - was done.

I was about to be handed back my own identity, to do what with, I had no idea and I was already starting to feel a little naked without my "Mom Armor" on. What was next? My whole life had been wrapped inextricably around and into this child, all of my energy and time had been consumed with shepherding this child through adolescence into a young man, I always knew that I had a purpose. I mean, if for no other reason, my purpose on this planet was to be if nothing else, Dereon's mom.

Maybe I should get a dog. A big ferocious dog. A dog that would never be able to fit into a purse. Maybe he would fit into a wheelbarrow, but never a purse.

Finally, the large man in the blue shirt finally located a seat and sat down, and the little gravy Mickey Mouse disappeared from view, the big blue wave collapsing over him.

Bye bye Mickey. Maybe I should have thrown him a lifejacket. Heck, maybe I should have thrown him a donut. I craned my neck around again, looking towards the entrance again, shaking my head, my lips twisting into a frown.

Where were these women?

A Little Seasoning....

Well, it is over, and I was exhausted, having clapped and cried until my hands and eyes were sore. Dereon did it, he really did it. I was now the proud parent of one high school graduate. Mama Jett and Sonni had shown up together, dragging each other through the throng of people, without Niecee.

Unfortunately, Niecee never made it as far as Kansas City International Airport due to some electrical issue with her flight out of Chicago, grounding the flight without the possibility of another flight out that could have gotten her here in time.

Understandably upset, she had apologized profusely, crying via telephone, heartbroken that she had missed Dereon's special moment.

"Niecee, you cannot possibly control everything," I had teased her, even though I knew that if she could have, she would have made it happen. If Niecee had her way and it were not illegal, being the control freak that she is, she would have nabbed a plane and pilot and would have ordered him to get her to Kansas City. Pronto!

After the ceremony, we searched for Dereon among the crowd of ecstatic new graduates, finding him amid the exuberant gaggle of young men and women who'd hurriedly shed their caps and gowns, to reveal the Capri pants, cargo board shorts, blue jean cutoff shorts, jerseys, jeans and the like that they wore underneath their graduation gowns.

What in the world any of these kids think is beyond me. I mean, back in the day when I graduated from high school — many, many moons ago — it was a requirement that the upperclassmen set the example for all who followed. This meant dressing appropriately with a "proper" haircut and "proper" attire... the young men were cleanly shaven with button-up shirts and ties, the young ladies would be dressed up in their Sunday finest complete with coiffed hairdos and makeup.

I looked around at this new generation, not a tie in the bunch. Plenty of Mohawks, fauxhawks, fro hawks, cornrows, "locs" and dreadlocks though – I guess that is what they call them anyway. I am sure that if Dereon took a second to pull himself away from this motley crew, he would tell me that I was wrong or that I was "old school" or something.

It's a new day after all and this new breed of young adults will do things their own way. All about self-expression, I don't know if this is what scares me about this new generation or if is that I am more afraid of the fact that this group of spiky haired rebels is the generation that is going to care for us "old timers" when we no longer can take care of ourselves! God help us! This group was ready to party — without the grownups lurking around.

Earlier that day I had suggested to Dereon that we should all go get something to eat afterwards to celebrate, but really, after the day I'd had, all I wanted at that moment was a nice quiet glass of wine in which to drown my sorrows. To his credit, Dereon had turned me down, gracefully, but still he nixed our idea in favor of going out to eat and celebrate with some of his own friends.

"I'll be home later, Mom, and maybe we can do something tomorrow, ok?" he had promised, not bothering to wait for my response as he allowed himself to be dragged away by the whooping crowd.

Pitifully, I gazed after him as he made his way toward freedom. Well, ok… maybe we will do something tomorrow. This day was becoming strangely reminiscent of the day that Dereon started Kindergarten, pulling away from my clingy mommy grip, kicking dear old mom to the curb to go and hang out with his new friends. No separation anxiety here, at least not on his part. I had to take the rest of that day off from work. Here is where the cord is cut, I guess. Dereon, tugging against the restraint also known as Mom, eager to run, pursue, and investigate all that he can. Me, I'm just trying to hold on to that cord for dear life while Dereon runs off and leaves me just standing there wondering what happened.

This morning I had looked at my stunned reflection in the mirror. Same face, same eyes, I did not feel any different, but somehow, the years were gone and this next milestone loomed directly ahead. What would I do? I, Mikki Robbinson, will be the proud owner of one life of one's own without a single clue what to do with it.

"Just think, girl," my friends told me, "you'll have all of that free time!" Great! Free time! Only I really did not have a clue what to do with it. My nest will be empty. Empty, just me and the great chasm called midlife looming directly ahead; I was being pushed, kicking and screaming over the edge, feeling like that coyote in the roadrunner cartoons, hanging in midair holding a sign that said "Yikes!"

"Just stop, Mikki," I told myself, shaking my head, this is a tad bit dramatic, even for me. Dereon was ready to do his own thing and me - I still wasn't sure what "my own thing meant". Sonni had referred to this day as training wheels for how it was going to be for me from now on.

Fantastic.

I stood with Mama Jett and Sonni as the crowd dispersed, a tired but happy smile on my face as I watched Dereon clowning around with his friends. Who was that girl he was all hugged up on?

I felt my brow rise. Could this be the mystery girl with whom Dereon always got all serious and everything whenever he spoke with her on his cell phone? Every time I walked into the room, he would begin speaking in low monotones that served as the red alert, "Hold up, girl. Mom's in the vicinity, I can't talk". Funny, on my end it sounded like a lot of grunts and grumbles, but I guess it served as a code or something. I am going to have to ask him about her, that is, whenever I can catch up with him. Obviously, that would not be today.

Mama Jett, with a shake of her head and a little smile on her tiny heart shaped mouth watched Dereon flirting with the pretty girl as she dragged him away, his attention somewhere else, not on his mother, his mother's best friend or his grandmother. She looked at me now and smiled. I shrugged my shoulders, my smile wry. I guess that it was just us "old timers" now. We are not nearly as interesting as little Miss Cutie Pie. Whatever. Mama Jett gently took my arm, turning me in the direction of the parking lot. Time to go.

"It's done, Baby," she told me. "He is a man now, you did good work." I adjusted the strap of my purse up on my shoulder, watching Dereon wistfully as his tall frame disappeared into the throng of teenagers.

I leaned forward and tapped Mama Jett gently on her temple with my index finger, mimicking a gesture that she'd always used for Niecee, Sonni and me.

"You are smarter than you know, baby," she would tell us with a tap on our temple. I guess this was her way of saying that everything I needed to know I already had in my head. I don't know if that's going to help me at this point, I hadn't really given much thought to this particular moment, this day actually happening. At least not until recently.

"No, Mama, we did good work." I said. Mama Jett nodded, and smiling she put her arm around my waist, hugging me tight.

"Well," Sonni adjusted the strap of her Coach shoulder bag higher onto her shoulder, pursing her trademark-glossed lips, her spiky hair not budging an inch.
"I'm tired of all of this working. Dereon just kicked us to the curb to go out with his little friends. This does not mean that we cannot go out to celebrate. Come on, I have to eat."

Fine, time to feed the cranky Sonni.

Somehow, we "old timers" made our way unassisted to the Red Lobster Restaurant, cool air caressing our faces as we entered the building, a techno styled Muzak version of Kool and the Gang's hit "Ladies Night" playing on the overhead speakers. In spite of the campy, tinny reproduction, I found myself humming along. Oh yes it's ladies night and the feelings right. How appropriate... I wondered whatever happened to those guys.

Sonni made it clear that her intent was to eat all of the crab legs that she could eat and, don't let the size fool you, this girl can eat some crab legs. My only intention was to find a little solace and sustenance at the bottom of a glass of a nice Pinot Grigio, only after that would I decide what I would eat.

Mama Jett and I both decided on a steak with the vegetable of the day and salad. I was going to celebrate our accomplishment by devouring as many of those delicious cheesy biscuit things as I could. Well, I am celebrating after all, let me have my carbs and no one gets hurt!

Sonni was determined not to let me wallow in my self-pity as she kept up her usual rapid-fire style of chatter, bouncing from one subject to another, from the temperature inside, to the graduation ceremony, to how cute our "little waiter" had been.
"Not bad for a fifteen year old," Sonni quipped as she surveyed the room. This is the point where I wanted to advise all mothers, with the exception of yours truly, to lock up their eligible young men. Sonni was in the house and no male was safe.

Mama Jett peered at the two of us over the rim of her eyeglasses, shushing us as we laughed and giggled like two little girls. Sonni apparently scored big points with our server when she'd commented on how cute he was, in return guaranteeing us primo service for as long as we were at the restaurant, which in turn, guaranteed him a good tip for "taking such good care of us ladies." Sonni's words, not mine. I think that child practically skipped back into the kitchen after receiving Sonni's high praise.

I shook my head, taking a sip from my glass of wine. Sonni is a shameless flirt, and never hesitates to pull this tool out of her arsenal whenever the occasion called for it. Getting a good table, getting an attentive waiter, whatever. In Sonni's world, every occasion called for it. She would flutter those long lashes of hers and get just about anything she wanted. I have to admit, this was a "skill" that I sometimes envied and wished that I could acquire. It seemed to work on men as well as women — nothing weird about it, men wanted to be with her, women wanted to be her friend. That is kind of cool, actually. Maybe I should get some lessons from her.

Apparently, in my quest to concentrate on my task of parenting Dereon, I had shelved my need to flirt and as a result, I lacked this particular social tool, heck, at this point, I think I have misplaced the whole darn toolbox. It's not like I totally lack this "skill" for pulling people in, it's just that, not saying that it was a bad thing, I don't think that I ever could use my "feminine wiles" the way that Sonni could. At this point, I was not sure that I even had one wily skill in my whole repertoire. It just did not come naturally for me; I had to work at it — hard. Sonni always teased me that all I needed was a little practice.

Practice? Please! I do not think all of the practice in the world could make up for what I lacked in that department.

"Leave that boy alone, Sonni," Mama Jett scolded half heartedly, causing us to giggle even more. The waiter hurried to place our order, nearly tripping over the enormous grin that he wore. Score another one for Sonni.

The seafood restaurant was a favorite of Mama Jett and Sonni, I was never much of a seafood fan, and it was just something that I never took a liking to. I preferred not meeting my meal or his relatives in the fish tank out front before the actual eating of the meal, preferring a meal that I did not have to fight or beat into submission. Besides, using an eating utensil that looked like an automobile tool made me a little nervous.

Sonni, I had decided long ago, would eat anything that would or could swim. She had never met a fish she did not like, be it battered, fried, broiled or otherwise.

I watched with a bemused smile as she cracked the crab legs with zeal, spearing the delicate meat with her fork and dunking it into the melted butter, her eyes drifting shut as she relished her meal. I stared at her wondering how someone so tiny could consume so much food without even breaking a sweat or even smearing her lip-gloss. I had to find out what that brand of super gloss is.

All I knew was that if I didn't "slow my roll" literally, I would wake up tomorrow morning dragging my backside behind me, my overindulgence in the cheesy biscuit things painfully apparent when I stepped onto the scale. Sonni continued to crack the crab legs with the swiftness and deftness of a surgeon all while talking what seemed like a million miles a minute.

My dinner or at least the crab leg that I had tried at Sonni's insistence was proving to be elusive to capture. I was not as adept at the art of mangling crab legs as Sonni was and proceeded to chase one lone crab leg all over my plate. Frustrated, I set the socket wrench/crab leg cracker thingy on top of the table. Forget it! I was just not that interested.

Grumpy, I picked up my wineglass, taking a big sip of the golden elixir, allowing it to warm its way down my throat. I was not going to chase down my dinner tonight.

"It's time, Mikki," Sonni jumped right in, interrupting my absent-minded daydreaming.

"Hmmm?" I swallowed my wine. Oh God, now what? I fidgeted in my chair, a nervous laugh escaping past my suddenly dry lips. Afraid I would drop it, I placed my wine glass on the tabletop.

"Ti --time for what?" I stammered, uneasy. I was always skeptical, no make that terrified, when Sonni began a conversation with a statement that made it appear as if this had been a subject we had been discussing all along. It kind of made me feel as if she had already figured out the highlights of the impending discussion and would be dropping some knowledge on the rest of us, finally clueing us in on what had already been established in her own mind.

Sonni smiled that sly little smile that told me that she had been working on a plan. "Trouble, warning, warning!" my mind screamed, bells clanging. Big trouble straight ahead! Years of experience as her best friend told me that when Sonni smiled that little smile, I was in trouble.

"Time for you to get out and meet some people, do some things. Maybe even do some people?"

I gulped, my breath causing me to choke and I coughed violently, my throat burning, my eyes welling with tears. My stomach began to flutter, and then lurch and I was afraid that I might actually throw up and I held my hand up as if to say "no more"! At Sonni's statement, Mama Jett gasped, putting her hand to her throat in what Sonni calls Mama Jett's classic "clutch my pearls" reaction, her reaction to all things ridiculous.

"Sonni! Girl, what is wrong with you! The things you say!" Mama Jett scolded half-heartedly.

Sonni laughed, knowing that Mama Jett was feigning her disapproval and that she had Mama Jett wrapped around her little finger as tightly as Niecee and I, having "adopted" Sonni long ago as if she were one of her own. Sonni grinned, her ornery little smile telling Mama Jett that she was just kidding. Well, maybe Sonni was kidding, maybe she wanted Mama Jett to think that she was kidding, but I knew better, there was that look in her eye.

Where was that little server kid? I might need to get my check and get the heck out of here.

"But really, Mama Jett," Sonni continued. "When was the last time that Mikki actually went out? With a man?"

"Hey, wait a minute!" I gasped, my throat still burning and I was unable to form words, my eyes tearing. I looked from one to the other bleakly, waving my hand in front of my face to fan myself.

These two were unbelievable, I mean, excuse me, I am still sitting here at the table, would anybody like to ask me when or who I went out with lately? When or who had I gone out with at any time?

I continued to cough shaking my head emphatically. I got out plenty, didn't I? I met plenty of people, especially in my line of work at GBGC. There were always guys around. Guys coming in from other divisions, other offices. We always had work functions, networking opportunities and the like. I met people all of the time — besides, I was just too busy being a mom and…uh oh…

I knew what Sonni was getting at but I just did not have time to meet someone new. And at my age, the whole bar thing was out, that was so not my scene.

"Sonni, no. "I tried, begging her to stop. "I appreciate what you're trying to do…"

Sonni brushed off my protest with a wave of her hand; her elegantly glossed now buttered lips pursed.

"Sure, you meet people every day, but only professionally, Mikki." Sonni put her own glass down, preparing to go in for the kill.

I am so screwed…
"When was the last time you actually went out on a real date? With a man? Who is not a customer or otherwise of your firm?" Sonni interrogated me.

Damn! She was way too good at this! I squirmed in my seat, feeling sweaty and disheveled as I looked in vain at my Mama for help. Nope, nothing there, I think she was kind of waiting for an answer as well.

What the hell! My brow rose slowly, not because I did not like her line of questioning, I had to admit, she had me on this one. But because in all honesty, I could not remember when the last time was that I had actually been out on a date. Well, there was that crazy time back when Dereon was a lot smaller when I had actually dated a man for like a minute. He had developed a case of cold feet and fled the scene once he found out that I had a small child, a son no less. If he wanted to get close to the mother, he would have to get close to the child. Minute Man actually told me that he was not prepared for a readymade family, that he was looking for someone with a lot less "baggage".

Readymade family? Baggage? It was just a date for Pete's Sake! No one was trying to drag his sorry butt to the altar! This man actually had the nerves to ask me at one point, "Does he always have to be here?" referring to the fact that as a young child, Dereon was always home.

With his mother.

I remember thinking, where else is he supposed to be? This was his home. I was his mother. I knew then that it was time for this man to go. Baggage was for trips and if anybody was taking a trip, it would be this guy. He was definitely a trip and I was more than happy to give him a one-way ticket out of my life. Dereon and I were a package deal, if you do not like the package, you can move on. Time is up, Minute Man.

Funny, I actually cannot remember that guy's name at this particular moment. He missed getting to know a really terrific kid, definitely his loss.

Surely there had been others? Wait, what about that one guy, it had to be many moons ago. What was his name? Craig? David? Kevin? Je, no, something plain and boring. Now that I think about it, I think that he had been from GBGC as well...

Ok, so there were not as many guys as I thought. Actually, there were not any guys, but I was not about to admit that to Sonni and add gasoline to the fire. She was nearly fully involved already, she needed no encouragement!

What had I been doing all of this time? Work, work, and more work, that is all I seemed to have time for. No, that is all that I had made time for. Work and raising Dereon.

"I guess you are going to have to stop hiding behind that excuse now." Sonni flicked my argument away with a sweep of her manicured hand as I voiced my objections out loud.

"Dereon's ready to have a life of his own, " She said. "And I can guarantee you that he is not going to sit back and tell some little cutie, "Oh, sorry, girl, I can't, I got to raise my mama."

I frowned at her, upset that she was all up in my business and not at all intimidated by my scowl. Sonni was taking no prisoners, a straight shooter as always.

I guess Mama Jett liked that one. She chuckled aloud.

"Looks like his Mom's going to have to do the same," she agreed with Sonni. I held up my hand to silence them both, exasperated. These two were not going to worry me with this craziness. I turned to look indignantly at Mama Jett who simply smiled that sweet little innocent smile that she always used when making a point.

Turncoat! What the heck? What was this, some kind of weird conspiracy? My own mother and Sonni against me? What was this, Get Mikki Day?

I picked up the crab leg cracker pointing it at both of them menacingly. "Don't make me have to use this," I muttered. Mama Jett laughed out loud, covering her mouth with her napkin. I frowned at her for emphasis.

"For real, Mikki," Sonni continued, undeterred by my wielding of a deadly weapon. She reached out, taking the tool from me, patting my hands between hers, and trying not to smear me with the butter from her crab fest. No respect.

"Mikki," she leaned closer, her eyes fastening full on my face. "I've known you forever, since the fifth grade. You know that I love you, right?"

Oh no… I nodded, my brain going to mush with this new attack of reverse psychology.

"But when was the last time you went out with a MAN and just enjoyed yourself? Sweetie, your child rearing days officially ended two hours ago."

Oh geez! Come on! I frowned, feeling self-conscious about her line of questioning. This was not going to go well for me. I laughed, a choking gasping little sound.

"Well, there was that time, on the tenth of never," I tried to joke in my own defense. I did not like where this was going, this was so bad, and I was getting the feeling that it was going to get a lot worse.

"Exactly," Sonni motioned for the cute waiter, requesting a warm towel or something with which to clean her hands, which of course he brought promptly, smiling broadly.

"It's time." She wiped her hands thoroughly, and then she wiped mine. "Mikki, Dereon leaves for college in the fall, then what?" Sonni asked her tone gentle.

Again, I shook my head, listening with my arms folded across my chest. I was quickly losing my appetite, really trying not to think about my impending empty nest "problem". Besides, why was it so much of a problem? What was wrong with being alone?

Sonni sighed. "I'm not trying to hurt you, honey. I just want you to be happy. You deserve to be happy."

Wait…I was happy, wasn't I? Why did people always think that they had to "fix up" their single friends? I shook my head, still listening but distracted looking everywhere but at Sonni and the uncomfortable truth that I was being forced to face. Since when was being alone a problem?

Sonni shook her head as well. "I have been reading a book by this author, Gail Sheehy, about a seasoned woman."

No, no, no! I rolled my eyes, exhaling with a loud groan. Great, here we go, I thought, Dr. Sonni was about to psychoanalyze me. This was bad, this was really bad.
At the mention of the book, even Mama Jett stopped wrestling with her crab leg, suddenly very interested. Oh God, this was really, really bad.

"A what?" Mama Jett asked, her voice going up an octave. Oh good, maybe now she would help me out. It is funny; this is the sound she makes whenever she was sure she was about to hear something totally ridiculous. Understood between us to be Mama Jett's "bullshit-o-meter," you can judge how whatever you were saying was being rated by the pitch of her voice.

Sonni laughed. "That goes for you too, Mama Jett," she teased. Mama Jett waved Sonni's verbal jab away as if it were an annoying fly.

"Honey, please! I'm more than seasoned enough already!" At that, Mama Jett fluffed her coiffed hair.

"Huh! This woman could probably learn a few things from me!" she sniffed.

I laughed at that, nodding my head. Yes, she probably could. Mama Jett was about as seasoned as they come, more spice than anything else.

Sonni grinned that grin that let me know that she was about to be ornery, and not even Mama Jett was going to escape her orbit this time.

"Gail Sheehy says that a woman of a certain age, which by the way happens to be our ages," Sonni motioned around the table. "She says that we are considered seasoned women. We are spicy because we have been marinated in life experiences."

Mama Jett chuckled, reaching for her fork. "Is that what they are calling it? Marinated in life experiences? Shoot!" Mama Jett laughed dryly, returning her attention to prying on the crab leg. Sonni continued, obviously liking the little tale that she was weaving.

"No listen, Gail Sheehy says that we are, and I quote 'a seasoned woman is like a complex wine, sweet, tart, effervescent, and mellow," and "a seasoned woman is maternal, playful, alluring and resourceful.'" Sonni nodded her head in Mama Jett's direction, seeking and receiving buy-in for her argument.

Mama Jett nodded her agreement to that, finally conquering the crab leg, cracking it into submission.

"According to her book," Sonni settled back into her seat. "A seasoned woman has no agenda for any of the men she dates because she is already doing her own things and loving her freedom. Maybe I'm paraphrasing but the bottom line is that once a woman reaches a certain age, she has already had her child — that's you Mikki - and is excited with the prospect of striking out to try new things."

I nodded like a puppet. Sonni continued. "She has no rescue fantasies; she's not waiting for Mr. Perfect to save her. She knows who she is and is living her life. Sounds good to me."

"Is that what we are doing? Living and loving our freedom?" I teased Sonni who in turn threw a mock glare of annoyance in my direction. Apparently, I, the student was messing up what Sonni the teacher was trying to teach. I waved my apology. I had to open my big mouth! Oops. My bad, sorry. Go on, Professor Sonni; tell us poor earthly beings what we are missing.

"Yes, you are, Mikki. You are a seasoned woman; you just haven't made the time to try to figure out what you want at this stage."

What did I want? I opened my mouth, wanting to speak but was shut down as she raised a hand to halt whatever protest I was going to make.

"I know what you are going to say, Mikki." I hated it when she knew what I was going to say even before I knew what I was going to say.

"I know you've been busy being a mom. Well, honey, it is your turn now. You cannot hide behind that excuse anymore; I'm not going to let you."

Now Mama Jett was interested. "What's up with these seasoned women? What happens with all of this seasoning?"

Sonni poked her tongue out at me, glad that somebody appreciated her well-read genius.

Obediently, I stayed quiet as "Dr. Sonni" bestowed her knowledge upon us. I am sorry, but this is weird! Just sitting at the same table with my mother and talking about sex kind of freaks me out a little bit. And the fact that Mama Jett wanted to hear about it just about sends me over the edge.

Obviously, she knows about sex, she has two grown daughters, for Pete's sake. But sex and your parents? Ack! Your parents having sex? Yuck! It is one of those things that if you even gave it too much thought, I think it could probably cause brain damage or something.

It's understood somewhere in the back of your brain that your parents are going to have sex or have had sex, but it's one of those things that you just don't want to think about.

Ugh! Now Mama Jett was sitting here, at this table, talking to us about sex. Double Ugh! I looked around for that cute little waiter; this talk was definitely going to require another glass of wine.

I had more than a little trouble separating "Mother Mikki" from "Sensual Mikki". Just the thought of it seems, I do not know, almost cosmically weird. Can a mother really be sensual?

As determined as I was to maintain the status quo, Sonni was just as adamant to throw me into the dating pool, kicking and screaming. Goodness! I was starting to feel like that little gravy Mickey Mouse again, hanging on to the side of the big blue wave.

"Mikki, you've got to do this," Sonni reasoned. "It's like you just received the keys to a brand new car, you've got to take it out for a spin." Sonni makes a gesture as if she were shifting gears, putting the pedal to the metal. What if I liked the old car?

"You get a do-over of sorts; you get to put the pieces of your life back together, little by little. Now comes the fun part, it's time for you to take the plunge into the world of dating again."

Ah yes…plunge, as in drowning? That I can understand, that was exactly the visual that I was getting. I was not nearly as thrilled about it as Sonni was. I do not care what she says; dating is not just like falling off a log, or driving a new car or riding a bike or anything like that. At best that I could remember, falling off a log was probably a lot less painful than dating. Riding a bike is simple, you fall down, you get back up, a little bruised but fine. Not so much with dating, at least not from my recollection. Besides, I hadn't been so great at riding a bike either, if I remembered correctly.

I have no idea what to do as far as dating. I had dated sporadically before Dereon, then little to not at all after Dereon. And now Sonni was telling me that it was time to get back into the game, this will be awkward, especially since I had no idea what the game was, let alone how to get back into it.

"There are steps, of course, Mikki, and we will take baby steps. But you have to take that first step, open yourself up to meeting new people." Sonni insisted. My goodness she was tenacious!

Waiter…wine…oh goodness, where was he?

"I don't know, Sonni," I hesitated, it all sounded interesting and scary.

Frankly, the struggle of mothering while working full-time had drained my energy and left me more than a little tired and with that energy went my desire for a life of my own. Why bother? I was not zeroing in on finding a husband.

"No one says that you're looking for a husband, Mikki, or even a permanent 'fling'." Sonni said. "We are not looking for that person who will be your happily ever after. Just someone who could "help you" with this transitional period. Someone fun, who can help you have some fun," Sonni asserted.

"Help me?" I threw her a skeptical look. "As in how?"

Sonni laughed then, shooting a quick look at Mama Jett. "There is a whole wide world out there, Mikki, think of it as a great big shopping mall full of new and interesting men." She fluttered her lashes suggestively. At that, I put my wine glass down, my hand going up to rub my eyes, laughing in spite of myself.

"Right, how about a great big nut bowl, with a few sweets tossed in to keep it interesting?" Mama Jett laughed too, shaking her head from side to side.

"There's nuts everywhere you go, baby," she reasoned. I shook my head; oh no! I was not about to talk about "hooking up" with my mother present! I just could not take this two-pronged assault.

"Oh, great, not you, too!" I exclaimed, throwing my hands in the air in mock surrender. I gave her a dirty look to match the one I had just given Sonni and as usual, this had no effect on Mama Jett.

"Well, this is true. But think about it, Mikki. What do you have to lose?" Sonni said. "You could have a little fun in the process. And girl, you do need to have some fun."

I was skeptical, questioning her reasoning. What do I have to lose? Well, let's look at the short list, shall we? Let's start with, oh, maybe my mind. Who had the time to try breaking in somebody new? Moreover, I still have my work. Maybe I could pick up a hobby or two. Throwing myself back out there into the dating jungle? That was not on the short list. Or the other list for that matter.

"Mikki, you're not looking for a father for your son. You're not looking for some man to take care of you, nor are you looking for a man to drag to the altar." Sonni kept going, hammering her point home.

True, true and true. At this point, did I really know what I was looking for? Sonni continued her argument, going for broke.

"Dereon ran out after his graduation like a man on fire. He could not get out of there fast enough to start experiencing a little life. I think it is his Mom's turn to do the same. You need to make a commitment to begin living during the second half of your own life now."

My second half? What was this? Was my life half over already? I am only forty-five, and Sonni is talking as if I had one foot in the grave! Well, it was not as if I had not had opportunities; I held my own pretty well. I still looked good. I dressed well. And it is not like there had ever been a shortage of male attention as far as I was concerned. I liked flirting as well as the next girl.

It was just, in the past; I just did not have the time to pay attention. There was always something to do with Dereon. Always some new emergency, always something to do to try to "keep the wheels" on our lives in order to keep it from spinning out of control.

But I had to admit, the idea of dating again had some appeal. A little! It could be fun to just relax a little bit. But I was hardly the sensual woman that Sonni was. I just could not see it. Sonni and I were polar opposites in this area. She was all sass and had the ability to draw a person into whatever tale she was weaving. Me, not so much.

As in the case of our little waiter, she had a strange power that seemed to send a man's ego into a tizzy. She was upbeat and loved her freedom and her independence. Sonni never had the desire to marry; she was content to maintain her own separate lifestyle, not willing to compromise her independence.

So what was Sonni's suggestion? The bar scene was just not for me and was not going to happen. A single's weekend? A - gasp! - Blind date? No, I don't think so.

Dating people at work were a definite no-no. Too messy. Too... I don't know, the word public comes to mind. Although there was an abundance of attractive men at GBGC, there was also an abundance of busybodies who seemed to know everything about the relationships of others at the firm.

No. Not for me. All of this time, after Dereon's dad, I do not know if I am ready for all of that again.

It wasn't as if he had been the great love of my life, no, he'd been nothing of the sort. I was just very conscious of the fact that I was not willing to risk being hurt all over again. Forget no pain, no gain; I am just not into hurting me.

Then there is the whole mingling thing. What would I do? What would I say? How many people were like me who had similar interests? I would have to teach myself how to small talk with people all over again. Oh geez! I may even have to initiate a conversation or two!

Sonni was on a mission to find a decent "friend" with whom I could "break the ice". I looked across the table at Mama Jett; does she actually understand what it is that Sonni is up to? What she actually meant by breaking the ice? That Sonni was suggesting that I actually look for someone to ... you know?

Eww! I cannot even think about that and my mother at the same time! Goodness! I do not know if I even want my mother thinking of me that way at all, that just makes it even more strange! I rubbed my brow; looking for a way out — any way out — of this conversation. Kitchen fire, alien invasion…anything would do right now.

"And what do you suggest, Sonni? How can we fix what apparently I'm not aware ails me?"

I regretted my question the second after I had voiced it. Sonni smiled slyly, removing her plastic lobster bib from around her neck.

"Online dating."

Crazy's Coming

I think that Mama Jett and I must have started choking at the same time. Our gagging in unison made curious onlookers turn around to look at us. Was there something wrong with the meal, they might wonder... no, just my crazy best friend!

What the... look, I know that sometimes Sonni likes to make statements purely for shock value, but this time she's got to be crazy! Online dating? Yep, she's definitely lost her mind. She is so cut off, no more wine for Sonni, obviously, she is drunk! Check please! Get me away from this madness!

"Wh--" I tried before my throat clamped bitterly around the wine that lingered in my windpipe. I coughed furiously, holding up my hand. Mama Jett obviously recovered with more grace than I had and sat mutely drinking from her glass of water, her eyes red from her exertion.

Will somebody please tell me why so many people are just so darn eager to introduce me to "the perfect person"? I mean, everybody seems to have a cousin, the friend of a friend or the brother of a friend. Next-door neighbor, associate getting out of prison on parole... everybody wants to fix you up with somebody. And why? Is it a cardinal sin to actually be alone and enjoy it?

Ugh! The mere mention of the word online dating sends thoughts screaming through my head and images too horrifying to ever let them out into the light of day. Opening myself up to someone, especially some online stranger would be frightening. And Sonni wants me to just throw caution to the wind and just throw myself out there like that? Well, why not buy me a ticket on the crazy train instead! This is not about to happen! That is it. Absolutely no more wine for Sonni.

I must have looked a sight because Sonni was laughing at me. Oh...I get it! She's joking, right? Oh you...you got me...

"Oh, come on honey, don't look like that! It never hurts to try the stuff you swore you never would." Sonni is relentless. I cannot believe this! Is Sonni honestly trying to sell me on the virtues of Internet dating? A frequent dater in her own right, my singlehood, or, ending my single status seemed to be at the very top of her list of "things to do". No way, baby! Find yourself another project!

So she tried a different tactic, flattery.

"Mikki, you are beautiful, funny, successful, and independent. What's not to love?" Sonni persisted.

"And busy!" I choked, reaching for my water glass. Very busy as I had to tell her time and time again. Who really has the time, not to mention the energy to spend on breaking in somebody new? Or just breaking in somebody? Geez!

"Sonni, aren't you the one who is always telling me that relationships are work? I already have a job, make that two jobs if you count Dereon."

Sonni shook her head, slapping down that argument. "Besides," she continued, "it's about time you learned how to be a woman again."

Wait! What? I thought. Learn how to become a woman again? Wasn't I already a woman? Geez, I was just maybe an hour or two into my new life without having to take care of someone else at every waking moment and already Sonni wanted to fill that time with someone new! I glanced over at Mama Jett, looking for assistance. I frowned at her silence.

Woman, put down that glass and do something in my defense! Mama Jett remained mute, instead training her gaze on her plate. Was she actually going along with this craziness?

"Look, I don't see a problem with being alone." I sputtered, taking my napkin off my lap to place it on the tabletop. Finally, my nest would be my own; I could do, or not do, whatever I wanted.

"Honestly, society as a whole seems to think that you cannot possibly be happy if you are single, which coming from you," I gestured in Sonni's direction, "is funny, you're not married, you never mention wanting to be married, you're not going to be complicating your own life anytime soon."

Sonni sighed deeply, placing her own napkin on the table. "I just want to see you with someone who will adore you, Mikki, someone who will treat you the way you deserve to be treated." She shrugged.

Well, I thought, that is fine, but how does complicating my life with someone else gel with what I deserved?

"I don't know, Sonni," I told her, I reached for my purse to reapply my lipstick — plain brown, if you must know. Nothing exotic for this girl.

"I don't want to rush into dating." I continued. "I mean, I am just getting to the stage where I am going to truly be on my own for the first time in my life. There is nothing wrong with that — being alone. I don't want to rush into anything before I'm ready."

Sonni gave me the look that I knew so well, the look that said that she was not buying any of the bull I was selling.

"Mikki, first of all, you never, ever rush into anything. That is what I love about you, you are always thinking. But sometimes, I think that you "think" yourself out of a lot of situations that you shouldn't."

"What's that supposed to mean?" I frowned.

"It means that you need to get out of your own head and get out of your own way." She stated simply.

I'm in my own way? Much to my amazement, Benedict Mama Jett nodded, clearing her throat when I looked at her, then looking back down at her plate.

I frowned, shaking my head. "No, there's really nothing wrong with focusing on me for a little bit, you know, getting comfortable with myself and who and what I want. Then I will be ready to tackle the whole crazy dating thing."

Sonni was not trying to hear any of my excuses.

"I can understand wanting to discover what it is that you want, Mikki, but I have also watched you become so reluctant to change a situation, no matter how uncomfortable that situation might be that you refuse to break out of it because you don't want to upset the status quo."

That shot across the bow got my attention and I raised my head defiantly. Sonni smiled sweetly, she was just enough of a friend to give it to me straight. She had been with me through the mixed feelings and emotions during my so-called relationship with Dereon's father and was not about to let anything like that happen to me again.

"You're hot, Mikki, and you know that you are."
I do?

"And I love you too much to just let you shut yourself away in your condominium. You deserve to meet someone who thinks you're as wonderful as we do."

Oh, Sonni was good, I mused silently, and she always knew what to say and when to say it. The little tart. I looked to Mama Jett for backup, a little help, to be the voice of reason. Come to the rescue of her baby girl... something.

"Count me out," Mama Jett said shaking her head. "That cyber dating thing is for you younger seasoned chicks. Older seasoned chicks like myself, we kind of like it quiet."

I rolled my eyes, shaking my head. Not quite the assist that I was hoping for. Quiet seasoned chick, hmmm, I don't even know how Mama Jett could fix her lips to say something like that. Especially about herself. I happen to know that her lawn man has been sweet on her for at least a couple of mowing seasons.

Mr. Green Thumb has yet to ask her out though. From Mama Jett I learned that he is a widower who owns his own small but successful lawn service. The man shows up to trim her yard every weekend and is still standing around chatting and smiling with Mama Jett an hour and a half later.

Tall and gangly with salt and pepper hair, Mr. Green Thumb remains sweet on Mama Jett, although she does not think I know about it. I cannot think of any other reason why a lawn service would show up without so much as a phone call to trim her lawn and beloved rose bushes and sends her a personalized card on her birthday and during the holiday season. But, that is just me; Mama Jett insists that he is just being nice.

Whatever. But her yard does look really nice.

"But you girls better remember," Mama Jett advised, having wisdom that comes with age and experience. "There are a lot of crazies out there. You have to be careful; it makes no sense to go looking for trouble. You might find it. Crazy lurking around the corners. Just because it looks good, does not mean that it is good. And even if it is good, it doesn't mean that it's good for you."

She leaned back in her chair, her expression one of firsthand well-earned experience.

"Just remember, when crazy's coming, you best cross the street. It is a lot easier to attract crazy than to get rid of crazy. You two have to be careful."

Becoming A Woman – again

I have to admit, I left our celebration dinner with a little bit of an attitude and had driven home in a funk. Sonni was actually suggesting that I needed someone, a man no less, to "help" me learn to become a woman again. Wasn't I already a woman? And if I wasn't, how on earth does one become a woman? I mean, aren't we all just born women — maybe not full grown women, but potential little women?

There seemed to be some confusion about becoming a woman. At least as far as I'm concerned, since when does being a woman or becoming a woman require the "assistance" of a man? But Sonni's persistent badgering about dating and the like really ticked me off; I wasn't sure if I was mad at her or just mad at her because she struck a nerve. Maybe I was just mad at her because she was asking all of the questions that I had already began to or was too afraid to ask myself. What did I want? What did I want to do next? Now I would have more freedom…to do what with, God only knows.

Peeved, I trudged upstairs to change my clothes, wanting nothing more from the evening than to curl up on the sofa and drift off into the blissful world of mindless television, ignoring Sonni's constant barrage of crazy talk about online dating. Apparently, in Sonni's world, one is not allowed at this juncture to decide what is best for herself, being single and enjoying it apparently is forbidden. One should kick up their heels and head for the nearest distraction — preferably male.

I tugged my old trusty nightshirt over my head and knee socks over my feet and up my calves, walking into my en suite bathroom. Why did it all have to come back to with whom I should decide to spend my newfound free time? What was wrong with just sitting back, taking it all in for a minute? Why was Sonni bent on throwing me out there to the masses?

Staring into the mirror, I shrugged, smiling wryly at my reflection. What was the big deal anyway? Overall, I was satisfied with my appearance. I wore very little makeup, my skin seemed so cranky lately that I really saw no need to aggravate an already precarious situation, one day my skin is dry, the next I am breaking out like a teenager. I leaned closer to the mirror, examining my face from all angles, yep, this is a dry day.

My hair was a different situation. Color me vain, but I actually liked my hair, a thick mane of dark curls that fell to my shoulders. How many times I'd envied Sonni's boldness for daring to make the break away from long hair to wear her honey streaked locks in the tousled pixie cut that looked so cute on her. Nope, I shook my head, there is no way that hairstyle would ever work for me, instead of tousled and cute, I would look like a porcupine.

I parted my curls with my fingertips, frowning as I studied my scalp. No, no grays yet, but my hair could use a little brightening. I pulled my hair back from my face, looking at it this way and that. Then I poked my tongue out at my reflection. Turning off the light, I headed downstairs.

Dereon was not back yet, he was probably still hanging out with Little Miss Cutie Pie. I glanced at the clock, it was nearly 10:00. Dereon has never had a curfew, I hadn't needed to ever "lay down the law" with him as he just seemed to know when to come home. I had no doubt that he would be responsible and do the same tonight, although I would grant him grace tonight, graduation night and all. Hell, one of us has to have a life.

I sank down onto the cool dark leather of the sofa, tucking my sock covered feet underneath my body as I searched for the remote control among the sofa cushions. I never bothered to look in the drawer where the remote belonged anymore because it never made it to the drawer; instead, it was like a treasure hunt anytime I wanted to watch television. Either it was in between the sofa cushions, or in the kitchen, or even in Dereon's room; tonight I got lucky as I found it with very little effort on my part.

"This is what it will be like," Little Mikki intoned. "More of the same and more nights alone. Are you ready for that?"

Be quiet, I told her sternly. You've done more than enough already. I shook my head, resigning myself to the inevitable. Might as well do this and get it over with, deciding against my better judgment to give in to Sonni's argument. Submission seemed a lot easier than subjecting myself to her persistent needling about the state of my so called love life. Wouldn't be the first time, the woman was pretty persistent. I knew that it I didn't surrender tonight, I would at some point in the near future.

Muttering to myself, I picked up the telephone and dialed Sonni's number. She answered on the second ring.

"Hey girl, what's up?"
I heard her phone do something funky and I realized that she had been talking on the other line. Oops! Which "lucky feller" had she been whispering sweet nothings to this time?

"Fine," I huffed into the receiver, pouting. "You win. We'll do it your way — for now. Let's sign up for the online dating service. I will give you sixty days, and then we do it my way."

***

"Mikki, you are taking this way too seriously, this is supposed to be fun."
I could hear Sonni fussing all of the way from my kitchen. It was Saturday morning and Sonni had cleared the entire day solely for the task of setting up my online profile.

Oh joy, and yes, I was having loads of fun right now, thanks…

She had been rummaging around in my cabinets for something to eat, anything that she wouldn't have to cook or microwave: a potato chip, a cookie, anything. No luck with that; Dereon is pretty good about cleaning out anything that even remotely looks edible. That's what teenagers do: eat, sleep, wake up, eat some more, make obligatory conversation with the parent figure, eat and sleep some more. That child was living the dream, such as it is!

Sulking, I sat cross-legged on the floor of my living room, wearing my most comfortable sweatpants and t-shirt, my tangle of hair held away from my face with a headband, my feet bare. I had dragged my laptop into the living room so that I could sit on the floor in front of the sofa, the computer warming my legs as I stewed over what I was being forced to do. Regardless of what Sonni thought of my efforts, I was trying my best to follow all of the "rules": I would keep my profile funny and witty. I would be unique and I would make myself stand apart from the crowd. No mom talk or ex talk — well, I couldn't see that this would be a problem, with the exception of Dereon's father, I was coming up a little short in that department.

Sonni continued to bang about the kitchen in her quest for sustenance. I smirked to myself as I listened to her grumbling, that's right sister, serves you right for making me do this. You're going to need your strength. I was not going to make this process easy for her, still hoping in the back of my mind that I would be able to dissuade her from this act of lunacy before it was too late.

"Does that kid ever stop eating? I swear, every time I come over here, your cabinets look as if they've been attacked by a swarm of locusts!" she protested half-heartedly. I could hear cabinets opening and shutting as Sonni searched for food. I knew that she could never be upset with Dereon for any reason, she loved that young man as much as any one of us Robbinson women.

"Locusts, Dereon, same effect," I laughed at her. "That's how it works, Sonni. Food comes in, food goes out."

I slid the reading glasses, an annoying appendage recently added to my mom arsenal, from my hair to perch them on the end of my nose, peering at the laptop screen. How else on earth was I supposed to take this internet-dating thing other than seriously?

I mean, look at me, a forty-five year old woman with a nearly empty nest letting Sonni talk me into putting all of my life, all of me, out there for everyone to see. Goodness, she was still getting me into messes, even after all of this time. I've known Sonni for what seems like all of my life and the adventures never seemed to end. I didn't know what in the world I was doing or even why I was doing it at this point. Oh, wait, yes I do. I'm doing this because Sonni said that it would be fun!

Right...

I had tried everything to talk Sonni out of this. I cajoled, I pleaded, I begged and I threatened to disown her as my best friend if she made me go through with this. Then I told her that if she really loved me, she wouldn't force me to do this. No deal. Sonni wasn't trying to hear any of it.

"This is for your own good, Mikki," she'd reasoned. I had sniffed at that. Funny how the things that others profess are for your own good are usually not!

"You have to get out there sooner or later. I prefer sooner."
Well, all things considered, I preferred much later but I guess that I really didn't get a vote in my own life.

"Just think of it, Mikki," Sonni called out from the kitchen. I heard the microwave start and the sweet aroma of popcorn wafted from the kitchen. Apparently, Dereon hadn't eaten everything.

"Sixty days to find Mr. Right Now. That still leaves you plenty of time to get Dereon ready for college this fall."

Whoo hoo! I mused. I can hardly wait! A whole summer to look for Mr. Right Now. A time to, as Sonni says "let our hair down and try something new". Two middle-aged divas burning up the town trying something new. Call me crazy, but right now, I just couldn't see it. Shopping for men seemed so out there, even for Sonni. I could think of a lot of other things that I would rather do with my summer and none of them included chasing men up and down the Internet Superhighway.

Sonni returned from the kitchen, a steaming bag of popcorn in hand, shaking her head at me. She plunked herself down on the floor next to me, looking over at my computer screen.

"I know that not everyone you meet is going to be a potential mate. We're not thinking long term right now, Mikki. If it happens, it happens." She paused in her musings to toss a buttery morsel into her mouth, grimacing slightly as it burned her tongue. She continued.

"We're just trying to have some fun. You don't have to date a different man every day. I just want you to open yourself up to the possibility of meeting someone new. Think of it as meeting a lot of new friends. Setting up a profile opens up a whole new arena for you. It forces you to step outside of your comfort zone."

Funny, but when she mentioned this new arena, I had visions of myself standing in the middle of the Coliseum with nothing but my laptop between me and the lions. And I actually liked my comfort zone; it was, well, you know, comfortable. I knew what to expect from me.

Sonni had lost her mind and was going to drag me along as comic relief. Online Dating? Was she kidding? I had heard both the horror stories and the great stories, keeping in mind that the "great stories" were usually sponsored and paid for by the dating services, television commercials designed to hype the glories of online dating with smiling, beaming happy couples gushing how this service or that one had matched them with their one true love.

I grimaced. Ugh! Was there really such a thing as a one true love? I remember once reading an article about a woman who had been on upwards of thirty or so online dates in a month — so far. Geez, she must have been averaging a date a day. How does one find time for that kind of thing? Either this woman was a total control freak and no one on this planet would ever be good enough for her, or she had incredibly high standards. Maybe she was extremely high maintenance and no one would ever be compatible with her. Or just maybe she was picky enough and brave enough to wade through the muck of "undatables" and had decided to hold out for "the one" who was really right for her.

Besides, weren't these online dating services for desperate people? Or for total nut jobs who lie in wait to pounce on the "innocents" who are only looking for a good man or woman and encounter these evil souls instead who are waiting, hands rubbing together, to kidnap them and do only God knows what to them.

Who was I fooling? I was so out of my league. But Sonni just kept pushing. I completed the lengthy questionnaire about myself and the type of man that I was looking for. I was beginning to feel as if I were completing an application for employment or something.

I was supposed to write a profile that captured the essence of who I was, a profile that would appeal to a potential love match. Love match? Who said anything about love? Ok, ok, whatever... I would relax and capture the essence of Mikki... that I can do. What was I looking for? Straight woman, looking for a definitely straight man. Make that a straight single man. Not enough?

Ok, Sonni said to avoid the mention of arts and crafts and any other topic that would make me appear to be too matronly, which is fine since I'm not particularly good at crafts or anything remotely close to crafty. She advised that I should avoid sounding too domestic and by all means, no negativity. No references to any past relationships or other entanglements. Not that I have much to compare…

"Ok, Mikki, it says here that you should never share your online horror stories. I guess we won't have a problem with that since you're an online dating virgin." She teased, laughing at her own joke.

Online Dating Virgin? Since when was that a bad thing? I scowled at her. She continued, ignoring my expression.

"When you send out your initial email to a potential candidate, it says that you should give the subject line some sex appeal. Be sexy but subtle."

My God, she was relentless! I flashed a dark look in her direction, wanting very much to strangle her, best friend or not.
"Could you at least share my popcorn with me?" I growled.

"Think sexy, Mikki," Sonni extended the bag in my direction, doing this thing with her eyes and eyebrows that made her look more silly than mysterious. I laughed at her in spite of my mixed emotions about this whole thing. Be sexy? What was this, an advertisement? A billboard? Hey all of you Internet weirdoes! Look at the Internet virgin!

Sonni! Tell me again how I let her talk me into this craziness! Oh, that's right. Because she loves me too much to let me be alone.

Fine, I would not begin my emails with the regular boring, "Hello, my name is Mikki." I would ooze fun and excitement. I would know who my "target audience" was, what kind of man I was looking for. I would sell the sizzle, not the steak. Steak, meat... How fitting!

"You know about these things, Mikki," Sonni chided. "You're in Marketing, for Pete's sake!"

Well, that was all well and good, but I've never had to market myself as if I were some product or commodity! I deal with greeting cards and gift-wrap, not this insane form of human sacrifice!

She gave me a look and I held up my hand, warding off a potential scolding. Fine! I would cooperate. It was only for the summer. And it was supposed to be fun, right? Then, once I had fulfilled my end of this wacky deal, maybe Sonni would give me a break and let me enjoy a little peace and "alone time".

Internet dating, I was quickly learning, was a visual medium and my photo had to be me at my personal best. Most people check out the photos first, if it is an unflattering photo, "shoppers" would move on to the next one. In spite of being practically forced into this scheme, I would play fair; I promised that I would try.

I would post a nice picture of myself, one that I particularly liked. I really did not have many photos of myself, at least none that I was willing to share with a cybermall of men. I had decided to go with the picture that was featured on our company website. It was professionally done, the lighting was just right and I remembered liking that particular photo the best of all of the pictures that had been taken by the professional photographer.

Oh no... That's when Sonni sprang into action.

"I know you are not going to put that work photo on your profile!" Her voice came sharply from behind me. She had wandered back into the kitchen for something to drink so I was not sure how in the world she had seen the photo from across the room. I looked at the picture, then back at Sonni.

"What? It's a good picture!" I told her.

She strode over and stared at the laptop screen. The picture was nice, I was smiling with my head tilted just so against the standard faded grayish background common for most corporate photographs. The lighting was good and just a hint of photo shopping had been applied to make me appear professional and appealing.

"Well, yes, it would be a great picture to use — if you were preparing a marketing proposal. You're trying to get dates, girl, not plot a corporate merger..." Sonni stated bluntly. I laughed then.

"Well, technically, <u>you</u> are trying to get me dates..." I said flippantly. Sonni shot me a frustrated look. Oh no... Well, that did it. Now she was in full swing makeover mode. Sonni left the room, striding purposefully in the direction of my bedroom.

"Get in here," she ordered. Yes, Master! Like a good zombie, I obeyed.

Sonni stood in the expanse of my walk-in closet chocked nearly to the brim with clothes that I seldom wore. Noisily, she began going through my clothes, her lips pursed, then curled.

"Do you have any sexy clothes?" She asked.   Sexy? What's that?

I shrugged, puzzled. What on earth was wrong with my clothes? I had a lot of good stuff in there.

"I have what you see." I told her. She frowned.

"Get your purse," she snapped. "We're going shopping."

***

So, to add insult to injury, my wallet was now singing the blues as I pulled out my American Express at one store after another, purchasing at Sonni's insistence new "modern" clothing and shoes and underwear, even sleepwear. What was wrong with my work clothes I did not know but I certainly was not going to get into this with Sonni. And I have to admit, the things that we picked out were really cute.

But why on earth did I have to buy new underwear? No one — and I mean no one — that I met in this cybermall was going to see any of that, I don't care what Sonni claimed was ailing me!

We ended our shopping extravaganza at the MAC Store on the Country Club Plaza where I endured a "makeover" by a young lady who quite frankly nearly scared the life out of me with her pale foundation, black, yellow and bright blue eye shadow and ruby red lipstick. Well, I guess she had all of her primary colors covered...

I had no expectations for a happy medium but found myself pleasantly surprised when the young lady turned me around to face the mirror, the woman in the mirror resembling a newer, fresher, prettier and yes, more modern version of myself. And yes, I walked out the MAC Store, two bags in hand full of potions and elixirs, shades, formulas and foundations that the young lady insisted would help me replicate her magic at home.

Returning to my place, we tried on outfit after outfit and took a number of pictures and poses with my seldom-used digital camera until Sonni decided on the perfect profile picture. Although I was not about to admit it to her, I guessed she was right again, the end result was a lot more fun and a lot more interesting than any old work photo.

Sonni went on to explain that it was common to find one's self in the situation of having too many online suitors and when that became the case, we would need to develop some sort of spreadsheet to use to keep all of my facts and dates straight.

Was she kidding? I admit I had to laugh at this one! A spreadsheet for tracking my many conquests? Geez! I had just set up my profile and already Sonni had me out on dates and logging them into a spreadsheet! This was going to be one long summer!

"Mikki, I'm not kidding!" Sonni was insistent. "You will need to know whose username belongs with whose picture. I'm not talking about starting an FBI file on any of these people. Just something to help you remember who is who, and most importantly, who you never want to hear from again, should the man prove himself to be some kind of weirdo."

Great, I had the feeling that this issue alone — the weirdo factor — would constitute one really large spreadsheet. Like I'm going to forget who's a weirdo! Sonni and I decided that we should spend no more than an hour daily looking for dates online. That was fine with me. The whole idea of wandering the virtual alleys of online dating looking for men made me feel really weird. Right, no need to chase everything that comes my way. Got it.

"You're so silly, Mikki," Sonni laughed at me, satisfied at last that I was making some "progress". "Nobody actually knows you're trolling the cyber alleys," she said with a wink.

Thanks. That really was not helping the situation. Sonni instructed that I should keep the first date short and sweet. That a person can usually tell within the first five minutes if they are interested in one another. Sonni said that we needed to pace ourselves. Got it, pace myself...

"If you're not interested, don't prolong the agony. Instead of meeting for dinner, meet for coffee, or a drink. If it goes well, you can always extend the "date". If not, then you can always cut it short and get the heck out of there." She instructed.

Sonni the matchmaker, yet another talent she kept tucked away in her arsenal. Maybe she should consider starting her own service?

"And," she continued, "If you are not interested in meeting, if he persists, you simply say that you are not interested, or you just don't respond at all." Sonni finished, her attitude nonchalant.

Obviously she's done this a time or two but this struck me as rude, honestly, what would be worse? Someone actually saying" I'm not interested in you, please move on?" Or someone simply not responding, ignoring you? The kinder, gentler response, I guessed, would be to not respond, this would at least leave you with your dignity intact.

Sonni cautioned me to not let this become too much like work, rather I should think of it as a fun new hobby and to not go overboard. Too late! She really didn't have to worry about that!

This was already becoming more work than I was prepared to do for the sake of a date.

Sonni finally decided to go home "where I know there is food to eat" she quipped and left me alone with my newly completed online dating profile.

"Don't you dare delete it, Mikki," she warned. "I will know if you do, you are a terrible liar." I stuck my tongue out at her at which she shook her long manicured finger, giving me the "I'm watching you" gesture.

"Go home, Sonni!" I groused.   I'd had enough for one night. Shutting the door behind her, I turned off my computer and turned in for a night of tossing and turning through dreams of fighting off one bad date after another in the arena as people cheered and booed intermittently.

***

The funny thing was after I uploaded my profile, by the very next day my email box was inundated with emails from so-called "eligible" men. After my long dry spell, Mama Jett would have said this was too much of a good thing as I seemed to be making up for lost time.

On my first day, my email inbox contained thirty-five hits! Things had changed so much since I had last dated all of those many years ago. It was a whole new world out there now; people had electricity, cable television, inside plumbing...

Well, ok, maybe it hadn't been that long, but long enough.

There was a lot of talk about profiles and electronic "winking," chats and rooms. I'd heard about these things all in passing of course, but I never thought that I would be one of the numbers who now met potential dates this way.

I could do things now that I'd never dreamt of before, virtually meeting ten or twenty men at a time, checking them out and not one of them would have a clue that he was being "shopped".

Sonni had called online dating a virtual shopping mall of men. I could literally sit in the comfort of my own home, wearing whatever I wanted to wear and sort through pages and pages of eligible men, which to my chagrin; I seem to get the hang of pretty easily.

Initially, the thought of being "shopped" made me feel a little uneasy. It was almost as if there were dozens of people looking through my window, checking me out and I had no way of knowing who they were, at least not until he emailed me or I contacted him. It's as if there were dozens of voyeurs swooping in to spy on me at any given time. Bizarre!

As far as eligibility, I was learning that being eligible was a state of mind, the definition of being eligible seemed to have changed quite a bit since I had been out on the dating scene. Meeting people online was easy, but I was quickly learning that meeting the right people would take work and time and energy.

Depending on how much time I wanted to invest into it, I could browse profiles to my heart's content. Short, tall, or so he may state on his profile. Handsome, successful. Some not so successful. Some of these profiles seemed to be total works of fiction worthy of a Pulitzer Prize.

Nobody noticed if you made faces or funny noises when you read the profiles. Some of them were just so ridiculous. Then there were the ones that read like love letters. Ah! That is another story all together.

Nobody noticed if you laughed out loud, it was all so blissfully anonymous! And if someone made a funny face at your profile or about something that you wrote, you really couldn't care less if they did. You could "kick the tires" all day long and it hurt no one. If you didn't find something you liked, well, you lived to shop another day.

I had to admit, I was having more fun than I thought I would.

Damn...

Getting Some

I glanced at him out of the corner of my eye as another loud clatter came from his direction, turning to see him drying my new Rachel Ray cookware as if he were mad at Rachel Ray personally. What in the world was wrong with him? Lately, he just seemed to be all out of sorts... maybe he was mad at Little Miss Cutie Pie.

"Is there a problem?" I asked, reaching into the hot sudsy water to pull the sink stopper, letting the dishwater out as I mentally added "call a handy man to fix the dishwasher" to my steadily growing list of things to do this summer.

Dereon grumbled something, reaching for another pan, drying the pot so aggressively, one would have assumed that it had wronged him in some way. Noisily, he stacked it with the others on the countertop to be put away.

Ok, definitely Miss Cutie Pie. I was not going to pry if he was not going to offer up the information. He grew more and more sullen as we cleared the kitchen.

"Is this about sex?" Dereon asked finally, forcefully blurting out the words. I was so startled by the question that I sloshed soapy water out of the sink and onto the floor. I grabbed a paper towel, bending down to clean up the mess I'd made.

"Wh—what?" I asked.

Dereon shrugged, turning his frustration onto the silverware, drying each piece and placing them in the divider in the drawer noisily. Here I was thinking that his moodiness was because I had asked that he help me with the kitchen chores by drying and putting away the pots and pans. Obviously Mr. D had a lot on his mind.

"All of this Internet dating stuff. Is this about getting some?" he snapped the towel out straight, flinging it over his shoulder, turning to look me squarely in the eye.

Getting some? Getting some what? Dinner? Where on earth had he gotten that idea? Getting some could mean so many things, although I knew in no uncertain terms what Dereon meant by "getting some".

"Sex?" I hedged, my voice squeaking and I laughed nervously. No, no, no! This was not going to happen, I was not going to discuss sex — or my not having sex — with my eighteen year old son! I cleared my throat, waving his question away.

He exhaled, exasperated, frowning across the small distance at me.

"Mom, I know what Aunt Sonni is trying to talk you into." He opened the lower cabinets, stacking the cookware in neatly, if noisily. I leaned against the counter, watching as he manhandled Rachel Ray into the cabinet.

"And what exactly do you think is going on?" I asked, intentionally evasive. Done with the cookware, he straightened to his full height.

"Mom, what do you know about all of this online dating stuff? I'm not being mean or anything, but you just bought your own laptop last year..." he groused.

I smiled at him. Point taken, this much was true. I had been more than content to complicate my life with technology only on an "as needed" basis, I'd never been a fan of surfing the web or anything else, nor had I an interest in lining up a bunch of friends on Facebook or tweeting or linking in or anything else. Who had the time? Only recently, I'd allowed Dereon to talk me into upgrading our cell phones for a couple of the new Smartphones that every one raved about. Seemed to be more trouble than it was worth at times. And email? No thanks; I had more than enough to do contending with the sheer amount of real mail and junk mail that filled my actual mailbox every day. Dereon was not about to let this go.

"Do you even know what kind of people hang out on these kinds of sites?" Dereon asked. He looked at me speculatively. Go ahead and say it, young one, I mused…. Even the man child knew more about internet dating than I did. Wait! Did he? And how did he know?

"It's harmless, Dereon," I stated. "Just a way to meet some people, to have a little fun this summer."

Dereon shook his head, his mouth pressing into a straight firm line, obviously not approving of this little summer adventure.

"Mom, I know that Aunt Sonni is behind this, you wouldn't have come to this decision on your own," he said, his statement matter of fact, and he crossed his arms in front of his chest, looking at me sternly. I frowned, shaking my head up at him. Does everybody think that I am an Internet Virgin? Even my own child? Does everyone think I am that naive? That clueless?

"Dereon," I began. "It's totally safe, I am just checking out what's out there, who is out there…"

"That's just it!" he answered, his tone sharp. He shook his head vehemently. I took a step backward, surprised at his reaction. Wait! Who was the parent and who was the child?

"There are all kinds of strange people out there, people who prey on people who have no clue what is going on out there." He continued. Wait! Was he saying that I was clueless in general or just about this? I crossed my arms as well, returning the scowl.

"Dereon, I am a big girl, I know how to take care of myself — and you for that matter."

Dereon was as relentless at pressing his argument as Sonni had been at pressing hers, at different ends of the spectrum, of course with her for and Dereon against.

"Mom, you haven't been on a date in ages..."

Ouch, right into the heart... Et tu Dereon? I rubbed my brow, perplexed. Now everybody was a critic about how I had lived my life these past forty-five years! As if I could not possibly take care of myself out there in the great big world of grownups!

"Things have changed out there since..." he began and then he flushed, his lips tightening down on the rest of his sentence. I cocked my head to the side, my brow rising as I watched him. Having never met his father, Dereon seemed ill at ease when expressing his thoughts about what had happened — or not happened between his father and me. I reached out, rubbing his arm, shaking my head.

"Since your dad... I know. But baby, that's why I have to get back out there. You're about to go out into your own life." I poked him in the ribs, smiling as he flinched away from the annoying finger, still miffed with me and not wanting to let the issue go.

"Besides," I continued, reaching around him to throw the paper towel in the trash. "If your mom has a life of her own, that gives you more time with Little Miss Cutie Pie without your mom — or her friends — constantly looking over your shoulder."

He looked puzzled then, appearing to not know what I was getting at. I poked him again.

"At your graduation? Don't think I didn't notice." I teased.

He flushed again, embarrassment touching his handsome man-child features.

"Jasmine," he muttered.

"Jasmine," I repeated, smiling at him. He poked me back.

"Mom, I just need you to be safe. You know that Aunt Sonni is on the wild side..." At that I laughed out loud.

"You think?" I chuckled as I looked around the now tidy kitchen. Sonni and wild, synonyms in the dictionary, to be sure!

"I will be careful, honey. You know me." He studied me for a long second, and then shook his head, his mouth a tight line though loosening a bit into a smile.

"And," Dereon said, making a punching move in mid-air, affecting an uppercut on some invisible foe. "If one of those clowns gets out of line, he's going to have to deal with me."

I laughed again at my sweet man-child. Always trying to look out for his old mother. I waved him off, laughing as he made a gesture toward me as if he would strangle me, deciding instead to pull a long curling tendril of my hair.

"Promise me you'll be careful..." He grumbled.

I smiled up at him. "I promise..."

He smiled back warily. "Ok." That seemed to appease him, if only temporarily.
"So," I began sweetly. "Tell me about Jasmine," I prodded.

At that, Dereon considered the conversation over and strode off to his bedroom, probably to call said Miss Cutie Pie Jasmine. I smiled at his retreating back.

This was going to be a long summer...

Family Man

Day one....

Ok, well, maybe this should be considered day seven since technically I was already a few days into my sixty-day experiment to find Mr. Right Now. Sighing, I placed my hand against my stomach, feeling sick as my nerves worked overtime. This was my first "official" date after my initial screening of would-be datables and I was more than a little uneasy.

I stood outside the restaurant, breathing deeply in and out as I wobbled in my new high heel pumps; uncertain if I even wanted to go in. Did I really want to do this? Could I do this? I had to; I really did not seem to have a choice since Sonni had made me "Sister-Girlfriend-Pinky Swear" that I would at least try this dating thing.

Already, I was breaking Sonni's first cardinal online dating rule as I had agreed to meet contestant number one at a restaurant rather than for coffee as Sonni had instructed. This was unchartered territory for me and I was sure that once I really had a chance to reflect on all of this I would probably decide that this was territory that should have remained unchartered. You have to crawl before you can walk, so Sonni says and I really had no clue what I was opening myself up for.

My "date" had emailed me within days after I'd uploaded my profile. On the surface, he was certainly handsome and from his profile I learned that he had a good job locally and he owned his own home. He was financially secure and most of all, he was single. He'd written all of the right things and had been extremely flattering although I had wondered how he could be so flattering having just "virtually" met me and all. And he was eager, almost overly eager to meet me in person. He loved kids and all things family. He liked the idea that I had a son. He pretty much thought that everything about me was pretty darn wonderful. Perhaps all of this agreeableness should have been the first red flag, as an Internet dating virgin, I really had nothing else to go on.

Ignorance is bliss.

Prior to our date, we had emailed back and forth and gradually moved on to speaking via cell phone. He seemed nice, even attentive so I suggested that we go meet for coffee some night after work, just to see if we clicked.

"Well, it's kind of hard to get away right after work." He had reasoned. "Sometimes I have to work late. How about if we set a time to meet for dinner sometime this weekend? I can meet you there."

And so here I stood, scared to death to go inside, my legs and hands trembling, feeling as if I could throw up. An older couple approached the restaurant arm in arm, smiling at me as I stood indecisive on the landing outside the restaurant.

Not too late to run, Mikki...

I returned their smiles, rushing forward to open the door for them, following them inside before I could change my mind.

Here we go...

Actually, my date had chosen a decent restaurant. I had been there a time or two before this evening with Mama Jett, Dereon and Sonni so I knew the place reasonably well. We had decided to meet at 6:00 p.m. on a Saturday night, not normally a time that I would have considered ideal for meeting someone new, but I figured, what could it hurt?

I had dressed nicely; family style restaurants did not call for silk or satin so I opted for a cotton wrap blouse in beautiful vibrant shades of turquoise, black and white and a slim pair of black slacks. With this I wore the new black Kenneth Cole Reptile peep toe pumps that Sonni had talked me into, as if it had taken much arm-twisting. My hair was pulled back away from my face and held in place with an elegant hair ornament and I kept my makeup simple, applying it exactly the way the MAC girl had shown me.

Smiling, I approached the hostess booth, giving the pretty young lady standing behind the small podium my name and the name of the party that I was supposed to meet.

"Of course, ma'am," she said and had another young lady show me to the table. Ma'am? Who the heck was ma'am?

I squared my shoulders, pinning a polite smile onto my glossy lips, wanting to make a good first impression. Nope. Not going to worry about being called ma'am tonight. I looked good and felt good. I was anxious, not really sure what to expect but what's the worst that could happen? We were just going to meet and greet, size each other up...

"Uh oh..."

My train of thought came to a screeching halt. Forget halt, my train of thought left the tracks and burst into flames. As I rounded the corner, the reasons for choosing this restaurant became abundantly clear. Apparently, my date had left a few things off of his profile, well, make that four little things.

Oh, I don't know, call me crazy but he might have wanted to mention to anyone who might shop his profile that he was part of a package deal. A very large package. Now, it's not like I have something against package deals, after all, I have a teenage son. But this, this was something entirely different.

This was no package, this was a caravan!

I had expected to greet him with a smile and an introduction of "Hi, I'm Mikki," but what became stuck in my mind was "What in the world!"

My date was seated at the table, leaving the chair beside him empty for me. Accompanying him at the table were four little pairs of eyes, all staring at me. And two of the owners of the pairs of eyes had to be less than four years old.

Oh...my...God! Now this ... whoa! This ... what? Nothing could have prepared me for this! I must have looked a sight as I stood still gaping at the children.

Family Man smiled broadly as he caught sight of me, pausing in his task of fastening a plastic bib around the neck of one of the smallest children to rise to greet me.

"Mikki! Hi!"

Opening his arms, he greeted me with a quick hug and a smile as if we were old friends. I swallowed, feeling myself shrinking away from him in surprise as I patted his shoulder awkwardly. I was speechless, my words stuck; I couldn't force them past the huge lump in my throat.

"Uh ... hi?" I tried again, the conversations in the restaurant seeming to fall away as all eyes seemed to be on me. The children stared at me. I stared at the children, not really sure what was supposed to happen next. Apparently, this was something new for all of us.

"Come and have a seat, Mikki," Family Man said with a big smile, pulling out a chair to seat me next to whom I guessed was the oldest girl. I sat down stiffly, clutching my purse like a lifeline. The girl stared at me and vaguely I found myself becoming uneasy with the directness of her gaze.

"Let me introduce you to the kids," he began, going around the table to introduce each of the children. The children continued to stare at me until one of the little boys, deciding that he was not going to wait for anyone else to eat, thrust his chubby little hand into the untouched breadbasket.

"Um," I tried again. "Yours?" I asked, motioning around the table. Family Man laughed the sound deep, smiling around the table at his brood.

"Yep, my own little tribe."

Ah yes, tribe. I gaped at the little group, I believe that this would have been the appropriate description. One of the little boys stared at me with big bright eyes, gnawing on the breadstick as if it were the first thing he'd eaten that day, pieces of the soggy bread hanging out the corner of his mouth as he chewed with his mouth wide open.

Oh, Mikki, what have you done? I tried to wrap my mind around all of this. So there were two boys and two girls. The two girls must have come first, then the two boys, oh, wait, the boys were twins. Twins ... oh…my…! Good heavens!

I blinked hard, fidgeting in my chair and I set my purse on the floor beside my chair, really not at all sure what to do next. This was not at all what I expected. How was I going to get out of this?

"Do it, Mikki! Run! No one's going to blame you! Snap out of it, Mikki! Get us out of here!" Little Mikki kicked her two cents into the internal debate.

I couldn't do that, common sense tried to reason. I could not just walk out, what would Mama Jett say? Hell, what would Sonni do? Who cared what Sonni would do in this instance, right now, all I wanted to do was to make it through this so that I could strangle Sonni when I next saw her.

All of these children, I could not, for the life of me, remember who was who. Family Man told me their names, but I think that I was just so shocked by all of this that none of the names had registered at the time.

The two little girls continued to stare at me and I began to feel as if I were starring in one of those creepy science fiction movies where the little girls hate to see their father with someone new. Anyone new. Their expressions were penetrating and I wanted to look anywhere but at those two. Simultaneously, the girls peeled their attention from me to look at each other then back at me.

"Hate her! Hate her! Must get rid of her! She's trying to take our daddy away from us. Must send her away! Kill her, kill her now!"

Ok, maybe a really bad science fiction movie. I felt self-conscious; did I have something on my face? Or, maybe my hair really was standing on end. That had to be it. The way they watched my every move was unnerving, those two Stepford Sisters were unsettling. I was totally caught off guard when the oldest girl suddenly smiled at me, her face going from serious to smiling in zero point three seconds. Weird ... I gasped aloud when she finally spoke to me.

"I like your earrings," she said. Her sister nodded in agreement.

"Thank you, honey," I said, goose bumps making my arms prickle painfully, grateful that I had been spared, for now I had caught a break with these two and they weren't going to kill me right away.

The boys were much too busy amusing themselves to worry about me, chattering with each other in this bizarre alien four-year old language that no one else at the table seemed to understand. Then, the littlest boy dropped his mangled breadstick on the floor.
"Oh no," the little boy whined, peering over the edge of his booster seat, his greasy little face crestfallen over the demise of the chewed up bread.

"Oh, I'll get it," I said, leaning forward to retrieve the bread. I was only trying to help, really I was. I leaned over to pick up the breadstick, now covered with dust and other odd and gross things from under the table and placed it on the edge of the table out of his reach. He reached for it again.

"Mine!" he whined, greasy little fingers reaching for the bread.

"No sweetie, that one is dirty; you need to have another one." I told him, reaching toward the breadbasket.

The little boy looked first at me then at the dusty, dirty mangled breadstick and began to scream bloody murder.

What the hell? I recoiled away from the child, my hand rising to cover my mouth, dismayed by the sounds of human suffering coming from such a small body. The child began to scream as if I had struck him with the dirty breadstick and believe me, the way he was screaming, I considered it, if only for a second!

Screaming and pointing at me. Oh...dear...God! I think that my eyes must have bugged right out of my head! Screaming and yelling something in gibberish about that dang breadstick.

Oh my goodness! I looked around, distraught. Please stop screaming! People in the restaurant were starting to stare, looking at me as if to say, "Who is this mean woman who is making this nice man's children cry?"

The little boy glared at me as if I were a wicked old woman for taking away his breadstick, stretching his little arm forward in the direction of the breadstick, tears streaking down his buttery greasy cheeks as he howled and moaned at the top of his lungs.

People began to shake their heads and whisper among themselves, eyes darting to the commotion at our table, then away again. Horrified, I had a thought. Oh my God! What if people thought that these were my kids? They were probably saying among themselves, "Why can't this woman control her kids!"

The little boy had now worked himself up into a state, screaming and flailing his little self this way and that in his little booster seat as if he were experiencing some kind of possession, reaching out again for this breadstick, pointing at it, then pointing at me, screaming "Mine! Mine!", kicking his little legs out straight, then banging them against the leg of the table.

His cry, this tortured strangled screaming, seemed to reverberate through the restaurant and I wanted to cover my ears. I looked at Family Man then back at the boy, wondering what to do now. Family Man did not even look in my direction. I was half tempted to give the boy the dirty bread anyway if for no other reason than to stop the screaming. To heck with the dust bunnies and various dirty things that coated it. A little dirt never hurt anyone.

It was then that the screamer's brother decided that I was pure evil, having harmed his brother in some way and he began to scream as well, alternately pointing at me, speaking in the alien gibberish while tears and spittle dripped down his little face as he stretched his little arms toward his brother, I guess to comfort him, or maybe just to save him from the evil lady who stole his brother's breadstick. I stared open mouthed, aghast as I looked around, my eyes coming to rest on the girls sitting quietly at the table.

Oh no...

The Stepford Sisters were looking at me again, this time, not as if I were some kind of child torturing killer, rather, the oldest sister shook her head, her lips downturned, a look of pure exasperation creasing her small face.

"Boys are so silly, they cry all of the time," the oldest Stepford Sister said with an exaggerated roll of her eyes. Her sister nodded her head in agreement.

The twin aliens continued to scream as Family Man tried to calm them down while the Stepford Sisters continued to debate between themselves the virtues of girl kind and how girls were so much better than boys.

"When we were babies like them, we never behaved like that," the older Stepford Sister said.

"No," the younger agreed with her sister. Of course she agreed...

Family Man had now given the upset child a fresh breadstick and one to his brother, wiping their faces with a napkin, calming them down.

Finally, blissful silence fell over the table as the boys demolished their new breadsticks, quiet at last. Now the Stepford Sisters felt slighted. I cringed, bracing myself for whatever new forms of torture I would be forced to endure at the hands of Family Man's "tribe".

"How come the boys get to have breadsticks?" The oldest Stepford Sister asked her arms across her chest, obviously displeased.

"Where is my breadstick, Daddy?" the younger Stepford Sister echoed, also crossing her arms across her chest.

"I don't want milk with my dinner, Daddy, can I have Coke?" The older Stepford Sister asked.

"Coke, coke!" The twin boys joined in, revitalized by their chewy breadstick snacks, no longer crying. They kicked their legs about, slamming the heels of their shoes into the fronts of their chairs, enjoying the dull "bump, bump, bump" sound that they made.

"Coke, Coke!" Bump, bump! I looked at Family Man, flabbergasted; the man had to be a marvel of human patience. How on earth could he be so calm with all of this insanity going on? Wait! Was he deaf?

"Babies don't drink Coke," the second Stepford Sister said to the "babies" which touched off a whole new flurry of pandemonium.

"We're not babies, we're big boys. Aren't we big boys, Daddy?"

Bump, bump, bump, bump! Those hard little shoes beat double time against the booster seats. Family Man smiled at the little boy, continuing to wipe at his tear and butter smeared face.

Oh sweet mercy!

"Of course you are a big boy. And everybody will have milk for dinner." Family Man said.

That obviously did not sit well with the self-declared superior girls, to which the first Stepford Sister was quick to assert that the boys always ruined everything. The younger girl nodded her head, agreeing with her sister. I began to think that she agreed with everything that her sister said. What was her name again?

I looked at Family Man, helpless. He simply smiled benevolently at the children. I cleared my throat, turning to glance in the direction of the front of the restaurant. Could I make it to the door in these shoes? What if I took them off? I could cover twice as much ground... I returned my attention to Family Man and his children. Leaning forward, I touched his arm gently.

"I can see that you have your hands full. Your children are hungry and they need you. I'm in the way." I smiled at him. I smiled at his children. Except for the Stepford Sisters, frankly those two scared me.

Family Man gave me a sympathetic look, nodding his head a bit. I should have been offended that he'd agreed that I was in the way, but at this point, I did not really care, all I wanted to be was gone! He smiled sadly at his "plight".

"Maybe this is too much for them. Maybe it's too early, their Mom's been gone for a little over a year now. I don't think they are ready for this."

They're not ready for this? I was not ready for this — whatever it was — either.

"She died a little over a year ago." He continued. "I thought it might be nice for the kids to meet somebody nice."

Goodness! Somebody nice? I think he is going to need a whole lot of somebody nice for his self-described tribe. All of his children, God bless them all, seemed very nice. But, if he was interviewing women for the role of stepmom using Internet dating, then I was going to have to take a rain check. Heck, forget rain! It would take a natural disaster knocking me crazy before I would ever get myself into a situation like this one.

"Yes," I agreed over the din of the confusion. I looked again at the children, nodding again for emphasis. "I'm going to go ahead and go. It was really nice meeting you and your family." I said.

I stood to leave, seeming to have been forgotten already, and honestly, that was just fine with me. Family Man was refereeing what appeared to be a verbal tussle between the second Stepford Sister and the twin boys. The older Stepford Sister sat with her arms crossed in front of her, a grumpy frown on her face.

"Go! " Little Mikki yelled at me and I picked up my purse, bolting to the front of the restaurant as quickly as I could. I don't think that Family Man and the tribe would have noticed that I had gone anyway.

I thanked the young lady at the hostess station and left the restaurant, teetering out noisily in the Kenneth Cole shoes, trying not to break into a mad dash out of the building.

Rushing to my car, I opened the door and slid inside, leaning my head against the headrest, terrified that one of the Stepford Sisters may have followed me. I closed my eyes for a minute.

Silence, blissful peaceful silence. No noise, no breadsticks, no screaming. I basked in the silence as I appreciated how very nice is to be on this side of the child raising game. Turning the key in the ignition, I steered my car toward home.

Geez! I'd heard of baby's mama's and all of that, heck, most of the daily television talk shows - Springer, Maury, Montel, almost all of the court shows anymore, that is all they talk about, who is the baby's mama or baby's daddy?

Everybody is looking for the baby's daddy. But this was a real twist. This man was looking for a mama for his babies. Four children! I think that maybe Family Man should put all of the time he was expending looking for a baby's mama into looking for a nanny instead.

I emailed him promptly, telling him that he was very nice, that his kids were cute but that I was sorry; this was not going to work for me. I wish him well and left it at that. He was going to need it!

Please…

Day thirteen…

Oh no! There it was again, yet another email from this guy… obviously he did not subscribe to Sonni's Rules for Internet Dating. This guy just would not take a hint! I tried the whole ignore him thing, ignoring his emails, pokes, winks and everything else but he just did not seem to get the message.

"Mikki," his initial email read. "I'm a local entrepreneur who would like to meet someone special to enjoy some quality time with her."

That was it. There was no con, no trying to impress me with "I'm so this or that." He mentioned the name of his company and it sounded vaguely familiar, I couldn't quite put my finger on it. He had not tried to impress me with the revenues of his company, nor did he try to quote some line to make himself seem witty or cool or hip. He was just plain and frank in his email, what a novel idea! There was no bragging, no hemming and hawing. He was very complimentary and seemed … I don't know … like a nice guy. What were the odds?

He was a local entrepreneur who had gone golden. His company had grown by leaps and bounds and now he had three different offices in Kansas City, Denver and Dallas. Impressive…

OK, so, I'm thinking in my mind's eye that when I opened the profile link from his email, he would be someone older with graying hair, a worldly man who may have seem some things, lived through some things.

What greeted me was not what I expected. The man was handsome. Forget that, this man was very easy on the eyes. He seemed tall, muscular with a killer smile, and dare I say, dimples to die for.

And young. Very, very young. He was a baby…

His profile was, well for lack of a better word, perfect. That alone should have sent me running. And, I want to say that for the record, on my own, I would have never contacted him.

I'd written my profile exactly the way that I was supposed to, certain that I indicated both my age and the age range of the men that I was looking for…um…interested in meeting. Someone older, settled, established in his business and in his life. Someone who was fun and did not mind exploring new things. Did I mention older?

After some of the knuckleheads I had received emails from recently, I think that I knew enough to know that sometimes, all right, most times the men I had exchanged emails with lately were more likely to put a picture of a much younger version of himself on his profile. Sometimes these profiles were downright deceitful works of fiction.

Again I looked at his picture, it was a good picture. Scrolling through the profile I noted that he was a self-made man, having launched his first company with only $100,000 of seed money paying back his investors in months rather than years and now his company, a local media and telecommunications company, was set to earn one million dollars in revenue this year alone, beating the records of a few of his competitors.

We seemed to have some common interests in advertising and media; just recently his company had introduced a technology and business magazine that seemed to do very well locally and he had capitalized on a trend that had quickly grown into a new media category and niche market. Ok, so the man had brains too. Brains and body, if the picture was really of himself, he seemed to be in good shape.

And now, his profile said, his company was dabbling in the technology and space industry, having been tapped to provide technology and infrastructure with a company in space technology.

Hmm… so this guy had a few things going for him. Keeping my own profile in mind, I'd said that I was looking for an older, settled man. The picture was definitely not older, and if that were the case, then I just did not want to be bothered. He had started this off on the wrong foot already by not putting a true representation of himself on his profile.

I scrolled back up to look at the picture again. Very, very nice but no deal. I deleted the email.

I Just Called To Say...

"Chitt!" I heard the mangled attempt at a swear word the moment the elevator door opened and I smiled. Today was starting just like any other day. I arrived at my office at GBGC, on time, as usual.

Upon entering my department, I heard the muttered swearing in heavily accented English and I knew that Karen the Temptress was in attendance and in rare form. I only hoped that I had arrived in time to prevent the dismantling of the department's one and only functioning copier.

Irritated, Karen yanked papers from the machine in spite of the arrow on top that suggested that the paper should have been removed from the opposite direction. I shook my head, how many times had I told her that violence and technology were not good bedfellows. Machines seem to work better when you love them. Don't love them...well, that is the beginning of a bad day at the office.

The Temptress wasn't in for all of that. She was showing the machine no love whatsoever. She attempted to smile as I walked by, the action tightening her bright red lips as she mumbled a grouchy "hello" in her thick native Brazilian accent. Stooping, she scooped up the mountain of crumpled paper at her stiletto clad feet.

"Meekee, the copier's down," she called after me in her singsong voice.

Big surprise there.

"Ok..." I murmured, distracted. I stopped at Karen's desk long enough to retrieve my little pile of messages. God, this woman's handwriting was horrible! Two returned calls, one - I really wasn't so sure what it said. Karen's handwriting, not the best in the world was about as indecipherable as her swear words most days. But hey, she makes a killer brownie — her saving grace —

and she got stuff done so I guessed that this would secure her place in my world, at least for this month. I hoped that the Temptress would have the copier situation under control with enough time to print out the materials for the departmental meeting this afternoon.

Karen, the temperamental Temptress, though I would never call her this to her face. But who knows, she might like it. Karen was an exotic Brazilian beauty with a hot Latin temper to match her sultry good looks. Tall, slim, blood red polished fingernails, heavily lashed dark eyes and an even darker curtain of thick hair that fell well past her shoulders, which she kept coiled neatly at the back of her neck in a fashionable chignon.

I often wondered how she did that. I'd seen Karen's hair unleashed from the restrictive style once when I'd happened upon her in the ladies room, working her magic on her mane. I remember being stunned that she could get so much hair up into that fashionable knot, held in place with only a couple of huge hair ornaments. Had to take practice. Me, I was lucky if I could master taming my curly locks most days.

Someone told me once that Karen had dated a prominent man in our fair city. Excuse me; make that a married prominent man in our city. I was never brave enough to ask whom the man had been and would not dare speculate. To tell the truth, it was those blood red nails of hers that I feared.

Today the Temptress wore a red knit tank dress with cute ruffles around the hem and a matching shrug, which was probably a good idea. We wouldn't want her to give anybody a heart attack at the sight of her super toned arms and ample bosom, wait, does anybody say bosom anymore? She still wore her standard four-inch heels — it was a work day after all, and there was no need to pull out the heavy artillery. I am sure that somewhere in GBGC's dress code this dress is in violation, but hell, who am I to tell her this? That dress is fierce and I am hating on it, wishing with every fiber of my being that I could pull off the look on any given day. As usual, her hair was a work of art and her makeup flawless. Yep, I'm hating, but in a good sort of way.

"I called copy man and he said to me one hour, give me one hour. Why it take him so long? Can somebody tell me this?" Karen was in full Brazilian meltdown and I just did not have the heart to tell her that while she had to wait for one hour for "copy man" to show up, everyone else in the building had to wait sometimes a full day for him to show up. I knew that he is secretly in love with the Temptress, poor thing; I just didn't have the heart to tell him that the line forms on the left...

I dropped my worn brown briefcase down on the floor next to my desk, putting the messages down on top of my planner, sighing as I tugged the edge of my linen blazer down from where it was riding up my back. Silently I cursed whoever it was who'd thought that all cute summer outfits should be made of linen. Linen always had a way of looking as if you'd slept in your clothes, yet, so many items among my wardrobe seemed to be made of this annoying fabric. By the end of the day, I would truly feel as if I'd slept in my clothes, wrinkled and all.

Groaning, my gaze swept over my desktop. Ok, where do I start? And like that, I worked for the next three hours, consulting what seemed like reams of information representing data about customers, storefronts, merchandise and floor plans and the like, sipping occasionally from a cup of cold coffee that remained just beyond my "spill zone".

I worked most days like this, head down, coming up for an occasional sip of coffee or when the Temptress had a question or a telephone call from someone who said it was "urgently important" that they speak with me. The way the Temptress stressed "urgently important" with that Brazilian accent always made me roll my eyes and the Temptress would do the same.

The telephone rang then, jarring me out of my reverie. I looked at the tiny screen on the telephone, not recognizing the number. I leaned over, looking out toward Karen's desk. I'd seen her leave a few minutes ago to direct the copier repairman to the ailing machine and she had not returned. The Copier repair guy was probably trying to score a date with the Temptress. Again. Most of the repairmen, deliverymen, window washers, whomever; all had tried to snare the Temptress. Unfortunately, none of them had the right pedigree, or they were so pitifully far outside of the Temptress' orbit that all they could do is watch this bright star from a distance.

Sighing deeply, I straightened my shoulders, working out the stiffness there and picked up the receiver.

"Good afternoon, GBGC, this is Mikki Robbinson, how may I help you?" I put on my best telephone voice. Countless training sessions as GBGC had pointed out that we should answer the phone as if we were looking into a mirror. Look, smile, transfer that smile into your voice. Great.

"Good afternoon Ms. Robbinson. This is Sheila from Dr. DeJovne's office," a disembodied woman's voice said. Who? DeJovne, DeJovne. Why did that name sound familiar?

"How are you today?" the bodiless woman asked, obviously remembering her phone training as well. Greet the caller, be polite, conversational.

"I'm fine, and you?" I asked. DeJovne. The name clicked. Oh goodness, my doctor's office! Why on earth were they calling? Had I done something wrong? Was something wrong with Dereon?

"I'm great, Ms. Robbinson. The reason I'm calling is that from our records, we show that you haven't been in for a Well Woman visit in quite a while."

Why? Of course I hadn't been to the doctor, I've been well, right? No need to go to the doctor if you are well. I hate doctors, not personally, rather the profession is what I hate was what I really wanted to say to bodiless woman. Every time I go to the doctor, I'm usually in trouble for something. Either I've waited two long between visits or I need to take a multi vitamin or cut back on the salt and sweets… It's always something.

"Mm, hmm," I said into the receiver instead, pulling out my planner. Hadn't I just seen the doctor for something?

I frowned as the wad of sticky notes and scraps of paper tumbled from the planner. So much for the Franklin Covey Planner System Classes I'd attended, courtesy of GBGC. I guess that the powers that be thought that perhaps a class in planning would make me more productive. Ha! Foiled again!

Well, I guess it would have worked if I hadn't been so busy at the time sticking everything else into the planner. Poor thing, stuffed to the gills with slips of paper, appointment reminders, business cards, and sticky notes. Not at all how the planner was engineered to be used, of that I was sure.

I flipped through the pages of my calendar, my fingers resting on the page in December where I had gone to Dr. DeJovne's office. And it was now June… uh oh…

It was on one of these sticky notes that I'd found the information about my last trip, I had managed to catch a nasty little upper respiratory infection and Dr. DeJovne had refused to prescribe me anything until I'd stopped by her office — and paid the required twenty-dollar copayment, of course.

"A couple of weeks ago, I called your office just to make you aware of some times and dates that Dr. DeJovne had available should you want to schedule an appointment. When looking at your records, I see that you recently had a birthday."

"Oh?" I asked. Dang! I remembered that call — vaguely. How could I forget? Yes, I did, my forty-fifth birthday, I wanted to snarl at her. Bodiless woman on the phone continued speaking as if I'd said nothing.

"Dr. DeJovne noticed also in your file that you've not had a mammogram and wanted me to stress to you the importance of having a mammogram annually. That it's vitally important that as women age they take advantage of this service ... early detection ... the procedure is covered by your insurance..."

Again there was that dig that I was getting old. What is up with that? Not like I needed a reminder! I frowned, my face twisting as if I'd eaten something sour. Mammogram. I'd heard about those things. Sonni had already clued me in to all of the high points.

Pain, agony, more pain, crying, gnashing of teeth. Then you wait while they read the scan of your now pancake-shaped breasts. That's all, everything is fine. We'll see you next year when we'll do this all over again. Whoo hoo! Mama Jett had been on my case to have a mammogram, as had Sonni and Niecee in spite of my assertions that I just did not have time.

"Dr. DeJovne would like to see you, she has some time available this afternoon, that way she can get you set up with the referral for the technician at the diagnostic clinic," bodiless woman said.

What? Wait a minute! What was the hurry? I mean, I had a ton of things to do today and being tortured was not on the list. Dang! I looked at the clock on my computer. I had the production meeting later this afternoon and from the sound of it; the Temptress had the copier back up and running.

"What you doing? There's nothing for you down there." I could hear her reprimanding "copy man" and I could only imagine what the poor guy had been caught looking at.

"Fine," I heard myself say. "I will be there." I finished up a few things, left a note on the Temptress' desk and left for my appointment.

* * *

"How have you been, Mikki?" Dr. DeJovne asked, studying my chart. "I haven't seen you for a well woman visit for a couple of years." She looked over the edge of her glasses, diverting her attention from the clipboard to me.

Dr. DeJovne was of Middle Eastern descent, I'd deduced, with beautifully even features, dark understanding eyes. The woman was a knockout and I could only imagine how she might have looked at the Temptress' age.

Doctors, I can't stand them. I mean, don't get me wrong, it's not the person the doctor is, it's the profession. They scare me; just the thought of going to the doctor does funny things to my stomach. Always has.

They stick me in a cold room, and then they poke and prod me. They ask me twenty questions, then look at me crazy when I can't remember the last time I'd done this, that or the other, heck, I can barely remember what I had for dinner last night, let alone what the day of my last whatever was.

When was the last time I'd had sex? Sex? What's that?

Then they stick me in a funky little gown with my butt hanging out and put my legs in stirrups and then wonder why I am uncomfortable. Really? Relax, they say, although I don't know how they even think this is possible, with my legs up in the air and my butt hanging out.

"How has it been going?" she asked conversationally, slipping on a pair of latex free gloves, obviously taking note of my latex allergy alert on my file. I look anywhere but at her.

"Great, although my body seems to have a mind of its own lately." I grumbled, trying to relax on the cold table. Poke, prod, geez! Really? And I'm supposed to carry on a conversation as well?

"Oh, how so?" Dr. DeJovne's lilting accent always made me feel as if she were about to start singing.

"Hot, cold, then even hotter still. It can't decide." I say, turning my head to look at a poster on the wall, again a smiling woman stressed the importance of early detection of breast cancer.

Dr. DeJovne laughed. 'That's perimenopause for you." She patted my leg. "You did fine. You can sit up now."

Peri-who?

"Well," I said, sitting up, pulling the gown over my legs as best I could without exposing more of my assets. "I don't know about that. Aren't I little young for that?" Just the question itself sounded ridiculous. Me, asking if I were too young for anything.

Dr. DeJovne shook her head, smiling a "you poor dummy" smile. "Not at all, it's common for women your age. This is when your body starts changing, all in preparation for menopause."

Women my age? Geez! Enough already! When had I been lumped into the "women your age" category? If one more person said this …

Menopause? If this perimenopause thing was the forerunner for the big show, I was in for a world of trouble. Why on earth do they call it menopause anyway? It should be called meno-blast. I just feel so out of it sometimes. Like a blast furnace is blowing through me, first on, then off, then back on and I become irritated, blasting everything in my immediate vicinity. As it was, poor Karen probably thought that I was already losing my mind. Putting my jacket on, taking my jacket off, only to put it back on twenty minutes later shrieking intermittently at times "is it hot in here or is it just me?" then at other times "who changed the thermostat in here, it's freezing!" By the time menopause rolls around, Karen will either have throttled me or quit. Then it's bye bye brownies.

"Well, how long does this last? This perimenopause thing?" It definitely could not be over soon enough for me, I am certain that the Temptress would agree.

Dr. DeJovne laughed. "It can go on for years until menopause sets in. It could go on for ten years before menopause."

"Ten years!" I snorted. "I could kill someone in ten years if this keeps up."

Dr. DeJovne laughed again, that husky tinkling sound. "You are still able to have your cycles; you are still able to get pregnant, if you choose." She looked at my chart. "Are you using birth control?"

I started laughing out loud and Dr. DeJovne tilted her head, gazing at me quizzically.

"Dr. DeJovne, I'm using the best birth control there is. I haven't had sex for many, many moons now. Abstinence works wonders." Dr. DeJovne smiled at me, that slow knowing smile that made me a little uneasy.

"Well, Mikki. You never know. You're an attractive woman, sometimes women in their forties experience a sort of reawakening in that area. You may meet someone."

Maybe, I thought. I could, but I could also win the lottery. Neither was likely but you never knew it could happen; nonetheless, I accepted the prescription for the birth control patch that she recommended. Just in case, as Dr. DeJovne had intoned, I was not in the mood for any "surprises", not at this stage of my life.

From Dr. DeJovne's office I drove over to the Diagnostic Center located strategically down the street from the doctor's office. The technicians over at the Center were able to get me in that afternoon for the mammogram, lucky, lucky me. After answering what seemed like a hundred questions, I was given yet another little gown, this time with the opening in the front and was told to wait for the technician.

I was instructed by a reasonably nice young woman to stand in front of a machine, a loud noisy contraption that whined and groaned more than Dereon did when I brought the wrong kind of cereal home on grocery day. I was not at all prepared for what happened next. She rattled off instructions like a drill sergeant, her voice soft, and her directions firm. The thought of another woman handling my breast kind of freaked me out a little bit but I obliged anyway.

"Turn, turn, turn. That's great," the young woman instructed. "Ok, I need you to lean forward. That's great." Standing on my tiptoes, the lab tech coached me on the perfect stance to take to insert my breast into said noisy machine.

"OK, Ms. Robbinson, I need you to remember to breathe through this." The technician turned away from the whining contraption and smiled at me, a kind of tiny little "it stinks to be you right now," smile.

And at that moment, I understood why she smiled. What followed was agony, pure torture as this machine turned pure evil, grabbing my poor defenseless breast and squashing it flat, opening slightly to pause for a beat only to flatten it again.

Oh sweet mercy! What manner of madness was this! I felt the blood drain from my face and I wondered if it were possible for the evil machine to rip my breast from my body.

"Breathe," the technician repeated over and over again, though all I could think of at that moment was throwing up. Throwing up and then passing out. Just when I thought I would do exactly those things, the machine released me, opening its evil jaws with a whine.

"Ok," the technician said. "I know this hurts."

"You think?" is what I wanted to say but I was afraid that if I attempted to say anything catty, that machine would reach out and snatch my poor breast right off of my chest.

"Now we have to take a picture of the other breast." The other one? I blanched as I struggled to hold myself still as again the machine whined and clamped its mean flat panels on my other poor breast.

Lord help me! I wanted to scream. Peter, Paul and Mary! Anybody! Help! When at last the monster machine released me, all I wanted to do was limp off into the corner to cry, dragging my flattened breasts behind me.

"Ok, go ahead and get dressed, a doctor will look at your scans and come in to speak with you." She smiled at me again, and all I wanted to do was sob like a little girl.

"Wouldn't it have been easier to just slam my breasts in the door?" I joked half-heartedly with the technician, cradling my wounded flattened breasts in my hands. My poor girls, I mourned for them. They would probably never be the same again.

"Probably," the technician said. "But then we wouldn't have the pretty pictures to look at."

I smiled a sick little smile in her direction as she left the room, poking my tongue out at her as soon as the door had closed behind her. Torture over, the scans came back fine and I could finally tell Sonni, Niecee and Mama Jett that the girls, though they felt much smaller and flatter than before, were fine and to never mention it to me again, at least not until next year. Maybe I would develop amnesia by then and forget all about the torture I had braved today. Not likely.

Back at my meeting back at GBGC that afternoon, I felt that everybody knew about my mammogram, they had to. I felt that everyone could see underneath the silky Ann Taylor blouse I wore. The girls felt as if they had been smashed as flat as two paperback books, two very small paperback books, underneath my shirt. My chest hurt and I couldn't raise my arms, just moving around was as painful as if I'd gone a couple of rounds with a prizefighter.

I was so very glad that the meeting ended without a question from the group, maybe it was because I did such an excellent job with the presentation. Maybe it was because it was getting late and people were just ready to go home. Maybe it was because I looked as if I were going to throw up.

Bidding the Temptress goodnight, I loaded up my briefcase, lugging the strap over my shoulder, careful not to disturb my breasts; I'd done them enough harm for one day. Time to go home. Thank God!

Lawman

Day eighteen…

I wasn't sure, but I was beginning to think there may have been one too many people along on this date, I watched the pale amber of my wine as I swirled it absently in my glass. Actually, I felt almost guilty, like a voyeur watching this intriguing love affair, but I cannot escape, I cannot tear myself away. The attention and adoration that one lavished onto the other was uncomfortably embarassing, the fascination with the details and the appearance of the other, the self-assured smile, the longing glances and an occasional "I love you" whispered by way of encouragement to the other.

Ok, maybe he hadn't actually whispered, "I love you" to himself, but I was beginning to feel as if I was intruding in this tête-à-tête between him and his ego. The date had seemed promising initially; silly me, I had begun to think that maybe there was something to this online thing. As an Attorney working towards Partner in a local law firm, he was an absolute treat online with a profile that read like a "who's who" in our city; it appeared as if he knew everyone and everyone knew him.

I should have known what to expect, this guy actually included pictures on his profile of himself with various local celebrities whom even I recognized: a picture with the former Mayor of our city, various city council people, and local athletes. His profile read that his aspirations included a move from the practice of the law to parlay his experience and his contacts into a career in politics.

Ambitious, bright and cute? OK, I would bite. What could be wrong with Mr. Wonderful? Initially, we traded emails, cell phone calls, and he seemed a decent enough guy, even if he liked to talk about himself a little too much as every conversation was peppered with his goals, his dreams, what he wanted to accomplish. The bright future that he envisioned for himself as he moved from practicing law to the political track.

Silly, silly me, I agreed to meet Lawman. I know that I should have known better, but nothing ventured, nothing gained, right?

We'd agreed to meet at a little bistro to have a glass of wine and to get a feel for each other although I had begun to think that I probably already knew way more about him than I wanted to know. I'd dressed professionally, opting for a simple cardigan in a soft peach color over a matching sleeveless blouse with a pencil skirt and beige pumps.

Lawman met me at the door of the bistro with a firm handshake, pumping my hand hard up and down as he spoke with a clipped tone, his exchange professional.

"Mikki. Hi. So good to meet you."

"You too…" I murmured in return although I don't think he noticed that I'd said a word as he continued to scan the room and I half expected a member of the press to step forward to take our photo, another snapshot for his "Who's who" wall of fame. Vaguely I wondered how in the world I was going to retrieve my hand from his iron grip as he continued to pump my hand up and down in greeting, his eyes flitting about the room as if he might miss someone who might be more important than what he was doing right now.

He would do very well in politics...

I frowned, pulling my hand away from his grip to shake it slightly in an attempt to restore the blood flow to my poor crumpled limb. Waving to someone across the room, he directed me to a seat at the bar where I ordered a glass of white wine, and he ordered some kind of scotch on the rocks; I cannot honestly say that I really noticed what brand of liquor he'd ordered, but from what I'd already gathered from him about himself, he spared no expense on himself, insisting on nothing but the best.

All I could think of at this moment was that Lawman was a little too smooth, a little too practiced, a little too … I don't know, a little too slick. Almost…oily. I don't know what made me do it but only too late had I'd noticed that I'd unconsciously began to rub my hand against my skirt.

I honestly could not say that I gained anything in the exchange with Lawman as the conversation seemed to consist of a running commentary on himself and his goals, an unending dialogue of "Ok, enough about me, let's talk about me some more."

In the end, I just wasn't sure if there was room enough for me, him and his ego in the conversation; he seemed to be perfectly happy entertaining himself with tales about himself. Blah, blah blah, a constant montage about him, him and him again.

I watched him steal one glance after another at himself in the mirror behind the bar and I realized that he'd already found his significant other in himself. I felt like the third wheel in this weird threesome of he, himself and me — the outsider in this relationship, the odd man…er…woman out in this meeting as he continued to glance at his reflection, his hand smoothing over his neatly trimmed mustache and goatee, licking his lips ever so slightly to moisten them, adjusting his obviously expensive tie.

Satisfied with his appearance, he spared me a glance.

"So, Nicki," he began. Oh, is it my turn to speak? Wait a minute…Nicki? A sound like screeching tires filed my head as in my mind, the conversation skidded to an abrupt stop.

Wait! Hold on, did he just call me Nicki? Who the hell is Nicki? What the … how are you going to agree to meet someone and then get her name wrong?

"Mikki," I corrected him. I looked at me, baffled, confused at my audacity to interrupt him. "My name is Mikki," I stated.

He smiled, not even having the decency to look embarrassed at his gaff.

"Oh, of course. Mikki."

No…

I knew right away that this was not going to happen I didn't need any warning bells or flashing lights to tell me that this was not going to work. I needed to cut my losses and walk out of there.

"Look," I began, but Lawman cut me off. "Mikki, I think that I know what you are going to say."

So now he was thinking for me too?

"I want you to look at something," he said.

He placed his manicured hand into the inside pocket of his obviously tailor made blazer, pulling out a folded sheet of paper, holding it out for my examination.

Tentatively, I took the paper unfolding it slowly, stunned to see that he had listed the time and date of every text message and every cell phone call that he had ever made to me complete with an approximation of how many minutes each interaction took from beginning to end as well as a cost estimation of each call or text message.

Wait! Was I a client being billed for his…er… services?

"Mikki, you seem to be a nice woman, very intelligent with a good head on your shoulders."

I frowned, moving back away from him. Was this supposed to be some kind of compliment? He continued, unfazed by my discomfort.

"You seem bright and ambitious. I can appreciate that." He shrugged, leaning forward. "Admittedly, this is an odd way to open a conversation. But, as you can see…" he gestured toward the paper in my hand. "I have already invested a lot of time and effort in meeting you and would love to continue to get to know you better. But I have to know that I'm not wasting my time."

Wh---what? I felt my mouth go slack. This guy was impossible! Wasting his time? Wasting his time! My eyes narrowed as I stared at him, for once in my life at a loss for words, something that rarely happens. This man had gall that was for sure. To present a potential date with a listing, a written computation of the investment of his time and interest. This was certainly a first for me.

I looked again at the "bill", pretending to study it carefully, nodding as I did so. Yes, fifteen minutes on Tuesday, another fifteen on Thursday and five minutes today to confirm our meeting for this evening.

"Hmmm, yes, I see." I said, feigning an interest in the notations and columns of numbers. He actually seemed pleased that I was taking the time to look at this garbage, nodding enthusiastically as he leaned forward to study the numbers as well. I looked up at him, his bright eyes crinkling at the corners.

Oh you, I mused. You could have been a contender… I cleared my throat, sitting straighter on my barstool as I turned toward him, leaning a bit closer.

"I can see that you have invested quite a fair amount of your time in this endeavor…" I stated. He smiled, looking at me — only me - I think, for the first time that evening. Picking up my wine glass, I finished the amber liquid, no need to let good wine go to waste.

Nodding, I tallied up the costs of the calls and the texts and for my drink this evening. Reaching into my purse, retrieving my pen after which I wrote on the paper "Paid in Full" and signed my full name, Mikaela K. Robbinson.

Reaching into my wallet, I pulled out a twenty-dollar bill, handing it and the bill to Lawman.

"This should cover your efforts and our drinks. Have a nice evening." I smiled.

I picked up my purse and left the bistro without a single look back. As I walked out, in the reflection of the window, I could see that his mouth had dropped open in disbelief and I wanted to laugh out loud.

Not only had Lawman lost the moment, he lost my vote for whatever office he was seeking.

A Little Birdie Told Me

"Meekee!"

"Oh no!" I whispered, looking up from my spreadsheet to cast a glance at the open office door. I looked around my office for an escape, nope, nowhere to run, no way out except the window. Hmm... If I jumped out, would I make it?

I looked toward my open office door again, frowning. Maybe I shouldn't risk it; I had way too much to do today to pay the ER a visit. Maybe if I stayed really quiet, she would think I was away at lunch. No such luck, I could hear the staccato of those crazy high heels barely muffled by the carpet as she headed my way.

What on earth had happened now? The way the Temptress drew out the pronunciation of "Meekee" I knew that something major had happened and I was about to get the great big Brazilian version of it.

Oh goodness! What did I do now? I watched nervously as Karen entered my office with a flourish; all ruffled blouse, pencil skirt, stiletto high heels and expensive cologne striding into my office in a huff, her full generously lipsticked lips tucked out in a perfect pout I knew without a doubt was because of me or something I'd done. Or not done.

"Meekee, how come you no tell me?" She asked, red nails flashing as she gestured toward her face, obviously worked up about something or another.

Huh? Tell her what? Unable to move, I shrugged helplessly, afraid to say anything out of fear that those red talons would seize upon me and rip me to shreds.

"How come I gotta find out from somebody else? How come you no tell me? Me! How long I work for you Meekee?" Petrified, I said nothing; honestly I had no idea what to say!

Frustrated, the Temptress gestured again, launching into a tangent unlike any I'd seen to date and I stared at her, my mouth dropping open as those red nails flashed with every wild gesture. I caught more than one "mios dios" and who knows what else she was saying. I held up my hand, attempting to jump into the one-sided conversation Karen seemed to be having with herself.

"What on earth are you talking about?" I asked.

The Temptress stopped mid-sentence and looked at me, her ample bosom heaving against the restrictive miracle fabric of the white ruffled blouse that she wore. Shaking her head, she plunked herself down in the chair across from me.

"I hear from strangers that you are...how you say...looking for love?"

Oh...my...God... I felt lightheaded as the blood seemed to drain from my face. Oh...my...goodness...this was really bad. I put my hand to my brow, pressing at the pulse pounding there. Looking for love?

This was bad, really bad. Is that what the buzz around the office is about? Wait, since when have I become the buzz around the office? That would certainly explain the crazy looks I've been getting lately. This... this was what I had mentioned to Sonni. GBGC was a big company, but apparently it was not big enough, in the end, everyone still knew all of your business. Now the word in the hallways was that I was, how does the Temptress put it, looking for love?

"Why you no tell me yourself?" the Temptress accused, her dark eyes flashing. "I work for you tree years and you no tell me?" Again, the hands went up to stab at the air. She pursed her lips together, making a small "tsking" sound as she did so.

Tree years...I smiled a little, Well, yes, it's been a little while but honestly... It's funny, but when the Temptress is all wound up, her accent takes center stage and everything starts to run together. I decide that is not at all in my best interests to laugh at her at least not as long as she sat across the desk from me.

"Where did you hear that?" I asked instead. The Temptress shook her head with a dramatic roll of her ebony lashed eyes.

"From that Hank the cow dog in the break room."

I shook my head, rolling my eyes dramatically. Ah yes, you can always count on the appearance of break room gossip. I swear the telecommunications industry had nothing on the grapevine at GBGC. Got a secret, it will be in everyone's email before lunchtime. And now, that lunchtime email tidbit was about me. Damn it! I thought that I had been so careful when I'd set up my profile on the dating site; it figured that someone would see my profile and that would be all she wrote...

I leaned forward in my chair, lowering my voice.

"What did Hank say?" I asked, my conspiratorial tone inviting the Temptress to divulge more info. I had no doubt that if anybody could get Hank the Cow Dog, nicknamed justly for his snorting, howling laughter, to talk it would be the Temptress.

Heck, I have no doubt that just a little attention from the Temptress would have encouraged Hank to put his own mother up for sale.

"Hank told me that he saw your profile on the dating website he, how you say, prescribed to..." She smoothed her hand along her dark hair.

I smiled again, the action disappearing as soon as it had appeared. Wait, Hank's on the same site? Yikes, how had I not noticed his picture in all of the ones I'd looked at to date? Ugh...

The Temptress pursed her lips again, wrinkling that beautiful nose of hers. "I told him, you must be crazy Hank, I know Meekee..." she looked at me pointedly and I shrugged my shoulders helplessly.

"Sonni made me do it," I offered up impulsively, more than happy to throw Sonni under the bus being driven by the stiletto wearing Brazilian. "She made me promise to give it sixty days."

Oh God! Now I'm doing it! Just one look from the Temptress and I'm spilling my guts. What was next? I wonder how Mama Jett would feel about being put up for sale? Geez, in this prizefight, I didn't know who I was more afraid of, Mama Jett or the Temptress!

The Temptress nodded her head solemnly. "Meekee, I understand. You are very beautiful woman. And I agree, it is time to meet somebody...but not Hank." She leaned forward again, her nails tapping on my desktop for effect. She sniffed then, sitting back in her chair.

I laughed, agreeing totally. No, not Hank.

"You have absolutely nothing to worry about there." I told my new protector. "Hank is definitely NOT my type!" I smiled across the desk at her. She smiled back, then she leaned forward, dropping her voice and I found myself leaning forward as well.

"I knew something different lately, Meekee. You seem ... how you say ... spicy..."

I frowned. Me, spicy? That's twice I've heard that lately.

"Spicy?" I asked. The Temptress shook her head, struggling to find the right word. "How you say... punky?" She frowned as she tried again.

"Spunky?" I tried to help. She snapped her long fingers then, smiling. "That is it. Spunky..." she rolled the word around on her tongue and I marveled. Geez, I didn't say it quite like that, it sounded so much better the way she said it.

"Yes, spunky. You wear makeup now."

Ok…

"But I always wear makeup," I said absently. Maybe I downplayed my assets but I always wore my traditional brown lipstick with a little black mascara. I mean, I'm no Temptress, but I'm not hideous either…

"No, now you wear makeup. You changed it, you look really pretty now, and your eyes, and" The Temptress made a motion upward at her eyes, her fingers making a "pow" motion for impact.

"They are very beautiful. You changed what you do. And," she leaned forward again, her words hushed. "And you are wearing better underwear…"

My eyes as well as my mouth flew open wide. What? How on earth could she know that? I sat looking at her, openmouthed as she continued.

"How do you know that?" I asked, laughing nervously. The Temptress laughed then, the sound husky. Seductive…my God! I have to learn how to do that!

"A woman knows, Meekee. Good bras make you walk differently," she motioned upward with both hands at her ample and dare I say perky breasts. "Everything where they should be."

I looked down at my own breasts, of course she was right but I was still a little weirded out by the fact that another woman had checked me out without my knowing.

"You must take care of the package, Meekee" the Temptress said unashamed at her forwardness. The package? The Temptress motioned, first at me, then herself.

"Your package. Your body. You must take care of it and protect it at all costs. You must dress her and love her. We owe it to ourselves to keep ourselves beautiful." The Temptress peered around quickly then leaned forward, again her voice hushed.

"How old do you think I am, Meekee?" She asked her voice dropping again to that husky whisper. I frowned, puzzled. I am so bad at guessing ages, but I thought that I could put the Temptress into her mid thirties easily. Like I said, I am terrible at this kind of thing, I would rather not speculate just in case I was wrong. I wouldn't want her to stab me with those nails of hers. She smiled at my bewildered expression.

"I am older than you think, Meekee. I am fifty-two..." she paused for a moment to let that sink in. Again, my mouth flew open and I am sure I must have made some sort of sound because the Temptress smiled, nodding sagely. No way!

"But, you look so young!" I sputtered. She smiled knowingly.

"It's the package, Meekee I protect my package at all costs and you must do this too. I expect and deserve only the best for myself. No one is ever allowed to misuse or mishandle the package." She sat back in her seat, her smile supreme.

"This package is priceless. Do you not think I know these men look at me? They are interested in the package. Men always want what they cannot have." She laughed then.

"They know they will never get the package, but chase it they will. The package is sacred. You must respect it and cherish it. Never ever let anyone make you feel less than you are. I take care of myself. I eat right. I no let the boys touch. They must be special. They must deserve to have me."

* * *

"And the way she said you must protect the package at all costs, I can certainly see where she is coming from." I said over my shoulder to Sonni who lounged on my bed, paging through my new InStyle Magazine to amuse herself as she waiting for me to pull some outfits out of the closet about which I'd wanted her input.

I had downloaded a new app called "Pinterest" to my new iPhone and damn it all if it hadn't put the idea into my head to try to put together a lot of new looks using the clothing that I'd stockpiled but never worn. I knew that Sonni knew better than me what was going to work so we were assembling piles of what would stay and what would be given away.

"Damn!" Sonni mused, shaking her head in disbelief. "I wouldn't have pegged her for fifty-two. She looks great! I would have put her at mid thirties at the most."

"Me too," I agreed, turning around to hold the red jacket up for Sonni's inspection. She shook her head no and sipped her wine. Shrugging, I put the jacket in the "go" pile. I had to admit it was kind of ugly

"She knew I had on new underwear!" I laughed from inside the walk-in closet, pulling three identical black blazers down from the hangers. When on earth had I bought all of these? And...I pulled them open to look at the tag...yep; all were from the same designer. What had I been thinking?

I held them out of the closet for Sonni's perusal. Surprisingly, she agreed that I should keep them. You could always find use for a black blazer, she reasoned. I returned the blazers to the closet.

"How in the world could she know I had new underwear on?" I mused aloud.

Sonni laughed. "I don't know, the woman is a freaking vampire, this just proves it. How does she look like that at fifty-two?"

I laughed as well. "Don't know. Maybe she's draining the life force from all of those poor besotted guys that follow her around like puppies."

I came out of the walk-in, walking on my tiptoes and sticking out my chest, vamping it up for Sonni.

"I no let the boys touch," I attempted with my best Temptress imitation. Sonni rolled over onto her back, laughing out loud.

"You're crazy!" she told me, rolling her eyes.

Up, Up and Away...

Day twenty-two...Up and away in my beautiful balloon, that is.

I was beginning to learn that there were a lot of things that really bugged me about the whole online dating thing but what bothered me in particular was when people put misleading photos of themselves on their portfolio. I mean, coming from a marketing background, there is this little thing called truth in advertising, a concept that seemed to escape the comprehension of many of the guys that I met. What I was left with was a bizarre type of bait and switch, you know, when the store advertises something for sale only to find out when you arrive to pick up your merchandise, "Hey, we're out of that, but look what we have here!"

When I'd established my online profile, I - silly me — had uploaded an honest and simple description of myself along with the recent photos that Sonni and I had taken of me after our impromptu shopping extravaganza.

My intro had been straightforward: a forty-five year old single mom, ready to have some fun after raising my only child. I noted my likes and dislikes and shared that I was looking for a stable middle-aged man who would like to do the same.

So, I don't know, I might have been incorrect, even a bit naive, but if you profile yourself as a fortyish year old, why on earth is the photo that you've uploaded a photo of someone who is NOT forty? Maybe twenty-five, I don't know. But hey, it could be that this is the picture that one holds of himself in his mind's eye — you know, maybe a sort of forever-young thing.

But let's be real, if you are forty, unless you are a very, very good forty, why on earth would you upload a picture of yourself leaning against one flashy car or another? Or even more interesting, you upload a picture of yourself from your glory days complete with processed curly hair or a muscled physique that you would be hard pressed to try to resurrect post-glory days. The first thought that comes to mind is "what is this guy trying to prove?" Is he having a mid life crisis of his own where he is stuck somewhere in the past where the much younger, much slimmer and much more attractive him had been quite the man about town, picking up numbers wherever he went but now, probably spends more time picking up fast food than telephone numbers.

Hey, I get it; none of us are what we used to be which was why I decided to give Bud a chance. Bud had viewed my profile and decided to drop me an email.

"Hi Mikki, saw your profile online. Would really like to know more about you. Your profile is great! It's nice to see someone with an outlook as refreshing as your own. I too like to travel, enjoy good food and company. Would love to meet, no pressure, just to share a meal and to talk. I could meet you or you could meet me. Let's meet!"

Hmmm ... ok, so I was intrigued and had clicked on his link, clicking through to more pictures. Bud was well groomed and he had a really nice smile with even straight teeth and dimples. I loved dimples. And his eyes seemed to smile. That I did like. You can tell a lot about a person just from their eyes. His were warm, as if he actually had a joke to share with someone. His profile looked promising, and his picture was nice, he actually looked forty-five, a middle-aged gentleman, nicely dressed in a dark suit and tie; with cute little crinkles around his eyes, the kind that you get when you've spent a lot of time smiling. Or laughing. Why is it that these same little funny crinkles on men are called laugh lines, on us forty-something year old women, I believe they are called crow's feet. No respect.

After a short series of emails back and forth, we had decided to meet at a restaurant in town, an all-you-can-eat buffet that Bud said was his favorite; it was close to where he worked and since he said that he would be working late that evening, I did not see anything wrong with meeting him there. Something impromptu with no pressure, no expectations. Just testing the waters to actually meet in person before an actual "date".

I had taken the time to freshen my makeup before meeting Bud, careful not to apply too much, keep it light and informal, but still wanting to make a good first impression. I had changed into a simple sleeveless blouse and skirt with a handkerchief hem. On my feet I wore a pair of high-heeled strappy sandals that would have made the Temptress proud. I had twisted my curly hair into a cute bun with soft tendrils around my face and was feeling pretty good about how I looked, not totally glammed out, as Sonni would have said, but looking good and feeling good.

Maybe he would be nice... I hoped so; I'd seen some really weird stuff lately.

I had no problem finding the place. Pulling up to the home-style restaurant, I checked my reflection again in the rear view mirror, making sure that I didn't have lipstick on my teeth and that the Midwest weather had not caused my forehead to be shiny.

All right, let's do it, I told myself, willing myself to climb out of the SUV. I felt confident as I entered the restaurant, smiling as an elderly man held the door open for me. I looked around the cozy restaurant, wondering if I would know Bud when I saw him. Maybe I should have worn my glasses, but in a moment of vanity, I had opted for the contact lenses that I despised.

That was when I saw him. Stunned, I blinked, once, then twice, my mouth going dry, my heart seeming to slam to a stop.

Bud? Oh...my...goodness! Bud, at least the man who was Bud from the neck up, waved at me from the head of the line of the all-you-can-eat place.

Apparently he had been waiting for me at the cashier's stand and had identified me the second I had entered the place. I cannot say that I would have done the same, but if I had...

Oh…my…gosh! Now I knew why the place was one of his favorites. It was obvious that Bud frequented the place often, probably more than anyone should. Bud was all of 300 pounds, at least. Equally as obvious was the fact that Bud was *still* wearing the same suit that he had sported in the photo uploaded to his profile; the suit was shiny in spots from being laundered and pressed one time too many and it was tight. The jacket, buttoned at his waist gaped open at the top and jutted out like a propeller at the back to make room for his immense behind.

I felt my breathing grow shallow as my mind struggled to calm down and think this through. Ok, ok, breathe...you can do this Mikki, I told myself. Just go ahead and meet the man. A meet and eat. Eat? I think there had been way too much of that going on already!

Mind your manners, girl, I could hear Mama Jett saying to me. There is no excuse for bad manners or bad behavior. You will make the best of this and behave yourself. Yes, ma'am. I pasted a smile on my face, moving forward to introduce myself to him.

"Bud?" I extended my hand, flinching a little when he took my hand between both of his thick meaty sweaty palms. "It's so nice to meet you in person," I told him.

Bud's face was just as shiny as his suit, it was clear that he believed in using lotion to its fullest extent because his face was shiny, as were his hands, almost to the point of being slippery. He grasped my hand tightly, shaking it up and down, a big smile on his big shiny face, greeting me as if we were old friends.

"Mikki. You made it!" he gushed. My smile was tight, forced and a little scared. He motioned me forward with one of those thick hamburger hands. "I got here a little early so that I could get us a good table. Come on, let's have a seat."

Nervously, I followed him into the buffet-style restaurant, seriously feeling a little overdressed as I observed restaurant patrons in various states of dress. Bud's idea of having a "good table" was having a table close to the buffet hot tables so that he could see when hot and new food items were added to the line.

Bud was a gentleman, after seating me in my chair, he plunked his heavy frame into the chair across from me with a groan, finally unbuttoning his jacket to make room for the huge tummy that had tried in vain to hide behind the shiny fabric of his jacket.

I have to admit that Bud was great company. During our all-you-can-eat extravaganza, he'd proceeded to ask about me and my work and to tell me all about him and his work as an Accountant with one of the city's larger firms. There did not seem to be anything that this man did not want to share with me, his hopes, dreams, likes, dislikes, everything. He obviously had no dislikes when it came to eating.

He talked nonstop while stuffing himself past the full mark with crab legs, chicken legs, roast beef, mashed potatoes, gravy, corn, green beans, pasta salad, red jello, cinnamon rolls, and hot rolls with real butter. Salad, just for good measure and to "get his greens in" he said with a wink. In where? How is it possible that there was room for anything else in there? I was getting full just watching him.

Bud was truly a nice guy and I assumed that the picture on the website had once upon a time been him. Since the date the picture has been taken, Bud had obviously lived a lot of life, possibly spending much of it parked at the buffet down the street from where he worked.

Discouraged and frankly a little nauseous, I bailed out of the meet and eat before he could mow his way through the dessert portion of the buffet. It too was all-you-can-eat and it was obvious that Bud was just getting warmed up.

I rolled myself into my condo that night, washing my hands and taking an antacid to beat back the heartburn that began to burn a hole through my chest.

Lying across my bed, I kicked off my shoes, making a mental note to add Bud to my rapidly growing spreadsheet of "undatables" as Sonni had called them. I think I was finally beginning to understand Sonni's insistence that I maintain the spreadsheet, there was no way I wanted to accidentally repeat any of the so-called dates I'd had so far. Frankly, I don't think my stomach could have taken another date with Bud.

Auto-dialing Sonni's number on my iPhone, I lay back against the duvet and closed my eyes, listening to the phone ring once, twice, then the third time.

"This is Sonni, not here, but would love to talk to you. Leave your number. Thanks." I groaned audibly into the receiver.

"Sonni, I honestly don't know how I let you talk me into this craziness. I just had the most bizarre date ever. Call me."

Ending the call, I groaned and rolled over on to my side, my tummy upset and rumbling. Let's hope that she was having better luck than I was!

The next day seated comfortable in the rich soft leather of her sofa, I recounted the whole date to her, right down to the piece of dinner roll that had hung in suspended animation from the corner of Bud's mouth as he had talked and chewed, chewed and talked.

Sonni giggled as she refilled my wine glass. "How late did he stay?" she asked.

I frowned, shaking my head, pausing in the discussion to take a sip of my wine, appreciating the warmth that soothed through me.

"Girl, who knows!" I ran my hand through my curls, lifting them away from my neck, a hot flash interrupting my train of thought. "I just couldn't take it anymore. The man just kept eating and eating. And talking. I think I just lost track after a while."

Sonni's crack of laughter made me laugh as well. I rubbed my forehead, grimacing, remembering the awful tummy ache I'd gone to bed with and awakened with the next morning. I shook my head, remembering Bud's shiny little face as he'd stuffed himself with abandon, as happy as anyone I'd ever seen.

"It was fascinating, actually. Every time he would lay his fork down, I just knew that he was finished, but then he would start looking around, saying, "oh, I just have to have their peach cobbler, it's the best in town." I laughed again, remembering how he'd practically bounced in his seat with excitement.

"He kept looking at me as if to say, eat up girl, that's why it's all-you-can-eat. Better get what you can." I shook my head ruefully.

Sonni laughed out loud at that.

Mr. Know It All

Day twenty-five…

"High School Principal at a successful area magnet school. A leader in the educational community and Shaper of a new generation".

Sure, why not? I accepted Mr. Shaper of a new generation's coffee invite without hesitation. I had always been one of the first parents to volunteer for whatever activities were going on at Dereon's school, having participated in as many parent-teacher opportunities as I could. You name it I've done it: I've sold trash bags, candy bars and cookies; I've even supplied goodies for bake sales to raise funds for band trips and the like. Mentally I made a note to find more things to volunteer for now that Dereon had graduated, no more bake sales for me!

On the surface, the Principal and I seemed to be interested in a lot of the same things, education is so important and I found myself looking forward to an opportunity to get to know other like minded up and comers in our community.

We had decided to meet for coffee at the Starbucks in the country club district of our fair city. I made sure to dress carefully for our meeting, steering away from anything flashy, opting instead for a soft blouse in a creamy beige silk that paired well with the taupe colored pencil skirt I'd chosen to wear with matching high heel stiletto pumps. I accented the outfit with a soft silk scarf tied casually around my neck in tones of beige, taupe and melon and my favorite earrings. No rings, Sonni had cautioned. I kept my makeup simple but elegant, I could tell that this was a serious man and I wanted to make a good first impression. You never knew what could happen… I looked together and professional, something I was sure that even Mr. Principal would appreciate.

Upon entering the coffee shop, I was relieved to discover that I was able to identify him immediately. Hallelujah! I sighed, a smile touching my lips. Finally someone who looked very much like his profile picture. This was a good start. He appeared exactly as he'd presented himself online; a middle aged gentlemen with handsome smooth features and hair that silvered slightly at the temples, giving him a sophisticated, professional appeal.

He walked toward me; his pace slow and measured and he stiffly extended his arm to greet me, his hand shaking mine firmly. Ok… good initial contact, no overly friendly groping and squeezing. That was something at least.

"Hello, Mikki, glad you could come." He said his voice deep and controlled. I smiled back. Ok, Mikki, a very good start.

"Very good to meet you." I said simply.

He forced a quick smile at me as a stiff self-aware greeting, the action seeming to be almost painful. When he managed to coax a smile forward, I noted that he had straight beautiful white teeth with nice lips. No dimples, well, at least as far as I could tell. No smile lines either, I noted, but that is fine I guess. Steering today's youth in the right direction is a serious job that called for serious people. I guess that I could deal with that.

He was very tall, much taller and slimmer than I'd expected him to be, which, after the incident with Mr. All-You-Can-Eat, was a welcome surprise. He was simply dressed in a dark pair of slacks, a tailored tweed jacket with leather patches at the elbows and a plain white shirt underneath which he wore open at the collar, an ensemble that seemed out of place considering it was nearly ninety degrees outside. Oh well, to each his own.

Wire-rimmed eyeglasses over which he peered from time to time to study people who walked in and out of the coffee shop framed dark intelligent eyes. Very somber and serious looking, his eyes, I noted were quick and assessing, looking around, not settling on anything in general but viewing and judging everything, dismissing whatever did not meet his approval.

I felt a twinge of uneasiness, wondering if this was what he'd done to me when I'd entered the building…. I guessed that I'd passed the test, for now anyway. He walked stiffly as he led the way to the counter, his stature ramrod straight and unyielding as his eyes worked the room from left to right. Sort of like a soldier, I thought. Or a cyborg. He seemed to be a little uptight and I wondered if this could be because of his profession. I found myself hurrying to keep up.

"What will you have?" With a stiff gesture of his hand, he indicated that I should order first. Yes sir…

I smiled at the ladies behind the counter; I think they must know me by now; this was quickly becoming one of my favorite places to meet my "dates". I decided to forego the slice of lemon pound cake that usually accompanied my coffee of choice, a Caramel Macchiato, Grande with an extra shot of espresso and full fat, I might add.

Out of the corner of my eye, I caught a quick movement. I know that it couldn't have just been me, the young lady behind the counter noticed the change as well, her eyes darting up at him then back at me and she looked confused, a small frown crossing her cute features. I could have sworn that a look of disapproval had swept over his face, it was quick, but it was there, a slight but brief down turning of his mouth that creased those smooth aristocratic features just for a split second.

I frowned as well. Maybe I had imagined it. I glanced at him sideways. But the look had disappeared as quickly as it had appeared. He ordered a green tea for himself with raw sugar. Extra hot, he requested of the ladies behind the counter. What exactly was extra hot anyway, I wondered. Too hot to drink? Hot enough to remove the skin from anyone passing by?

He held himself rigidly, seeming to angle his frame away from me ever so slightly. Oh… I get it; maybe he had some kind of allergy to cream or something, a bizarre lactose intolerant thing. Maybe this was why he had disapproved of my choice of drink.

With a point of his long index finger, he directed me toward the back of the coffeehouse, suggesting that we retire to a corner to talk and to get to know each other. Now it was my turn to frown.

Pointing? Really? Dimly I heard the beginning tinkle of the warning bells way back in the corner of my mind. Maybe it was just me. Sitting down, he relaxed — well, if you could call it that — in a corner armchair with his scalding, hot as the sun green tea. I, with my Macchiato in hand, perched on the edge of a chair across from him, waiting for him to speak.

What was up with the whole brooding silence thing? Unbelievably, I was nervous, unable to relax back into my chair, and I began to feel awkward, a little weirded out even as visions of being pulled into the principal's office threatened to take over. Little Mikki began to squirm anxiously in our chair.

"Mikki." Mr. Principal would have droned in his serious tone. "I brought you here today to talk about what's been going on in your Biology Class". To which I would have retorted in my obnoxious snarky way that was so typical of Little Mikki, "Well gosh, Mr. Principal. I don't know what you are talking about."

I shook off the vision, trying to concentrate on what he was saying. Or not saying. The man was a Sphinx; he sat stock still in his chair, silently studying me across the increasing distance. I could understand how he got into his profession, beating the student into submission with the heavy club of silence that sat between the two of them, making the student sweat until he or she finally cracked under the pressure, confessing to just about anything. "I did it! I admit it! I hid Mrs. Percy's lab notes!'

So, ok, if he wouldn't start the conversation, I would but the minute I opened my mouth he began to speak. I would soon learn that the man, in addition to being intelligent and handsome, had an opinion about everything and would not hesitate to educate any and all who crossed his path.

Mr. Know It All crossed one of his long legs over the other and looked at me over those glasses, his perusal quick and assessing as he pulled a mini note pad from the breast pocket of his tweedy blazer.

Wait! Really? What was this, an interview? With his notebook and pen poised at the ready, he almost appeared to be a reporter, staring at me down the bridge of his nose as he waited for me to say something prolific.

Umm… I've got nothing…

"So, Mikaela," he began. "Tell me about yourself."

Mikaela… I frowned. It *was* an interview! Would the questionnaire and application come next? What if I got the questions wrong? Would I flunk? Would I be forced to slink out of the coffee shop in a walk of shame?

Mikaela - what was up with that anyway? Not even Mama Jett called me Mikaela, er…at least she hadn't lately, not unless I was in trouble... He called me Mikaela like I had been caught doing something I should not have.

"Well Mr. Know It All," I wanted to say. Those warning bells that had previously been relegated to the back of my mind were now front and center, clanging louder than a Salvation Army bell ringer at Christmastime.

Mr. Know It All began firing questions at me in rapid-fire succession like a machine gun. What are your likes, your dislikes? What brings you here?

When did you start online dating? How many dates have you been on so far?

How long have you lived here? Does your family hail from these parts?

How many in your family? Are you the oldest? Have you ever been married?

You have a son. What is he like? Is he involved in any sports, or extracurricular activities? Is his father in the picture? Why not?

You do know that it's very important that young men his age are involved in this, that or the other.

I'm assuming that there are male role models with whom he can relate, since you are a single mom and such.

Blah, blah, blah. My head was swimming as he peppered me for more and more information about all things Mikki. Ok, interview over, I was exhausted from all of the questions, now it was my turn. I threw myself into the one-sided conversation kamikaze style, artfully dodging yet another round of penetrating questions.

"So tell me about yourself," I began but did not manage to get in another single word. Apparently this turned out to be exactly the opening the Mr. Know It All needed, for he was more than happy to talk about himself, his ideals, and his opinions. And boy, did he have a lot of them.

Listening to him ramble on and on about one subject or another, it became apparent that he was the self-described authority on everything and anything when it came to world, local, national and international events.

I mean, really, this man put CNN, MSNBC, Court TV, National Geographic, the History Channel, Talk Radio, Public Broadcasting, 60 minutes, Imus, Rush Limbaugh, Kelly and Michael, The View, The Chew and everybody else to shame when it came to his facts and information.

He knew a lot and wanted to be sure that I knew that he knew a lot. He was more than happy to open this vast warehouse of knowledge to the not as knowledgeable, the unlearned, and me. I guess earning both a Bachelors and Masters Degree was not enough anymore, not when it came to Mr. Know It All.

Within the span of our hour long conversation, please note, the longest hour of my life to date, I knew everything about everything from global warming, the causes, the effects, the cause for the wildfires in California, the flooding and landslides in Colorado and what measures would need to be taken to get these natural disasters under control.

He was more than happy to offer his opinion on the Demi Moore and Ashton Kutcher fiasco — his words — and why an older woman/younger man relationship would never, ever work and the facts and statistics that pointed to their demise, spouting something about the "half-your-age-plus-seven" rule of thumb which defined whether the age difference in an intimate relationship is socially acceptable.

Socially acceptable? Who comes up with this stuff anyway?

I also learned from him what it would take to end the strife in the Middle East and bring peace to the region. I knew whom and why the Axis of Evil was who they were and what needed to be done about them.

It was also pointed out to me — no, perhaps dictated to me is a better description — why I should work harder at minimizing my carbon footprint and I "must think about the children," that I must use less, and become "more green".

In a single hour, I was educated in the reasons why the youth of America were so poorly prepared to move into a successful future as leaders in the new economy and how they were so poorly trained for the workplace and how we as parents were doing such a disservice to our children when we allowed them to pollute their minds with Nickelodeon, Disney Channel, VH1, BET and any and all music channels and videos.

Did I mention that Mr. Know It All had no children?

I learned about the fallacy of depending on Social Security to be there in the event that I would need it when I was ready to retire. Especially if I was depending on the poorly trained workforce, represented by our children that we as parents were spewing out left and right. Spewing out, he said... just the way he spewed out the word "spewing" made me want to laugh out loud but I decided against it.

Mr. Know It All even suggested that the products that I used, even to the extent of my choice of personal feminine hygiene products that I used and the makeup brands that I preferred could possibly be harming our world and that I should change my ways and not buy into the propaganda machine otherwise known as the beauty business.

Obviously in his world, beauty equals evil. I think that maybe fashion equaled evil as well in his eyes as I studied his tweedy jacket, noting more than a little wear on the leather elbow pads of his blazer.

The fate of the world rested on my silk covered shoulders it seemed as well as depended on the brand of lipstick that I chose to wear. I have to admit that initially I thought, wow, this was cool, this man had standards, and this man knew some things. This man was motivated. This man had a mission. This man was on a crusade. Heck, he was just plain mad as hell and he was not going to take it anymore!

Only I learned that this man was not just mad, he was mad at the world altogether for screwing up things for him and everybody else. Damn you women for wearing makeup! Things must change, he said time and time again. And we must begin with ourselves. Heck, I thought, let's just get a drum and beat on it and shout it to the world, "Change or die!"

I stared at Mr. Know It All, bewildered, and I began to think that this man was just plain wacky! I mean, he had taken the weight of the responsibility for the whole world on his bony shoulders, and though it was true that we all could and needed to make some changes, I was just not ready to be one of the many who goes about offending the rest of the world by throwing paint on fur coats or riding on a boat somewhere out in the gulf protesting oil drilling. What in the world did they think powered those huge boats anyway?

Obviously I had not realized that because I'm a woman, because I choose to wear cosmetics, without regard to all of the testing that goes into making my favorite lipstick or blush, I'm part and parcel responsible for some of, if not all of, the ails of the world.

Who knew?

But the one thing that truly rubbed me the wrong way was when he pointed that long skinny finger directly at me, and said "and you Mikki need to start doing your part..."

My head snapped back as if he'd jabbed me on the forehead with that bony cyborg finger and I wanted to jab him back right between those beady eyes. Ok...now, the interview really was over.

I smiled as stiffly and as politely as I dared, minding my manners. I rose to my feet, tugging my pencil skirt into place, straightening my scarf around my neck and pulled the strap of my purse higher onto my shoulder.

"Well," I began, pushing my shoulders back to stand taller. "Thank you for the coffee, it was really nice to meet you." I extended my hand, shaking his robot hand quickly; muttering something about it was both a pleasurable and informative meeting and got out of there faster than I could say Caramel Macchiato with an extra shot.

I could tell from the look of confusion on his smooth robot face that my actions "did not compute" in that ever-evolving highly functioning mind of his. I laughed. No, it probably didn't compute at all.

Call me selfish, but I just was not ready to take on the responsibility of the world tonight *and* switch from my favorite brand of cosmetics. On my way out of the coffee shop, I purchased a slice of my favorite lemon pound cake for the road. Maybe I did it just for spite.

I drove home to enjoy my one-woman rebellion in the peace and sanctity of my own home. Maybe the story of the woman who'd dated over thirty online candidates knew something that I was soon going to find out. Play the field, have some fun. Even if you never found Mr. Right, at least you'd find so many of the Mr. Wrongs that you'd pick up on it faster and not spend so much time and energy on working my way through the undatables.

My spreadsheet was filling up faster than I thought…

Incognito

Day twenty-seven…

Tucking my portfolio under my arm, I managed to pull the heavy coffeehouse door open without dropping everything, the heady aroma of coffee beckoning me into the building. I had arrived a good half an hour before the time that we were supposed to meet. On Saturday nights, the place seemed to be populated for the most part by the noisy throng of the skinny jeans and Dockers hipster crowd with their fedoras, converse tennis shoes and thick-framed eyeglasses.

I had dressed casually this evening, opting for comfort over glam, wearing a white belted sleeveless tunic over a pair of skinny jeans, my favorite pair of leopard print loafers on my feet and thick chunky jewelry to complete the ensemble. Cute but comfortable.

I had smiled broadly when my favorite barista had smiled at me, nodding his head as he had motioned toward my ensemble saying "How cute! Don't you look classy!"
Yes, I am so feeling myself this evening.

Taking a cue from Mr. Know It All's knack for studying others without being noticed, I spied a small table and chair against the far wall, purchased my cappuccino and sat angled strategically so that I could view — incognito — anyone who entered the shop.

I had brought some work home in a small portfolio that I kept with me in the car so I would have something to keep me busy while I waited. I thought that it might be a good idea to sit where I could look around the place, just another face in the crowd. Maybe check him out before we actually met.

I smiled at a gentleman at the next table who seemed to be intently studying anyone who entered the room. Meeting my eyes, he in turn, hurriedly buried his head in his newspaper. Ok, so maybe not him.

I really had no idea who I was looking for. When I had emailed the "gentleman" I was supposed to meet, he had written in return that he did not have a recent digital photograph that he could send to me. He had seemed like a really nice guy, we had spoken briefly on the telephone a few times. He sounded fine, there was no slurred speech, no noticeable speech impediments, he used the proper pronunciation of words, etc.

But something told me ... well anyway, being the online dating virgin that I am...er... I was, I just did not put too much thought into it at the time and against my better judgment, I said, that was fine. I had agreed that I thought it might be a good idea to meet over coffee.

I had asked what he would be wearing and he had been cagey, finally letting on that I should look for a gentleman in a blue suit with a white shirt and a patterned tie.

Ok... I looked around, cautiously. Not a tie in the bunch but in this crowd on a Saturday night, he would be fairly easy to pick out. There were not many men who would hang around the coffeehouse on a Saturday night dressed in suit and tie.

At promptly 7:00, I noticed that a "gentleman" had entered the coffeehouse. No one in the coffee shop could have missed his entrance, it was as if the energy had been sucked out of the room; you could feel his presence before you actually saw him. Perhaps this was because of the reactions of the people who took notice. I too allowed my gaze to follow the looks of others, halting in stunned horror at the spectacle that had entered the establishment.

Oh... my... goodness...!

At that moment, it became blindingly clear to me that the one caveat about online dating should be when a person neglects to put his or her picture on their profile, there is usually a very good reason.

The man wore a suit that was not only blue, it bordered on a cobalt royal blue kind of blue. I could say sky blue, but even that would be an understatement. This was a color never to be found in nature. He wore a white shirt underneath the blinding blue ensemble, not just a white shirt but a shirt with one of the biggest, widest collars that I had ever seen. I swear the tips of the collar touched the points of his shoulder blades.

And his tie! Oh my goodness! His tie! I don't think that I had ever seen anything like it! The sheer size of it reminded me of a large patterned sail of red, yellow and dark blue flowers. On the outside of his wide collared shirt and ultra bright tie, he wore a thick gold rope chain with a huge gold medallion that looked like something he'd stolen from an old school hip-hop rapper. To complete the dapper ensemble, on his head, he wore a wide brimmed hat angled just so to make himself appear to be suave and debonair. And he wore gold rings on every finger — every finger — and the biggest gold hooped earrings on his earlobe. A little rainbow pirate…

He swept off the big hat as he entered the building, one bejeweled hand rising to pat his damp shiny brow then up to smooth down his processed hair, dark waves of shiny, sticky looking processed hair that grazed the collar of his jacket. Lowering his arms, he snapped his sleeves, repositioning the toothpick that he held at the corner of his mouth; this was when I noticed the gap.

Pleased that he now had everyone's attention, he smiled at the awestricken crowd, revealing a huge gap between his two front teeth big enough to hold another tooth or two. He sauntered into the room, walking with an exaggerated swagger, his gait halting and jolting as if one leg were shorter than the other.

Oh my ... please God! Please say this is not him! Please say that this is not the man that I'm supposed to meet! Mr. Hip Hop strutted around the coffeehouse, looking like a blue, red and yellow peacock as he studied the faces of the women in the coffeehouse, who in turn looked away, terrified. I felt a cold trickle of terror as

I've never known seeping through my limbs. Numbing me, paralyzing me, a dull buzzing filling my ears, seeming to deafen me.

Sweet Mother Mary! Horrified, I remembered that my picture had been on my profile! No! Oh no! Arms! Legs! Please move! He would recognize me, of this I was sure. What the ... oh no! I had to get out of here! Must escape! Must escape now!

I ducked my head down as far as I could without crawling under the table. He was heading my way; did he recognize me from my profile? My heart hammered loudly and that shiny greasy head turned my way as if he'd heard its desperate staccato and he seemed to look directly at me. No! Please help! Anybody? Could I run? Would he chase me?

I tucked my head down again as I stuffed my things into my portfolio, then leapt up from my seat, hitting the table with my hip, causing my cup of cappuccino to rock back and forth on the tabletop. My hand went out to steady my drink to prevent upending it onto the table.

You've got to calm down girl, I told myself, trying to shush Little Mikki inside who by now had dissolved into a full blown panic attack. Ok, breathe. Keep your head down, Mikki! Don't even look at him! Try not to call too much attention to yourself. Stay calm!

Stay calm? I felt myself bordering on hysteria. Little Mikki was already there. How in the heck does once stay calm in the face of impending doom? All I wanted to do was run out of there before Mr. Hip Hop wandered over to me. Where was my purse? I looked around frantically, I had to have my purse, the keys to the getaway car were in my purse! Oh...ok, good, there, there it is, I had dropped it on the floor when I had jumped up from my seat. I swept the purse from the floor, never taking my eyes off of Hip Hop for one second as I thrashed my hand inside until I found the oblong key fob.

I peeked up through my lashes, managing to stifle a little scream. He was heading my way! Oh God! He is coming! OK, hands stop shaking. You got it? Keys, coffee, portfolio, must go now.

"Now!" Little Mikki screamed.

Mr. Hip Hop stopped a couple of feet away from me; from my location with my head in the down position, I saw that on his feet he wore shiny patent leather shoes. Oh my gosh! Could this get any worse? The man was wearing black and white wingtips! And they went with absolutely nothing that he was wearing.

I stole a glance upward as he stood mere inches away from me looking around. His forehead was gleaming; I had no way of knowing if this was from perspiration or if it was from whatever it was that he had put on his hair. He frowned, looking over my bent head. Then he removed his toothpick from his mouth. I gulped.

That's it, he saw me…

"Are you Mikki?" He said. I felt my heart plummet to my knees and I wanted to crawl out of there, crawl away into a corner and die. I looked at him, not daring to say a word, not daring to even breathe. Then I noticed that he was not looking at me.

He was not looking at me? Thank God in heaven!

Out of the corner of my eye, I noticed a pretty younger woman standing almost directly behind me. She had been standing, waiting for someone, maybe for her own online date. I didn't know and I was not going to stick around to find out. I saw the young woman look around, then look behind her, hoping that Hip Hop was talking to anyone but her.

"Are you Mikki?" he asked her again.

The pretty woman stammered, flustered, a look of panic crossing her pretty features.

"No, I'm sorry sir, I think you must have me confused with someone else," she stammered, her face blanching, then flushing.

"Huh ... are you sure?" Mr. Hip Hop asked her, convinced that she was not telling him the truth. "You are an awfully pretty young lady. What's your name?"

The girl made a strangled sound, her shaking hand going up to clutch her throat.

Oh, poor girl! I groaned audibly from my spot on the floor. I knew that I was going to hell now as punishment for this crime against womankind. A woman should never leave another woman behind but I had no choice! I had to save myself! I should have thrown her a lifeline, taking her aside as if I were the friend that she had been waiting for. But I couldn't, my only goal at that moment was to escape unrecognized by Hip Hop. I flashed her a pitying look. I'm sorry… I backed away from the scene unfolding before me.

The poor woman looked as if she was either going to throw up or burst into tears. Looking as if she had been pushed out into oncoming traffic, the expression on her face was one of complete awfulness. Coffeehouse patrons stared aghast at the bereft woman, probably wondering if they were together, staring aghast at the scene unfolding, something too horrible to imagine.

Oh…my…gosh! I was not going to stick around for the rest. Go! Go now! I forced myself to leave the building on wobbly legs, not daring to look around, not looking back. I stumbled through the side door, down the steps and onto the sidewalk, sticking the landing and walking as quickly as I could, keeping my eyes straight ahead.

I had scary visions of Hip Hop bursting through the doors of the coffee house to pursue me. Stop that woman! We have a date! Hold it right there! I know who you are!

I did not slow down until I reached my SUV, pushing the buttons on the key fob a number of times to open the door. Sliding behind the steering wheel, I slammed the door behind me, ducking down a little. Only then did I notice that my legs were shaking, not because I was afraid, but because I just could not control the hysterical laughter that erupted from me once I'd entered the sanctuary of my SUV.

I knew that I should feel bad, I mean, I just stood the poor guy up. No, I'm not saying that I was proud of myself; in fact, I was a little ashamed at my response for what I had just done. I know! Shallow, shallow Mikki!

But in my own defense, I had been lied to as well! I mean, he did not actually say that he was tall, dark, handsome and well dressed, but he also did not tell me that he was going to be dressed like a pimp out on a Saturday night. Unfortunately, the young lady that had been standing behind me had to deal with the repercussions of my actions. In my own defense, I was not what he was looking for either, I mean, really, I was standing right in front of him and he had looked right past me, which was fine with me.

I drove home as quickly as I could, stopping only at red lights and at my favorite Chinese takeout restaurant for a little fried rice and crab Rangoon therapy. I would salvage this evening somehow.

Upon entering my condo, I immediately queued up my laptop, determined to block any further emails from Hip Hop.

Dang! I stared at the screen. Obviously I hadn't driven home fast enough. Hip Hop had already managed to get in an email.

"Mikki, I'm so sorry that we weren't able to meet at the coffeehouse. I was really looking forward to meeting you, from your emails, I could tell that getting to know you better would be fantastic. Maybe we can arrange another get together, maybe out to dinner this time, you and me. I would like that very much…"

No, no, no! Hell no! I stopped reading after that. Was he kidding! I had seen enough, more than enough! I felt sorry for the young lady who had been mistaken for me, remembering the look of trepidation and confusion on her pretty face. But there was no way I was going to get in front of that train, I would just have to say a lot of prayers or do a lot of good deeds or something later as penance for my transgression.

I deleted the email, adding his phone number to "block contact" on my iPhone and made a mental note that I would have to ask Dereon or Sonni later how to block any further attempts to link up!

McScreamy

Day twenty-eight…

Hmmm… I leaned in closer, squinting as I studied the tiny face on the screen. Sighing loudly, I rolled my eyes at my own narcissism. Perhaps now would be a good time to banish my vanity and invest in a good pair of readers instead of the cheap drugstore variety that I seemed to purchase by the dozen. I didn't seem to be able to see anything lately, especially on this little laptop screen. And had I held it on my lap the way it was intended to be used rather than on the countertop, I wouldn't have been able to read a word.

Never needing glasses previously, since becoming a woman of a "certain age," I found that I needed quite a few more things than I'd needed before. Things like reading glasses. More bathroom breaks. More sleep, though once my head hit the pillow, sleep was anything but a reality as I spent most of my nights tossing and turning, kicking the covers off only to hug them back up to my chin minutes later, seeming to freeze to death.
Damn hot flashes.

And damn! Internet dating was becoming more and more time consuming. Lately the majority of my time online was spent sorting through the mountain of garbage that filled my box, messages consisting of propositions for various and unmentionable things from "Hey would you like to…" or "You look delicious, why don't we meet to…" or "Hi, you look great, would you send me some private pics, wink-wink" or "Hello, Lick sent you a special photo". Or one of my all time favorites, "Hi M, would you like to see my…"

Um … no, I don't think so.

This latest profile seemed interesting though and the gentleman seemed to be saying all of the right things. Feeling adventurous, I clicked over to investigate. I nodded slowly, my lips pursed. Good picture, he seemed to be just what Dr. Sonni would have ordered, nice looking, clean-shaven, with a nice smile. I scrolled down to read the rest of the description.

If his profile could believed, and I only say this because of the number of works of fiction I'd read lately on the service's website, but if the profile was correct, the gentleman had a responsible job in Hospital Administration with one of the area's largest hospital groups. Sounds promising.

I hesitated for a second, my fingertips drumming against the countertop. I'm a successful forward thinking woman, right? Maybe I should email him first, you know, just as an introduction. Sonni would be so proud, look at me, all "growed up" making the first move and all.

But wait …, Was there really anything wrong with my approaching him first? I wondered if he would be receptive to that kind of thing. I sat on the barstool in the kitchen, running my fingertips through my hair as I thought out loud. In spite of what they say, I was learning that men could be a little strange about women who approached them first, I mean, even though they say that they appreciate a woman who is bold enough and is willing to go after what she wants, I am learning that what they say they want and what they really want are two different things. Then again, I didn't want to reek of desperation. I mean, this is me, chasing a guy around. Did I really want to be "that woman"?

I groaned aloud sitting back on my seat, rubbing my tired eyes. Ok, I'll bite, I decided, continuing to surprise myself with my newfound forwardness. This is a new day; I can do this, I'm successful in my own right. I have my own job, responsibilities, and a mortgage. If he is as forward thinking as he says he is via his profile, and as forward thinking as I thought myself to be, then he would not be intimidated by my emailing him first.

So, I did it. I emailed him. God help me…

"Hey, enjoyed your profile," my email read. "Looks like we might share some of the same interests. Would like to meet for coffee to find out more about you."

Bam! I hit enter key, feeling more than a little proud of myself. Smiling, I sat up straighter on my seat, stretching my aching back muscles, my fingers reaching for my drinking glass. I was feeling quite pleased with this "New Mikki," even if the "Old Mikki" was having a little trouble getting with the program, continuing to jabber repeatedly and endlessly about the lunacy of this new program.

Wh-? My attention was drawn to the little message indicator that popped up in my box almost immediately. What was up with that? It was as if he'd had the dating site cued up waiting for that little electronic wink to pop up in his box. Waiting...

Anybody? Anybody? Should that worry me? I was beginning to get that "stalker vibe," but headed it off. Give him a chance, Mikki, it could be that he happened to be online checking at the same moment... He invited me out immediately.

"Hi Mikki," his email read. "I liked your profile too. Rather than meet for coffee, how about we do dinner?"

Dinner... I hesitated, my fingers hovering over the keyboard as I worried my lower lip between my teeth; long seconds ticking by as I deliberated. A meal, not coffee... I frowned. Meeting a potential date for a meal flew in face of all of the "dating rules" that Sonni had made me all but recite back to her verbatim. And, call me crazy, but I still could not get the "date" with Bud the eating machine out of my mind. If I had to do a repeat of that one, I would have to ... I shuddered, rubbing my hand across my midsection. Ugh! I just could not think about it, my stomach just could not handle it. Besides, I think I may be out of antacids...

Yes or no? Come on Mikki, what happened to the adventurous Mikki of a moment ago? A woman's got to eat, right?

OK, dinner it is. Why not? I relented, slowly typing my response as I ignored Little Mikki's nattering in the background.

"Would love to get together over a meal." I responded.

Remembering Mama Jett's warning to never allow a stranger, no matter how nice he appeared to be, to pick me up at my home, I fired off an email agreeing to meet him at a specified location at 7:00, regular people time.

* * *

At 7:30, a half an hour later, I was still waiting in the parking lot of the restaurant he'd indicated in the email, my car running with the air conditioner working overtime. Kansas City summers were hard on a girl's hair and makeup and I did not want to show up at our first "meet" looking as if I'd run a marathon.

I spied him across the parking lot, noting that he'd parked in the fast food restaurant's parking lot rather than the parking lot of the restaurant he'd chosen.
What the …

He looked around the parking lot, his brow furrowed as he visually checked each car in the lot, spotting me an instant later from where I watched him. Frowning…. Smiling, I raised a hand tentatively as a greeting. His frown seemed to deepen. Ok…

"It's not too late girl," Little Mikki whispered. "You could put the car in gear and burn out right now."

Still frowning, he motioned with an exasperated wave of his hand for me to come to where he stood waiting. I felt my brow rise as I studied his face across the lot, his handsome features screwed up into something like frustration.

Not too late…

"Ok, keep calm, Mikki," I cautioned myself aloud, still wanting to give him the benefit of the doubt. Maybe he's had a bad day, maybe that is why he is running late, and maybe he had been concerned that we would miss our reservation.

After one last look in the vanity mirror, I climbed out of my car, taking care to straighten my pencil skirt and blouse. Here we go.

I headed in his direction, vaguely wondering why he remained where he stood, not bothering to meet me even halfway in the parking lot. I was more than a little surprised when he walked ahead of me into the McDonalds restaurant.

Fast food... McDonalds? Really? You have got to be kidding!

No, really, we were going to eat fast food for a first date. What am I, seventeen years old? I looked down at the first date outfit I'd put together with painstaking care; the sleeveless poplin blouse I'd paired with a slim pair of ankle pants and a pair of cute sparkly bejeweled sandals that showcased my fresh pedicure in OPI Big Apple Red. Hardly McDonald's attire.

He stepped inside the building, holding the door open for me with one arm stuck behind him but only barely. Ladies first... I followed him inside, grabbing the door so that it would not fly back and hit me on the heel once he'd released his hold on the door. Such a gentleman.

Groaning inaudibly, I could feel my brow rising so far that it could now be a part of my hairline. Entering the busy restaurant, we were greeted with all manner of acts of mayhem occurring simultaneously.

A sweet little girl, all pink cheeks and curls... and mud and grass, bounced around the lobby, jabbering nonstop about "French fries! I want French fries mama!" while her mother, oblivious to the racket, stood nearby studying the menu, an infant in a hand-carried baby seat balanced precariously in the crook of her elbow as well as a large bag that probably served as purse, baby bag and whatever else.

"I know honey, just wait," she advised absently. Obviously Little Honey was not big on the whole waiting thing and continued to bounce to the mantra of "French fries, French fries," fascinated as the blinking lights on her tennis shoes kept time as she did so. Oh Lord, I cringed every time those little light up tennis shoes hit the ground, flashing pink lights blasting in my direction from *My Little Pony's* blinking eyes and nose.

A teenager stood impatiently next to his grandmother as she deliberated quite loudly with the female team member behind the counter about what comes on the Big Mac.

"What's in that special sauce anyway?" she asked and the teen rolled his eyes, earning a smile from the teenage girl behind the counter. Yep, this is why I use the drive thru…

And my so-called date … I huffed, annoyed with the direction in which this "date" had detoured. Once inside, he never even bothered to introduce himself, simply saying "Hi Mikki" as a greeting, then walking ahead of me up to the counter. Yikes…

We placed our order with the girl behind the counter, a super-sized extra value meal for him and a regular size value meal for me. Don't get me wrong, McDonalds is fine, it is edible and will do in a pinch, but it was certainly not my idea of date food. I made a mental note that I would save my calories for something much tastier later.

The young lady read the total due for our meals. My date made an earnest show of searching his pockets for something, appearing confused when he could not find what he was looking for and I realized what was happening. Oh no he did not! He was actually going to pull this? He turned in my direction, smiling sheepishly at me.

"I … I don't know what happened. I must have left my wallet at work. Mikki … would you mind?" He asked, putting on a good show of appearing to be exasperated. Sure, the old "I must have left it at my desk" trick. Or my other suit, or whatever the line was. Fine. I frowned, reaching around to fish in my handbag for my own wallet. Furious, I paid for the meal. Di—sas—ter.

"Thanks, Love," he said with a wink. "I'll get the next one."

I laughed out loud at that. The next one? Right. Hell no you will not! I returned my wallet to my purse. There will be no "next one," of that I was sure.

The instant our food was placed in front of us on the counter, my date grabbed his sandwich from the tray, tearing the wrapper open to stare down at the sandwich as if it had slapped him. Then he glared at the girl behind the counter, his face seeming to turn at least three shades of red as he tossed the sandwich back onto the counter.

"Look at this!" he screamed. I stared at him. The girl stared at him. Everyone in the restaurant stared at him as a hush fell over the lobby. Even Little Honey stopped jumping up and down. He picked up the burger, ripping off the top bun, then he slammed both halves down onto the countertop, the pickle flying off of the sandwich as rehydrated onions littered the cold stainless steel surface. He launched into a full frontal attack on the young lady behind the counter who cowered away, not understanding why he was upset. Well, maybe upset was not the word; she did not understand why he was acting crazy. I didn't either and found myself taking a step away from the crazy person as well.

"No onions!" He screamed at her. "I plainly told you no onions! Is it so hard to get a simple order right? It's not rocket science, sweetie, it's just a sandwich!" He threw his arms into the air, stepping away from the sandwich melodramatically.

"I … AM … ALLERGIC! What if I had not looked at my sandwich? What if I had eaten those? I would die! You are trying to kill me! Is that what you want?" He shrieked, his face seemed to purple from the neck up over the collar of the business shirt and tie that he wore.

Well, I mused silently. If he had eaten the sandwich, we would not have been treated to the spectacle of his little performance.

He slammed his hands down on the counter for emphasis. "No onions, that was all I asked for! Nothing special!"

He continued to berate the young girl on her sandwich order skills and inadequacies and I stared in confused horror as it became blatantly clear to me why my date was still on the dating circuit.

McScreamy was an angry man. Well, I don't know, maybe angry was a little too vague; McScreamy was a furiously terrifyingly angry man who obviously had a problem controlling his anger.

I stood stock still, horrified and mortified. Oh God, how could I get out of this? How could I leave the building before anyone figured out that I had come in with this lunatic? I wanted to back away from the scene and bolt from the building, to hell with the meal I had just paid for. The girl behind the counter paled visibly and I felt as sick as she looked.

It's ok, Mikki, I cautioned myself. Let's just eat and then I will go home — alone — and forget that any of this happened! Thankfully the manager intervened and presented McScreamy with a sandwich more to his "specifications". Silently, I wandered deeper into the restaurant to find a booth. Anywhere that would allow me to escape the pitying glances of the other people in the restaurant.

McScreamy followed me to our seat in the corner, choosing to behave as if nothing had happened. No, I mean really, he gave me a little smile and a shrug, then proceeded to dig into his meal with the concentration of a starving man. I don't know if he even noticed me sitting across the booth from him.

I made a half-hearted attempt to start a conversation with McScreamy but those attempts were met with one-word answers or grunts or simply a stare that indicated that I was interrupting something very important. Oh no… Maybe I'd better not interrupt, he might throw his sandwich at me next. Then, there would certainly be something for the restaurant patrons to see as I would be forced to choke him out afterward. Heck, the other folks in the restaurant would probably throw me a parade after the way he'd behaved.

I rolled my eyes, giving up, there was going to be no dinner conversation with McScreamy. Apparently his mouth only served two purposes, eating and belittling those he felt were beneath him. When he was not screaming at scared little girls, he was shoveling food into his trap as quickly as he could. It was probably for the best anyway. If he had started screaming at me, well, let's just say I would not be responsible for what happened next.

Just when I thought that this fiasco could not get any worse, it did. McScreamy, without skipping a beat, reached across the table and began to eat my fries.

What the hell?

Without skipping a beat, McScreamy finished off my fries in addition to the super sized meal he had ordered for himself — at my expense. He then shook his now empty cup and looked pointedly at me as if to say "are you going to finish that?" his eyes darting down to look at my untouched cup. He reached forward, his intention clear. He was going to take a drink out of my Coke!

Oh no! Hell no! I whipped my cup off of the table and beyond his grasp. I don't think so! This meal was over and so was the so-called date. After the strange meal, I said all of the usual proper things: goodbye, it was nice to finally meet, knowing that for me, this would be the end of it.

McScreamy, finally remembering to be a gentleman, followed me over to where I had parked my SUV, whistling at my choice of vehicle, commenting something to the effect of "that's a big car for a little lady".

I pursed my lips, shaking my head, not caring what he thought or what he said, I just wanted to get away from this nut and find something to eat, especially since I hadn't had the opportunity to eat my own meal.

"So, Mikki, why don't we go back to your place and get to know each other better," he said. In my mind, I heard to squeal of brakes as my train of thought came to an abrupt, clattering halt.

Is this guy crazy? Well, skip that, I knew he was crazy after what had just gone on in the restaurant. Was he honestly going to consider this a successful first date and try to take it to the next level?

I opened my car door, tossing my things inside and turned to look at him as he stood nearby, smiling. He actually had the nerve to wink at me. Yuck! As if I would to invite him back to my place for coffee or something. There would definitely be no "or something"!

I am certain that my look of disgust must have conveyed the proper message because he eventually took his leave, stomping back across the parking lot to his own car. He would probably find a dog or cat or something to kick on his way home.

By the time I'd wandered home, McScreamy had already left me an email, thanking me for dinner and asking when we would do it again!

Delete, delete, delete!

Meet Me...

Day twenty-eight...

Again? I'd retired for the evening, changing into my uniform of sweatpants and one of my oldest, softest college t-shirts. Lying across my bed, the only thing on my agenda for the rest of this evening was to catch up with my favorite television shows that I'd recorded on my Tivo. So when the email pinged, I was more than a little peeved as I'd had to press the pause button yet again.

Yet another email! From him! Stalker guy just would not quit! I scanned the newest email quickly, yet another invite for coffee or dinner or whatever.

"Mikki, what do I have to do to get a chance to meet you? Just meet me, once, in public at the place of your choosing. Broad daylight, just meet me for coffee, bottled water, whatever. I really would like to get to know you."

Ok, I thought, this was strangely bordering on stalker. He was persistent, I would give him credit, but what was this, the third...fourth email? Should I report him? I mean, it's not to the point where it could be considered a nuisance, but it was certainly strange. I mean, how many times do you have to say no before someone finally gets the message that you mean it?

No, stalker guy, I huffed. Not only are you interrupting my television time — how dare you interrupt Scandal - I will not see you. I will not meet you. Either he is persistent or just plain crazy and crazy was not what I needed right now. Maybe I should report him. But why? He really wasn't saying anything weird or wrong. I read the message again, skipping over to look at his picture again. Still very handsome...and so polite. Actually he was very polite and well spoken. How would that look? Yes, I'd like to report this guy because he seems like a nice guy but I am just not into him?

I pursed my lips wryly, the administrators probably more than had their hands full with all of the legitimate complaints that they probably already received day in and out because of some of the crazy messages. Trust me, I'd received more than my share of those already with the number of propositions I'd received during my short time on the site. Why add to the insanity? No, I would just ignore them; eventually he would get the hint and go away.

I was going to delete this email with the others... wait, what was this? Out of sight out of mind, I thought that I had deleted the others already, but there they were, winking at me like guilty little secrets in my email inbox.

What ... well, I should have deleted them a long time ago. But, I could not, I found myself strangely, I don't know, flattered I guess. How long had it been since I had been pursued by anyone? And no, a hungry teenager wondering what was for dinner did not count.

In a weird kind of way, it was kind of a turn on. This man, a successful man, if even a minute of what he had written was true, was after me. Sending emails, practically begging to meet. Ok, maybe begging is a bit strong, but it was still a big boost to the ego.

Maybe I should email him back, I mean, maybe he had the wrong email address. And, I could just nip this in the bud. It seemed a shame to allow this man to waste so much of his time on something that was not about to happen.

So, I emailed him. Short and sweet, "Maybe you were trying to reach someone else, or you've mistaken me for someone else. Thanks but no thanks". That should do it.

His return email came three hours later, and I have to admit, I was a little surprised, and a little disappointed that it took him so long to respond. So much for flattering myself. No, he was not mistaken, he'd said. He had meant to contact me and still wanted to meet.

Absolutely not, I decided, sending his email to join the others in the delete folder.

Mr. Clean

Day thirty…

I smiled absently, stirring my cappuccino as I watched my newest coffee date. This was going well, I mused, a self-satisfied feeling enveloping me.

This time I had been more selective. I had vowed to myself that I would not simply look at a nice picture and decide from that whether he was a good guy or not, nope, this logic had failed me way too many times already.

This time I would be more discerning; I would read the profiles much more carefully. I would correspond, via email, at least three or four different times before deciding to meet. I would select the place where we would meet. This time I would be the one who would gauge his responses to my questions. And heck, I wasn't even going to get started with the dimples thing.

I was learning that online, every guy can appear to be Prince Charming, it's only after you've agreed to meet them that you figure out a toad is still a toad, no matter how nicely dressed or well spoken. You've screwed up. Again.

I smiled slightly, you would think that in my line of business, I would know better, the profiles I've read to date could be considered a few of the most successful advertising campaigns I've ever seen, selling the sizzle, not the steak; it's only after you've made the investment of your time and your emotions that you discover that your initial "purchase" was not nearly what you were expecting. The sizzle was all there was.

Had I chosen wisely this time? I looked across the table, sipping my coffee. Only time would tell, but we were certainly off to a good start. Maybe I was getting this thing down. Lord knows I'd run into more than my share of nuts in the past weeks. I smiled across the table at him. He beamed at me. I crossed my long legs. He smiled even more. Ok…this just might work.

His profile had been interesting. No alarms had gone off. Again I'd chosen to meet at the coffee shop. After McScreamy and the Eating Machine, I was not going anywhere near a restaurant, certainly nowhere near food of the "all-you-can-eat" variety. I would keep it simple, just coffee, that's it. I had planned to sit tucked away in the corner so that I could watch the door but was surprised to be greeted at the door by a well groomed man with a broad smile on his face. He'd obviously been waiting for me.

He was not short or tall. He was just kind of a medium build and was medium looking. Just an average guy. That's fine. Average is fine. His mustache and beard were neatly trimmed and his suit was of a good quality; his trousers were nicely pressed and creased and his jacket was a good fit with no shiny spots and as far as I could tell, it did not hide any surprises of the oversized belly kind.

He stood apart from the crowd, rubbing his hands together vigorously; initially, I thought that it was because it felt chilly inside, then I realized that he was rubbing hand sanitizer on his hands. Ok…that is fine, I guess. The man is into hygiene; this was definitely not a crime, especially considering some of the things that I had seen lately.

He had smiled broadly as we shook hands, introducing himself and suggesting that we place our orders. He did not bat an eye when I placed my order for my favorite coffee, full fat, and non-sugar free. Good start…

"That sounds good." He had stated enthusiastically and proceeded to order the same. When I reached for my wallet, fully prepared to pay for my own drink, he stopped me with a gentle hand on my elbow.

"No, Mikki, this is my treat. How about something to eat with your coffee?" he suggested.

Hold the presses! He actually wanted to feed me? This one might work! I ordered my lemon pound cake and he decided on some kind of raspberry crumb cake thing. Ok, we were off to a very nice start.

We'd sat down at a small table out of the flow of traffic, a quiet spot to sit and speak for a bit and I was surprised to find that he was very attentive. From our conversation so far I found out that he was a civil engineer for the city government. He was intelligent, had a lot of things to say, and he did not knock the choice of my brand of cosmetics nor did he demand that I save the world tonight. He seemed genuinely interested in my stories and laughed often. Alas, no dimples but no matter, I guess there would have to be a tradeoff somewhere.

I was having such a nice time that the usual hour that I allotted for these initial meetings came and went with little notice. He was funny and smart, he seemed genuinely interested in me, and to his credit he did not flinch when I mentioned my teenage son, the true test for any of the men I would meet: would he balk at the mention of Dereon? That was the deal breaker.

He cleared this hurdle with flying colors, asking about Dereon, his interests and what he intended to study when he went away to college in the fall. Engineering, I told him, feeling more than a little proud of my offspring and he nodded his head agreeably, relating easily to Dereon's choice; commending me on the job I did raising a son as a single mom and my accomplishment of sending him off to good college. No quips about the under trained workforce from this one…take that Mr. Know It All!

Mama Mia! I thought. Could this be true, could this really be happening? Already, I was thinking ahead to how this might end. I liked him. He liked me. We seemed to hit it off just like that. We were into the second hour the date; I think you could officially call it a date now, right?

Careful girl, I could hear Mama Jett's deep assuring voice cautioning me. "Be careful. Everything that looks good..."

"Mikki," He began, his voice going deep and quiet as he leaned forward, staring deeply at me as if he were about share one of his deepest, most intimate secrets with me. "Can I ask you a question?" He asked, his husky voice drawing me in.

"Sure," I responded, smiling as I leaned forward as well to better hear what he was about say, several scenarios playing in my head.

"Mikki," he would say. "I have had such a delightful time. Would you want to come have some dinner?" He would ask to which I would reply, "Why, yes, of course, dinner would be nice".

This could be fun. Maybe we would go to hear some music down in the Jazz District of the city. Maybe, just maybe this date would stretch on into a second date, maybe even a third. Just maybe, this would work, so what if he did not have dimples. So what?

"Sure, go ahead," I smiled, tilting my head to the side to study him. He smiled sheepishly and then he moistened his lips with the tip of his tongue, my eyes following the action as I waited. He leaned closer, looking me directly in the eyes. And, I leaned closer.

"Do you shave?" He asked.

Wh—wh—what? My eyes flew open wide and I am certain that my mouth followed suit. What? The activity inside the coffeehouse seemed to drift into a slow motion crawl and I stared at him, not sure I'd heard what I thought I heard.

"What?" I choked the word out. Surely I'd heard him incorrectly. Was he actually asking me about shaving, like two hours after having met?

'What?" I sputtered again. Mr. Clean seemed unapologetic, having no qualms with asking the question again.

"I asked if you shaved?"

Well, there it was; there was no question that I had understood him correctly.

"My…my underarms?" I tried, tripping over the words. In spite of myself, I found myself pinning my arms close to my body, needing to restrict him should he have the courage to decide to visually investigate for himself.

Mr. Clean smiled a deliberate knowing smile, his brow rising as he made a downward motion with his head.

"Everywhere."

Oh…my… wha…

"I'm sorry?" I heard the words squeak out of my mouth and I stared at him, a flush covering my face and I felt as if my eyes were bulging out of my face.

Really?

I'm sure that my jaw had to have become unhinged and was hanging open. Horrified, I looked around to see if any of the nearby coffee drinkers had heard this bizarre question. Who asks a question like this, especially on a first date! No, skip this, now I was absolutely not going to refer to this as a date! This was quickly turning into a... a… a disaster!

What was wrong with this guy? Crazy was not coming, he was already here, dressed very nicely, and saying all of the right things, well, at least he had been up until ten seconds ago!

As I so often do when I am at a loss for words, I started laughing, first a choking sound, then a nervous giggle, my eyes burning as I desperately gazed into the frothy top of my cappuccino, willing the words to magically present themselves in the foam that would enable me to answer appropriately. Was there an appropriate response?

All I could do is stare at him, my eyes watering as I choked and laughed. To my absolute astonishment, Mr. Clean kept going, not missing a beat in his quest for information.

"You know. Mikki," he continued, "I don't mind my women a little hairy actually. I kind of like the natural thing."

OK, now I was going to choke and die. Mr. Clean looked at me across the table, the congenial smile seeming to have been replaced with an oily smirk. Frowning, I pushed myself back into my chair, feeling both grossed out and desecrated. He smiled, looking around the coffeehouse then back at me, even white teeth shining in his shiny face.

"I dated a woman once who did not shave her armpits or her legs. It did not bother me one bit. I find it all a little primal; I thought it was kind of sexy. And raw. Nonetheless, I can also appreciate the smooth feel of a woman who shaves. I'm just saying. If you don't shave there, it is fine with me."

Shave there? His women? A little hairy? When he says hairy, is he talking like peach fuzz, or more in the line of Sasquatch? Yuck! He was never going to know the silky feel of this woman that much I knew for sure!

That was it, the straw that broke the camel and all of that; this "date" was officially over. For once, I was grateful for the outlay of cash I constantly doled out to my aesthetician to keep my legs and my armpits hair-free. But was I going to share this little tidbit of information with him, with this little freak? I think not!

Mr. Clean never noticed my discomfort, nor did he seem to care. This man apparently had no shame.

"I was only wondering if you do," he concluded with a shrug. Shrinking back into my chair, I watched as he took a tiny tube of sanitizer from his pocket, applying more to his hands and rubbing them together briskly, the gesture making me a little nauseous. I wasn't sure if he was OCD or just a neat freak but I had no intention of figuring it out.

This guy was just plain freaky…no…he was not freaky. He was just a freak! And creepy! Just when you think you've met your quota of crazies, one more comes along to add to the rest of the nuts in the candy bowl.

Well, that was enough for me. I reached for my purse, careful not to touch him or to put any part of my body anywhere near him. Since I was actually wearing a silk halter blouse with a matching skirt, he would have to deduce the answer to his own question.

Rising from my seat, I staged my exit, "Oh, well, would you look at the time," and stated that I needed to get home. Any excuse would do right now. I had a breakfast meeting tomorrow morning and would need to get an early start. Nevertheless, thanks for the coffee. Maybe we could do it again some time.

Heck no, not only no! There was no way on this planet I was ever going to see this strange man again! All I knew was that I needed to get out of here before I poured my coffee over Mr. Clean's head, imagining how satisfying it would feel to watch it drip over that cheesy smile of his.

Something Stinks…

"Something smells fishy…" Sonni stated from the kitchen, the sounds of the refrigerator door registering dimly as it opened and then shut as I continued to stare intently at my computer. This girl was constantly looking for food and I wondered vaguely how she was able to maintain her slim figure eating the way that she did.

"Huh?" I asked, absently wondering what on earth she was talking about now. I knew for a fact that she couldn't smell fish in my fridge because I never ate the stuff. I know, shame on me as all of the beauty magazines attest that fish is full of good stuff that is good for you, especially for a woman "at my age," or so I am told. I just never warmed up to the delicacy that Sonni seemed to enjoy so much.

Nope, no fish in my place, that is unless Dereon brought something in. Wait, does Dereon even like fish? I shrugged at nothing in particular. I had to wonder. Lately I really had no idea what that young man liked, he had changed so much lately, and I honestly could not say that I had a clue if he'd pick up this habit.

He seemed so strange lately with everything that's been going on ever since Little Miss Cutie Pie Jasmine entered the picture. I swear this child has never had a curfew before, at least not one that I ever had to enforce because he just always was aware of the fact when to come home. But ever since Miss Cutie Pie entered the scene, Dereon had begun staying out late, talking on the telephone until all times of the night and just in general, acting weird. I wasn't going to lay down the law yet, but Mister was cutting it really close.

And then there was his recent obsession with hygiene, although, I can say that from a Mom's point of view, this is a very good thing, to go from having to remind him to brush his teeth and hair to having to take a number for my own bathroom. Change is a good thing when it comes to hygiene.

Do males go through PMS? I grimaced and shrugged again, perplexed. Who knew? That kid was acting really weird. I guess it was possible, he was certainly showing all of the signs, maybe it was the whole puberty thing, you know, hormones, girls, moodiness. Girls...

"What are you talking about, Sonni?" I asked, pulling my nose away from the screen of my laptop and away from yet another row of "eligible" Internet bachelors that I had been studying. Geez! I was fed up with this exercise in futility. Out of the corner of my eye, I could see Sonni entering the living room and I straightened up, concentrating anew on the screen. Fine, I would play fair. Just a few weeks to go...

Sonni returned from the kitchen empty handed, a frown on that perfect face of hers. No food. Sorry babe, I mused silently, smirking. It's your own fault. I just hadn't had time to go to the store lately what, with work and trying to find out what was going on with Dereon all while fighting off one dreadful date after another. I would need to make a concerted effort to take care of things at home that I'd begun to let slide, beginning with a trip to the grocery store to stock up.

I glanced up at her, all at once taking in the outfit that Sonni wore, a fitted short sleeve perforated black blouse with a black bustier underneath and a slim fitting black skirt that showcased her toned legs with sky high stilettos. As ever, her hair and her makeup were flawless.

Where was she going dressed like that? And with whom was she going? Was she stopping by or was she staying? I don't know, Dereon wasn't the only one who's been acting weird lately. Sonni was actually seeing someone, well, maybe not actually "seeing" someone, but for the first time that I've known Sonni, she had actually "seen" the same man twice in one week. Hmmm...

And for the first time that I can remember, I'd called Mama Jett on her cell phone and she was out with a friend, an unnamed friend, and said that she would call me later. What in the world was going on? Had everyone lost their minds? I shook my head.

"Well," she began. "Maybe I should have phrased it differently. Maybe I should have said that I smelled a rat."

What? I turned to look at her, returning the frown. A rat? Here? Sonni leaned forward, taking the laptop from my hands to glare at the faces on the screen.

"Why are you doing this?" She asked, motioning one red-tipped manicured hand toward the little row of candidates on the screen. Well, duh... why else?

"Um...because you're making me do this..." I sassed back, flinching as Sonni's frown turned into a full on scowl...Yikes! Ok...maybe not the best response.

"No," she growled through clenched teeth. "I mean, look at this. Look at these guys, Mikki," She motioned again toward the little heads on the screen. I followed her look.

Yeah, so? I shrugged my shoulders, not understanding what she meant. Sonni shook her head vigorously, her spiky hairdo not budging an inch. She returned the laptop to me, placing that manicured hand on her hip, tapping the fingertip against the fabric of her skirt.

"Mikki, you know that on any given day, you would never, ever give any of these "gentlemen" a second thought."

I looked at the pictures again, feeling guilty. Well, I had to agree with her on this one, not one of the "gentlemen" I'd met so far had been my type. If I had a type, that is.

Sonni's "Summer of Love" challenge had creaked its way through the halfway mark and I still had nothing to show for it, no satisfactory dates, that is. And I was fine with that, really. I just wanted this craziness to be over so that I could go back to my nice quiet, uneventful albeit boring life. After some of the crazies that I'd met recently, a boring evening had a really nice sound to it right about now. Just the way I like it.

"Are you even trying?" she asked pointedly and I found myself bristling at her interrogation. What was she insinuating? I was doing everything that she told me to do, following all of her rules, sort of...

"Ye...yes, of course I am." I stammered. I was trying; I just was not good at this kind of thing. I raised my hand in an apologetic, helpless gesture, rising to my feet to place the computer on the countertop.

"I am trying, Sonni." I heaved a sigh. "This is just not working for me."

Sonni grunted, stalking over to click through the profiles with the practiced ease of someone who's done this a time or two.

"None of these guys..." she pinched her lips together, shaking her head with frustration then turned to look at me. "I smell a sabotage," she stated, those dark eyes fastening on me.

"I think you're setting yourself up to fail." She turned away from the laptop and in my direction to stare at me. "I think that you are doing this, maybe not intentionally, but nonetheless doing it in an effort to protect yourself."

Doing what? What was I doing? I looked at her blankly, unnerved as the little bells began to tinkle at the back of my mind. The gig was up. Sonni knew me better than anyone on the planet and she understood what I had only just discovered I was doing — just going through the motions.

"Do you love me? Do you love Mama Jett? What about Dereon and Niecee?" Sonni asked in rapid-fire succession. I turned to face her, feeling angry and cornered as I angled my body away from her, beginning to feel irritated by her line of questioning.

"Of course I do, you know that I do. I would do absolutely anything for any of you." I bit out, my irritation driving me away from her to pace around the room. I began to feel caged and trapped by her interrogation.

"What about you?" Sonni sank down onto the couch, watching me, not approaching me. Not yet.

Me? I turned to look at her. What the hell was she going on about now? What about me? Sonni fastened her gaze on me, refusing to back down.

"Do you love yourself, Mikki?" She asked, her eyes intent on me, the hunter keeping her eye on her prey. At that, I groaned out loud, exasperated, throwing my arms up in a mock surrender. Now Sonni was going to go all Dr. Phil on me?

"Oh course I love myself." I flashed back, my temper rising. I did, didn't I? Sonni shook her head, her eyes a little sad.

"I think that you don't feel that you deserve to be happy. After the Darren thing." She stated her words matter of fact.

"The Darren thing? Is that what we're calling it?" I sniffed, shaking my head, as I pushed my hair away from my hot face, a flush covering me from head to toe. Oh, that's right. That little thing where I had the affair with the older married man with the hopes that he would choose me … and he didn't. He didn't choose me, and he didn't choose his baby.

His baby…my baby.

I looked about the room, looking at nothing in particular as I thought about those circumstances that seemed to have kept me frozen in time. The Darren thing.

I had allowed myself to be sucked into the allure of being involved with, no, infatuated with an older man. For me, the young newly minted college graduate, just the thought of being involved with an older man was heady stuff, a huge boost to my young ego that an older man found me to be exciting. The sensation of this obsession was as heady as a fine brandy as I'd relished in the thought of being the recipient of this older man's attention, causing me to feel worldly and mature as I crossed the threshold from college student to real grownup.

He had been sweet in the beginning, playing into my young girl dreams of Prince Charming, and I into his façade of student to his teacher. Though I was never permitted to call him at home, he soon swept me away with messages "just because" he was thinking of me. Bringing a single rose from the gas station whenever he came to visit. I was easily impressed then...

He appreciated that I was a good listener; I made him feel good, important, and special. Cherished. When he broke the news to me that he was married, I didn't even bat an eye. Oh, it was a heartbreaking story, they weren't happy; his wife was inattentive and didn't understand him. They hadn't been together in months as husband and wife. She didn't listen to him and was much too busy for him because she was so busy with her work and her friends.

We would walk along the tree-shaded paths of the campus, talking about any and everything. He seemed fascinated with everything that I did or said and oh how I'd loved to see that smile on his face, his eyes crinkling when he laughed as I regaled him with tales of my life during my college days.

He just seemed so lonely and said that I made him feel alive again, that I'd returned the smile to his face. He said that I treated him so much better than his wife did and assured me that I was everything that she was not. And that was enough for me at the time.

We would meet at different places, always varying the locations in the nearby college town where I'd graduated, far away from the prying eyes of anyone who might see us together and recognize him, reporting back to his wife. At least here, the likelihood of running into anyone who knew him was slim, while I was forced to come up with alibis to explain who he was to my friends. Never my guy or my boyfriend. Just my friend. My friend...

And the sex was so sweet. He was more than happy to sneak in stolen moments with me. And I thought we had been careful...until we weren't. I could remember the day as clearly as if it had occurred only yesterday.

With shaking hands, I'd sat on the cold hard toilet lid in the bathroom of my tiny apartment, staring down at the blue stick of the second home pregnancy test I'd taken — overjoyed when the stick confirmed what I had suspected for weeks. I was pregnant and terrified. What would he think? What would he say? Did he even like kids? I knew that he had no children of his own with his wife — too busy, she'd always been too busy, he'd said to bother herself with a family.

This was our chance. He would love this baby. He could finally leave his wife, leave that loveless marriage and start over fresh with our baby and me, the family he longed for. Our little family. He would be excited. I just knew it. He didn't love her anyway and this would be the fresh start he'd said he'd always wanted. His chance to be happy. Our chance to be together. Finally, no more hiding.

I'd sent him a cryptic message, saying it was about work, should his wife ask. I'd asked that he meet me at the quiet Mexican restaurant where we'd met so many times before. I'd dressed carefully that evening, flat ironing my tangle of naturally curly hair into a long shiny ebony curtain that hung past my shoulders because this was the look that he preferred. Straight black hair with his favorite dress, a long black wrap dress that accentuated my youthful curves. This I wore with my simple gold hoops, again because this look was what he preferred.

I sat in the corner furthest away from the door; he would know where to find me because we'd frequented this restaurant so many times before. My stomach churned as I waited, rehearsing over and over again in my mind how I would break the news.

"I'm pregnant. You're going to be a father. We can be a family..." I hugged the nugget of my news to myself, terrified but happy.

Darren had entered the restaurant, looking bristly, distracted and anxious. I smiled as he made his way to our usual table in the corner away from everything, the action fading as I noted the frown that marred his attractive features. He was late by nearly forty-five minutes and he appeared to be upset about something, the frown only seeming to deepen as he surged towards our table. I smiled up at him as he sat down; watching as he impatiently waved away the waiter, turning down the offer of a soft drink to opt for "only water" instead.

Ok... Darren was not in the mood for small talk, preferring to get directly to the point.

"What's going on, Mikki? I got your message while I was at home; my wife was standing right there..." he began, his tone abrupt. I frowned, puzzled. So? He'd had a problem with it before. What gives now? Had she become suspicious? He hadn't seemed to care when the messages came in before...

I fidgeted in my seat, perturbed, an action that drew another frown from him. As much as he appreciated my youth, he hated it when I fidgeted "like a child" — his words - it was "unladylike" and he expected nothing less than ladylike behavior when we were together.

Whatever.

"I need to talk to you, Darren. It's important," I said, my voice wavering. The waiter brought his water and he took a sip, his dry lips crinkling around the straw. Again he shook his head at the waiter, declining a menu.

"What is it, Mikaela? I was on my way to something important for my wife's job." He snapped.

Mikaela? I felt my brow rise at his use of my given name. When had my identity in this relationship devolved from the familiarity of Mikki to the formality of Mikaela? And since when did he attend functions with his wife, especially for her work? He'd never cared about any of that before. He'd told me that he'd preferred not to have anything to do with his wife's work since according to him; her work was the very reason why they didn't get along. Her work and her dedication to her work was the primary cause — also according to him — of their lack of marital bliss.

"You're not staying for dinner?" I asked. He scowled, his lips turning downward as he looked anywhere and at anything and anyone but me.

"No."

Ok...I cleared my throat. Unsteadily, I pushed a long strand of straightened hair behind my ear. Still, he refused to look at me.

"Darren," I began, my fingertips going to toy with the straw in my water glass. "I'm pregnant."

Time seemed to scream to a stop in that corner of the restaurant as his gaze slowly returned to me. Gone was the warmth that used to encompass me and in its place was a glacial iciness that deflected any warmth, especially any warmth from me.

"You're pregnant?" He repeated his eyes hard dark pieces of flint as he stared at me. He pushed his water glass away, his breath escaping from him in a long bitter hiss.

"I see." He stated. I fidgeted again and those hard lifeless eyes seeming to pin me into place.

"Yes," I said in a whisper, my hands falling to rest in my lap. He continued to glare at me, dark, brooding, and mad as hell.

"I thought you were more responsible than that, Mikki," he said, leaning back into his chair, angling his body as far away from me as he could.

"I was," I said softly, "It just happened. I'm sorry." I whispered.

His mouth turned down in a snarl as he shook his head, his hand rising to push aside my argument.

"Nothing ever just happens, Mikki. You're a smart girl, you know how these things happen, but now, here you are with a problem."

Wait? Here I was with a problem? How was this only my problem? I seemed to remember him actively, even eagerly participating in the creation of this "problem" as often and as many times as possible. Hadn't seemed like a problem then…

"My problem?" I frowned back at him across the table. "I believe this "problem" is yours as well." I snapped back. He glared at me across the table, his expression ugly and mean.

"Mikki." He pushed his chair back. "You have a big decision to make. I'm not ready to be a father. I don't want children, not now, not ever."

I sat back in my seat with a thud, my shock apparent as I tried to muddle through what he was saying. He never wanted children? Then what had all of those long heart to heart discussions been about, the ones where he mentioned how important family was to him? Indifferent to my feelings, he pressed forward with his argument.

"Either you can make this problem go away, or you will need to figure out how to deal with it by yourself. You have to decide how to this is going to play out — for yourself, for your life. But I don't want any part of it."

I stared back at him across the increasing distance, my face stinging as if he'd physically slapped me. He didn't want this baby, not now, not ever. He wanted nothing to do with this baby and he expected me to make a decision — alone — that would change my life forever.

Then what? If I "made it go away," his words, then what? We would continue on like we always had with him hiding me away from his wife and his life, expecting me to continue to do the same? I realized then that I would never be first in his life, not ever, always resigned to be the "woman on the side".

The cold finger of the reality of what was going on prickled slowly up my spine to clasp the back of my head, forcing me to focus my attention clearly for the first time in months. Gone was the fuzzy glow of my little girl dreams, my Prince Charming was nothing but a two timing manipulator who, if he would cheat on his wife with me, he would cheat on me with someone else...if he wasn't cheating on me already...

That thought caused a wry smile to cross my lips. The cheater who cheated on his wife with me was possibly cheating on me with someone else? How ironic. I looked at him, seeing him clearly for the first time. Was he already seeing someone else?

"What about your wife? What would she think?" I asked my tone snippy. I knew that the hard edge of my voice would irritate him but I no longer cared what he thought about my tone when I spoke to him. I was done playing the obedient little girl to his overbearing "Papa Bear".

At the mention of his wife, he lunged toward me in his chair, leaning forward until his line of sight was level with mine, those nasty little eyes tearing into me, his face dark, and his voice darker. His hand came up to slap flat against the tabletop, causing the lit candle in the center of the table to jump and rock. I'd flinched as well, afraid that he would strike me out of anger. Then he pointed one bony finger in my face, his expression murderous and unyielding.

"Do…not…mention…my…wife." He ground out between clinched teeth. "She will never find out about this." He stopped and he looked around, his tone lowering, his mouth twisting as he glared at me. "What? Did you think that if you told me that you were pregnant, I would just drop everything to be with you?"

His sharp crack of laughter caused other restaurant patrons to glance curiously in our direction. His face twisted into an ugly mask as he mocked my childish dreams. He leaned closer, his voice quiet and ominous, his lips curved into a cruel smile.

"Listen to me, Mikki and really hear me." He ground out between clinched teeth. "I am never leaving my wife. And if you ever figure out a way to mention any of this to her, I will deny everything. And if that doesn't work, I will expose you as the home wrecker that you are. I will destroy your reputation to anyone who hears about any of this. I am not leaving my wife. I will never leave my wife."

His eyes flicked derisively over me as he rose from the table, staring down at me, pulling his jacket into place, raising his hand to smooth his beard, neatening his appearance.

"Do not contact me again, Mikki. This…" he waved his hand for emphasis. "Whatever it was, it is over. It's done. You do whatever it is that you have to do. Keep it, get rid of it. It's up to you. But this is over."

And with that, he left the restaurant. I'd watched him leave, unable to cry, unable to do anything but watch him go. Frozen…

Remaining frozen. Even today, I remained emotionally frozen in that place. Unable to love to that magnitude again, unable to allow myself to be loved by a man. I would not allow anyone in and I was unable to let myself out. I could not, would not expose myself — or Dereon – to this kind of thing ever again, choosing to raise my son on my own. He would always know love and acceptance, something the man who fathered him could not bring himself to do.

"Damn," I muttered, dashing away the tears that rushed down my hot cheeks, staring at my wet fingertips in wonder, then hugging my arms around myself, shaking my head to clear away the memories. I had never cried over Darren and I damn sure was not going to start now. He was not worth it, not then, not now.

"I cannot believe I'm crying about this now…" I muttered, irritated with myself. Sonni sighed deeply and I looked at her, wiping at my cheeks.

"Sweetie, you're not crying for him, you're crying for you and I say that it is long overdue. It was a mistake, Mikki," Sonni said, her voice breaking. "A mistake. People make mistakes; everyone makes them. " Sonni said softly. "You've got to stop punishing yourself for this one."

"A mistake? Is that what we're calling it?" I laughed sharply, my hands going up the rub at the tension bunching in my shoulders as I watched her from across the living room, my look wary, her answering look determined. I swallowed hard against the lump that had suddenly appeared in my throat, my chest tightening.

Though I never regretted having Dereon – not for one second — my actions denied him the father that every child has the right to have. No, not my actions, my choice was not father material, he never wanted to be a father and told me in no uncertain terms. It was my choice that denied Dereon the father he deserved. I'd chosen unwisely, and Dereon had paid the price.

"You didn't make a mistake, Sonni." I said. "Not like this." I turned away from her, looking out the window, my shoulders sagging, my spirit lagging. God, I was so tired of carrying this brick of disappointment around.

"My mistake totally changed everything and everyone, especially Dereon." I turned away from the window to look into the room, staring at nothing, the magnitude of the actions of my past paralyzing me now just as it had every day since. Sonni's sharp laugh caught me off guard and I looked in her direction.

"Honey, I have certainly made more than my share of mistakes." She rose from her seat, walking toward me. She continued. "But one mistake with a married man does not justify putting your entire life on hold. It's like you're subjecting yourself to this bizarre type of penance to compensate for the one mistake. You don't feel worthy of your own happiness."

I looked at her, shaking my head as my hand rose to push away the hair that curled at my temple. My smile wry as a bitter taste filled my mouth. Curly hair, the way I preferred, not straight as Darren had preferred.

"Sonni," I said, my voice breaking. "I was young and stupid. When I learned that he was married, I continued to see him. I was trying to break up a marriage. I just wanted to break it up because I wanted him for myself. I was determined to do what I wanted and have what I wanted. At whatever the cost." I shook my head again, closing my eyes as my hand rubbed at my stiff neck.

"And Dereon is still paying the cost for my choices." Sonni muttered something under her breath. I flashed a questioning look at her. Sonni shook her head, her lips tight with aggravation for her friend. For me.

"But you didn't break up that marriage." Sonni said, coming closer. "Besides, this wasn't all you. There were two of you involved in this thing. That man knew that he was married from the beginning. And Dereon," she reached out, placing her hand on my shoulder, forcing me to turn around to look at her.

"Do you know how wonderful you are, Mikki? Do you know what a phenomenal mother, what a phenomenal woman you are? In spite of everything, you have given that child everything, not just material things, but a real chance at a real life. Dereon is sweet and smart. Hell, look at him, he's a hottie and he won a full ride scholarship to a kick butt college. You did that, Mikki. Nobody else."

I laughed, a hiccup escaping as I did so. "Well, I had a little help from a bunch of strong women." I said.

Sonni laughed as well, giving me a little shake, looking me in the eye, forcing me to really hear her. "*You* did it, honey. Your child is successful and has grown up to be a successful young man. You've got to give yourself a break!"

Damn it, I was crying again, but this time, I allowed the tears to come. I laughed, a little choking sound as I looked away, my throat tightening on any response I would have made. Sonni the Conqueror peered up into my face, patting my cheek.

"It's time you let somebody love you too."

I shook my head, my lips twisting as I fought to contain the tears that burned my eyes, flooding onto my burning cheeks.

"Sometimes, I feel like I just don't deserve to have that, especially after trying so hard to break it up for someone else." I whispered. Love? God! I just could not get my mind around that thought! Love! I was certainly not ready for that! The whole idea of opening myself up again to that kind of thing. Ugh! I think I'd rather have dental surgery before I did that! Hell, I'd rather have any kind of surgery before I signed up for the whole love thing again.

"Mikki, you have to let it go. Darren is not worth your sacrifice. That's what you're doing, sacrificing your own happiness. If you stay alone, he wins."

He wins … Darren wins… the thought churned through the cloud of confusion. He wins… I turned to look at Sonni, my back stiffening. Hell no.

"No." I said again out loud. I've allowed him to take enough from me. I've given up enough for him. Not anymore. I squared my shoulders, my action resolute.

"Fine, I will try harder." I muttered. Sonni smiled a reaction to my declaration that should have scared me witless.

"I know you will honey, because I am picking the next one."

Winking at me, Sonni returned to the laptop, scrolling through the messages I had placed in the delete file. Logging in to one, she dashed off a response with a few quick keystrokes and clicked send.

"There, it's done." She stated. I nodded. It was done.

Excuse me Miss, Is Your Husband Married?

Day thirty-three…

"Mikki," his email began. "I'm new to the service, having recently lost my wife. I'm a forty-seven year old man, in good shape, looking for a settled fun loving woman with whom to share some good times and good conversation. I would love to meet some time, you sound like an intelligent woman who I would be pleased to get to know. Email back if interested in talking, we can meet for coffee."

I frowned. How sad! Putting himself back into the wacky world of dating was commendable, had to be tough enough losing someone, but being brave enough to jump back into the shark tank of dating had to be scary.

Meeting for coffee? Goodness, I'd had so many coffee meets lately! I think that maybe the local coffeehouses should begin sending me thank you notes! But he sounded nice, as if he had a good head on his shoulders. And his picture was nice and he seemed totally age appropriate at forty-seven years old. From his profile, I learned that he worked in IT for a local bank and had been employed there for a number of years. Some kind of supervisor or something.

His marital status had been left blank, but as he had explained in his profile, he had lost his wife recently. Poor thing, maybe she had been sick, he hadn't said in his profile but I guessed it wasn't the sort of thing you wouldn't include, especially in the beginning.

We exchanged email addresses and cell phone numbers. Hmm…no home telephone number, he'd said that it was easiest to reach him only via cell phone between the hours of 9 and 5 p.m. and that he was unavailable by email and cell phone anytime before 9:00 a.m. and after 5:00 p.m. That was fine, I guess, maybe he worked an overnight shift at work.

The meet seemed promising online. He contacted me first, his emails were well written, no typos, his picture appeared to jibe with what he said his age to be. We shared quite a few instant message conversations. Spoke via cell phone, or by email — always at work, mind you. We just seemed to click.

We decided to meet for coffee during the lunchtime hour on a Thursday that week, he really wanted to meet but just could not get away at any other time because of his crazy work schedule, things were hectic at work with an upcoming systems conversion; he may be working a little later than usual since he was in IT and all. Perfectly understandable, I knew from firsthand experience how computers could be difficult. I fought with my company issued laptop on a daily basis and seldom emerged as victor.

On the day of our coffee meet, I was dressed in business wear, a simple tailored black blazer and slim skirt, a brightly colored scarf looped around my shoulders and my new stilettos that added a full four inches to my already five feet seven inch frame.

I walked through the revolving doors of the building that housed the Bank where he worked, noticing the tall handsome man standing next to a coffee cart in the bustling ground level of the building. He checked his watch then, catching sight of me as I entered the building, he smiled.

Handsome, no dimples, but he was well dressed, his clothing was nicely coordinated and appropriately ironed and starched. I couldn't say why but something seemed off from the beginning. We never sat down, we just sort of stood off to the side out of the crush of people entering and leaving the building. Every now and then he would see someone who he knew from work, extending a pleasantry or two before returning to our conversation.

During our "coffee break," he referred often to a woman named Jana and my warning bells began to jangle ever so slightly. Jana this or Jana that. So, of course I had to ask the question. Who is Jana?

Jana, he'd replied smoothly was the woman that he lived with. The woman that he lived with? What was this — a sister, a cousin? I voiced my question aloud.

"Jana is my wife," he'd replied without batting an eye.

His wife? What the... a dating married man? How are you going to be married and going out on a date? And what was all of that about "losing" his wife? Where had he lost her? Did she know that she was lost?

"It's just a technicality," he said to me. "We are separated, but she cannot afford to move out on her own yet, so we still share the condo."

Was this man crazy? Did I actually have stupid written somewhere on my person? A technicality? Since when is a wife a technicality? Did Jana, wife of Mr. Dating Married Man have an inkling that she was being explained away as "a technicality"?

Separated? Who determines the rules of separation anyway? Obviously Mr. Dating Married Man forgot to mention the fact to Mrs. Jana Dating Married Man. Big time lesson here. If a man says that he and his wife are separated, run! Run as if you are on fire!

I have always had a problem with this term "separated". Are we talking separated for a month, a year? Are we talking separated for a week while she is out of town visiting her mother? Are we talking separated for the eight-plus hours daily that your employer requires of you in order to earn a paycheck?

Or hey I like this one! We are still living in the same house, but we haven't been together in months. Now who do you think you are kidding? I know very few men, normal red-blooded men, who are living in the same vicinity of a living breathing female body who is going to let this one float. Not going to happen, for some, just being in the same zip code as an attractive woman, or any woman for that matter, is enough to throw this little theory out the window.

Dating Married Man was adamant about the "fact" that they were no longer sleeping together; they shared a home only. And a last name as well. Hmm... It was then that I noticed the ever so faint tan line on his ring finger. A ring had very recently sat on that finger and I was willing to bet, that same ring was currently sitting in his pocket, waiting to take its rightful place on that finger before Mr. Dating Married Man ventured home once his "coffee break" was over.

Here is a technicality for you, Mr. Dating Married Man. Technically you are still married. You know what, contact me when your situation changes. Better yet, don't contact me. Ever.

The fact that he was married more than explained why he only accepted calls or emails during specified times. Mr. Dating Married Man was definitely married and would continue to be married. I made a new note to myself: I would never agree to meet anyone else until I had regular telephone contact, both mobile and home. If a man tells you to call only on his cell phone, only at specified times, if he is not free to meet you, the signs are there. He is married; he may have temporarily forgotten this little tidbit. Nevertheless, I guarantee you that I know what to look for the next time around.

Separated is still married — until it isn't.

Rockabye Baby

Day thirty-seven...

"Hi Mikki," his email began. "It was good to hear from you. I apologize for not getting back to you sooner but I was away in Denver for business. I'm looking forward to meeting you. I know the perfect place. "

Wait! What? Wait a minute! I'd never agreed to meet him...had I? I chewed my lower lip, thinking hard. Things were moving so quickly now in my life with everything that went into preparing Dereon for his departure to college in the fall and everything that was going on at work. Had I inadvertently responded to his email by mistake?

My hands trembled as I entered my password and logged on to the site. I honestly could not remember responding to this email and I clicked over to search through my email box, finding nothing at all until I switched over to go through the messages hiding out in my deleted folder.

Oh...dear...Lord! I gasped aloud, covering my mouth with my hand, my heart seeming to slam to a stop as what had happened slowly sank in. No...no...no! Please say this is not so! Holding my breath, I quickly read through the email, shaking my head.

"Damn, damn, damn!" I said out loud. I looked at the date of the email — the one that Sonni had responded to. Un-freaking-believable! Stalker guy! Sonni had responded to Stalker Guy's email on my behalf!

I couldn't meet Stalker Guy, what was she thinking! Had she not read the profile? He was...well, there were so many things! I grunted my frustration out loud, standing up to pace around in front of the laptop, stopping again in front of the computer to read the email that Sonni had sent.

"Hi, sorry, been a little busy, but would like to meet."

Simple, but damning.   I fully planned to choke Sonni out later.   But right now, I needed to get out of this mess that she made.

Exhaling loudly, I covered my eyes then raked my fingers through my hair, shaking my fists in the air.   This was crazy!   I couldn't get out of it, not without looking like a jerk.   How would that sound, oh, sorry Stalker Guy, I can't go out with you, my best friend — make that soon to be ex-best friend — thought it would be a good idea to respond to you on my behalf, but I'm not going to follow through with it... sorry about the misunderstanding.

Right, real smooth!   Damn it!

"I don't know girl," Little Mikki said sagely. This guy really could be some kind of psycho who grabs Internet virgins and makes them disappear. Or he could be exactly what he said, but what was the likelihood of that? Right, I knew that I had to see this through.

Resolute, I emailed him back.

He emailed that he was now in Dallas on business right now and so we began this email "tag, you're it"... kind of thing, I know, call it juvenile. But, during the course of our many emails, I found that he just did not seem to be just another smooth talker, er ... writer like some I had traded emails with lately.

He actually had things to say, interesting things to say and I found myself actually looking forward to his notes in my inbox.

And then, I did it. I agreed to meet him in public. At a very public place, a really nice restaurant that he'd mentioned was one of his favorites as well.

All right, Mr. Perfect, let's see who you really are.

***

We'd agreed to meet that Saturday evening and I had to admit, I was looking forward to it. I had taken considerable time getting ready for our first meeting that evening. I had just gotten my hair done that morning and in spite of a closet full of clothes, I'd actually gone shopping and bought something new, a sexy little knee grazing gold crocheted sleeveless curve hugging tank dress with tiny little glittering strands of gold that shimmied when I walked.

In this dress I channeled my own inner Temptress, wearing a pair of four-inch heeled strappy gold beauties that showcased my legs. If he was short, he would just have to deal with it. I would certainly give him an eyeful of what he was definitely going to miss. My hair I let fall in curly dark shiny spirals to the tops of my shoulders. My makeup I kept sultry in shades of bronzes and dark browns, my wide dark eyes lined with dark kohl eyeliner, my lips full and lined with the unstoppable, unsmearable burgundy lipstick the scary MAC girl had recommended that I purchase. From my earlobes I wore long dangling gold earrings.

I smiled at my reflection in the mirror, hardly recognizing myself. Maybe he had lied on his profile, but I was definitely feeling all that I said that I was on mine and more! I left my house, feeling good, feeling sassy. Feeling punky, the Temptress would have said. I have to admit, she would have been very proud of me this evening.

My favorite station had been playing old school music tonight, what seemed like all of my favorite songs one after another on my drive over and I was feeling good. I entered the restaurant, totally glammed from head to toe, feeling confident and totally full of myself as my own background music filled my head.

The restaurant he'd chosen was one of the best in Kansas City, one that I knew well from infrequent visits made to the establishment when wining and dining our bigger clients. Only the best…

The restaurant had recently won many fine dining awards and accolades, the atmosphere one of refined sophistication featuring historic architecture and exquisite finishing touches of rich mahogany, deep warm leather and flattering lighting which seemed to set the mood.

After turning over the keys of my SUV to the valet to park my vehicle, I sashayed into the restaurant, giving my name to the maître d' at the door; he nodded his head, and seemed to know exactly who I was here to meet. He smiled approvingly, his gaze flicking down to check out my long legs in the gold dress. Oh yes, I was feeling it.

"Of course, Miss, right this way, the gentleman is expecting you in the Wine Room." He stated crisply, smiling at me warmly.

Miss? Why yes, I will take that. We were dining in the Wine Room, a private, quiet, intimate setting surrounded by an elegant backdrop of rich mahogany and wine cellars. Oh yes, I can be wowed!

I shimmied behind the maître d' to a very nice, very secluded table tucked away into a little alcove. There was a man sitting at the table, I could only see his profile, he was studying the wine list.

Nice, I mused. A man who knows wine. Very nice. When he noticed our approach, the man placed the wine list on the table and stood up. And up. And I'm sure that at that moment my eyes probably popped out of my head like some kind of crazy cartoon character. I stood speechless, staring at him.

He was exactly as he had appeared on his profile. And tall. And ... oh...my...goodness! I was going to hell! Smooth skin, even white teeth and dark intelligent eyes that crinkled ever so slightly at the corners evidencing that he laughed often. He was tall with a muscular build, his suit no doubt tailor-made as it molded his wide shoulders. His shirt also fit to perfection hiding from view what had to be a well-defined set of washboard abs. And his trousers…

I shook my head to clear it, forcing my eyes back up to his face, that undeniably attractive face and I swallowed. Hard.

"Mikki," he said, his voice as smooth and as rich and as dark as chocolate. Yes, I'm going to hell, right after this date. Just the sound of my name on his lips made me long to hear it whispered against my neck when he…

Mikki stop! I silently reprimanded myself, peeved that I was behaving like a teenager with a crush. I made the mistake of looking into his eyes and was hit by a wave of desire that I'd not experienced in many, many nights, the rush of the sensation actually seeming to steal my breath away.

The man was beautiful! And young! He had not mentioned his age on his profile, mentioning only his accomplishments. I had assumed, mistakenly, that the picture he'd put on the site had been a hoax.

He held out his hand, and in a trance, I placed mine into his open palm, allowing him to pull me forward. When his palm slid across my hand, I felt my brow rise in surprise at the electrical current that seemed to shoot through me. Everything about the man from the masculine cut of his jaw to the tilt of his head as he watched me made him unbelievably handsome. Was I staring? I could not speak, oh my God! Was I even breathing?

When he chuckled aloud at my startled gaze, I knew that he'd felt it too and I felt my hand tremble on its own accord within his hand as he tightened his hold on my hand, watching my eyes as my breathing grew irregular. My gaze lowered to our still joined hands and I cleared my throat, opening my mouth to speak and was unable to say anything at all.

Releasing my hand, he smiled, pulling out my chair, settling me into it before returning to his own. I sat stock-still, my face on fire, my hand trembling, still warm from his touch. I forced my gaze to meet his own; aware of the buzzing that filled my ears as I tried to rationalize what had just happened. I could feel my heart pounding and I felt my skin feeling red and hot, my thoughts confused as I tried to make sense out of what was happening. What was happening?

His eyes were dark on me as he took note of my expression and I was sure that he could see the war going on inside of me. What had I been thinking? Why in the world had I come here tonight?

"I'm glad that you came," he teased. What was that? Did I actually say something? Or maybe I just thought that I had. Oh God, now he probably thought that I was some kind of crazy person! I stared at him from across the table.

"Surprised?" he laughed a little at my apparent disbelief. That was when I knew for sure that I was going to hell. This man — man? Could I honestly say that? This man was practically a child, at least from my side of the apparent age gap. And what did that make me? A dirty old woman? Hey kid, come here, do you want some candy? Gross!

Back door, yes, there had to be a backdoor to this place. Maybe through the kitchen? I could make up some excuse and sneak out.

I shook my head. Mikki! What is wrong with you! This man, this sexy as heck man, looked barely old enough to be out on a date. Hell! He could have practically been a play date for Dereon but really, all I could think of when I looked at Baby was a play date for me!

He was too young, way too young! Were there not enough eligible men to go around without my having to descend on some poor young boy, looking and acting like some crazy old lady?

Come here sonny, come to Mama, I have a new game to show you!

I shook my head again, feeling sick, my stomach queasy. What had I allowed myself to be talked into? I should have just deleted his emails but no...what had he said on his emails?

"I know that this is probably not your kind of thing," he'd said, "but I would appreciate the opportunity to meet you just once, to talk, to introduce myself. I would really like to meet you. Someplace public, your choice. You say when and where. I look forward to hearing from you soon."

Oh goodness! Whatever little bit of common sense Dereon had not knocked out of me during the years of raising him, was now officially gone.

"H--how old are you?" I whispered.

He smiled, the dimples deepening into grooves on either side of his mouth. That mouth, those lips ... damn, damn, damn! Why did he have to have dimples?

"How old do you think I am?" He asked. I raised my hand, helpless. I was stumped. I could not even begin to guess. Maybe I was just plain afraid to guess. Sixteen? Nineteen? Ok, let's try a different tactic. I exhaled shakily, trying to calm myself.

"How young are you?" I asked. He smiled again, his dark eyes fastening on my face.

"Thirty-five."

There. There it was. I rolled my eyes, yep; make that the fast track to hell for me... I really was going to be sick. You've got to be kidding! He was practically a baby.

A baby! And I guess that made me a kidnapper! Wait, no, this had to be some kind of joke. I got it! Any second now Sonni was going to jump out from behind the maître d' and yell

"Gotcha"!   But no, there was no Sonni lying in wait to spring something on me. No gotcha.

I felt sick. I wanted to excuse myself to go to the ladies room. Would he notice if I did not return? God I felt dizzy! I shut my eyes for a brief second, rubbing my forehead.

Thirty-five... a very mature thirty-five, but still thirty-five. My head began to swim, my heart seeming to flounder in my chest. Was this it? Was I going to have a heart attack and then die?

"Is that a problem for you, Mikki?" he asked, his voice deep. I looked up at him, my breathing shallow.

Problem?   Problem? Hell yes, I would say this is a problem. He was way too young! It finally clicked where I had seen his name and the name of his company as I remembered that he had been profiled in a recent article that I had read. "Thirty under Forty" of the brightest individuals of their generation, all top business people, all innovative thinkers and leaders in the technology industry, all age forty and under.

And under...

"Would you like something to drink? This restaurant has an excellent wine list," he smiled at me from across the table, the action sensual, his lips curving up into a lopsided grin to showcase...oh no... those dimples again.

Drink? He was barely old enough to drink! I was old enough to be his mother, well, maybe his older sister but still!

"Wine, yes, wine would be great," I heard myself say from far, far away.

Why was I not surprised that he was on speaking terms with the Master Sommelier of the establishment, I watched impressed, taking a minute to compose myself, as they discussed the wines and the foods that paired well with each wine, finally settling on a vintage the Master Sommelier was sure would meet Baby's expectations.

"I thought," I began, my voice failing as a server returned with our wine, pausing to pour a little into Baby's glass. I worried at my lower lip with my teeth, not sure what to say. I watched as he tasted the wine, and then nodded his head. I stuffed my napkin down into my lap and twisted it with my fingers, not trusting myself to keep them on top of the table for fear of upending what apparently was a very expensive bottle of wine.

"I thought that the picture was a joke," I blurted out once the server had disappeared out of earshot. Baby, to his credit, laughed out loud.

"What, you did not like my picture?" he grinned. Straight even white teeth, perfect. I pinched the ridge of my nose, exhaling unsteadily. And dimples ... sweet mama ... I shook my head, chiding myself silently. Must stay focused. Must keep a clear head.

"Your picture is perfect," I stammered. "I mean your picture is fine."

He chuckled and I flushed, embarrassed.
"You have no idea how many people put a much younger picture on their profiles." I tried by way of an explanation.

I sat back in my seat, my hands falling to my lap, my fingers twisting the gilded fabric of my dress.

"Why didn't you tell me how young you were?" I whispered in a hushed stage whisper. He studied my stricken expression, leaning back in his chair, his brow raised. He reached for his wineglass, slowly raising the glass to those lips...those nicely shaped lips...

I shuddered, shaking my head to scatter those thoughts. I had to keep it together. Focus Mikki! I scolded myself. It's been a long time but you have to keep it together! He studied me over the rim of his glass.

"Would you have come if I had told you I was thirty-five?" he asked, sipping his wine. I shook my head, confused.

"No, I mean, I don't know," I shook my head again, my hand rising shakily to my temple. I did not know what I was talking about, what I was thinking; I just could not seem to form a coherent thought. Geez, everything was just so confused up there right now. I exhaled again, shaking my head, my own brow crinkling into an exasperated frown.

"No, you would not have. That's why I did not tell you. Because I wanted to meet you." He stated smoothly.

I rolled my eyes, frustrated. "Why?"

He smiled then, the corner of his lips curving upward. "I'm interested in you Mikki, and I want to know more about you."

I held up my hands in mock surrender, shaking my head.

"You do know how old I am, don't you?" I asked. He had the grace to shrug, my eyes following the movement along the solid line of his shoulder, watching the play of the muscles underneath the fabric of the fine suit that he wore. Uh … right … what was I saying?

"You're forty-five."

Ewww! It sounded so … *old* coming from his handsome *young* lips.

"Oh my goodness! Come on! Don't be such a fuddy-duddy!" Little Mikki griped. Apparently she was ready for some fun. But, there is fun and then there was just plain crazy, and this was certainly stacking up on the crazy side of the table. I rubbed my temple, my head beginning to pound in earnest now.

"Exactly!" He seemed nonplussed by the age difference. "That's only ten years between us, Mikki," he said.

"Ten?" Again with the stage whisper. It might as well have been a hundred years! I looked around the restaurant, oh no! Had anybody else heard that? Ten years! I think there is a word for that — a cougar. A cougar! Oh my God!

"That's an entire decade!" I tried to reason.

He smiled at me, his gaze flicking down to my lips then back up to my eyes, speaking volumes with his look.

"I think older women are fascinating," he said. Baby ticked off his reasons for wanting to date a woman older than himself. He preferred older women. I could not help but wonder how many older women he had dated.

"It's simple, Mikki," he continued, his eyes resting full on my face. I felt myself flushing again under his intense gaze. "I find that an older woman usually has a lot more going on than the women my own age."

I groaned aloud. Women his age… He continued his eyes fastened on my face, watching me intently.

"And, truthfully, I find that younger women are looking more at my wallet and my earning power, they are thinking about what I can do for them rather than at me the man."

I frowned, not sure at all how to respond, the man himself was so very easy on the eyes.

"Younger women are looking at my net worth, looking at me as a catch and a proper mate with whom they can settle down and have kids. That's not what I'm looking for right now." I pinched my lips together, not sure how to respond to his frankness.

"Do you make it a habit of dating older women?" I blurted out the question. At that he laughed.

"Not usually, Mikki, I have to admit, you would definitely be my first." At that, I rolled my eyes. Great! So this was an experiment, he was looking for something novel to brag about to his friends? The man who seemed to have it all was looking to try something new? His maturity no doubt was attributed to the fact that he was a business owner, a serious business owner who had no time to mess around with the frivolity of young women and the drama they brought with them.

"Where many of these women are going, I have already been," he reasoned. "Their whole mentality is about things that are of no concern to me at this point in my life." He stared at me, his eyes fastened on my face, the action unnerving. Then he smiled, the corner of his mouth turning up as his gaze flicked down to my lips, then back up to my eyes.

Sweet mercy...

"That would certainly not be the case with you, Mikki. You are independent. You have your own career, your own life. You seem to be smart and funny; you know your own mind and what you want."

I do? He leaned forward then, his eyes sincere and intense.

"We are free to just be there for each other. To explore new things together. I really want to get to know you, Mikki."

Oh dear God! Slow down...must slow down! The things I could explore with this man ... I stared at him, not sure if I was even breathing at this point. I certainly wasn't thinking straight. A strange churning began in the pit of my stomach and underneath the table, I pressed my thighs together, uncomfortable but fascinated by the new heat that throbbed through me.

"I'm comfortable with my own identity. I'm looking for a woman who is confident in herself, what she wants and where she is going. You just don't find that in women my own age."

"But, I'm old enough to be your mother, well, not really." I reasoned, or I tried to reason. I waved my hand helplessly. I was making such a mess of this. I couldn't actually be his mother; it was only ten years…ten years! Who was I trying to convince, him or myself? I was at least old enough to be friends with his mother. Oh God…I'm going to hell… He smiled, the action sensual, enjoying this banter immensely, pleased that I was genuinely flustered.

"But you are not my mother, Mikki," Baby countered smoothly, smiling.

"I don't want to be mothered; I want a woman who knows who she is, sophisticated, attractive, and sensually aware. A strong woman, someone to have fun with." He looked at me then, dimples cutting grooves into his cheeks.

"We could have fun, Mikki." he said, a little smile playing along those beautiful lips. Oh, I was sure that we could! I raised my eyebrows.

"Don't you think I'm a little too old for you?"

Forget it, Mikki, I told myself; people would see as some creepy old lady preying on innocent boys. The kind of creepy old lady who lives in a dark house and stares at you from behind the drapes.

"Too old for what?" he asked, laughing, dimples cutting deep gashes into his face and I imagined tracing those dimples with my fingertips, following the lines down to those firm lips…

What was I thinking? When I was his age, let's see, he is thirty-five, oh my God! That means that he is seventeen years older than Dereon. He could be a friend of my son! I felt sick. I felt nauseous. A vision of my life passed before my eyes, I think this is what they say happens in near death experiences. I was surely dying, or I was surely going to die because Baby's mother was going to kill me!

"I'm thirty-five and you're forty-five," he said and I made a shushing sound, waving my hand for him to keep it quiet, an action that made him laugh again.

"Not so loud, someone might hear!" I shushed him, cringing back into my seat. His head tilted a bit as he studied me.

"You're an attractive woman and I can think of nothing that would please me more than getting to know you better." He grinned across the table at me. "Much better."

I squirmed in my seat, the heat creeping through my limbs. This was it. I was going to die, and then I was going to go straight to hell. Punished for being some demented she-wolf. Not only was I robbing the cradle, I was kicking that sucker over, stealing the young and running out into the wilderness with him, waiting for the town to turn out en masse with pitchforks and blazing torches to hunt me down.

Absently I rubbed my temple, my thoughts racing, my heart thudding crazily. Valium. That is what I needed. They say that it calms you; I had no idea if this was true, but I think right now, I would have taken just about anything! Shakily, I reached for my glass, pulling my wine forward and taking a big sip from the glass, fighting the urge to drain it dry.

My heart thundered in my chest and again, there was the strange clenching in the pit of my stomach as a strange wonderful warmth began to course through me. I thought it might be the wine, but I knew better.

This sensation was strong, sensual and seemed to rush through me like a brush fire. What on earth was going on? I hardly knew this man but my senses were working overtime.

I do not know how I made it through dinner, or how I made it out of the restaurant for that matter. He turned out to be the perfect dinner companion, making me laugh often as one glass of wine turned into two, keeping me entertained with stories about his business and his clients as we made our way through appetizers of prosciutto wrapped mozzarella with vine ripened tomatoes — no fish because he'd remembered this from an earlier email — dry aged sirloin steaks with shallot butter and flourless chocolate espresso cake followed by the most exquisite coffee I'd ever had. My head was spinning and I don't think it had anything to do with the wine we'd enjoyed with our dinner.

I felt pampered and spoiled — and terrified of what would come next. As Mama Jett had always said "there's no such thing as a free lunch baby"…er…dinner and I prayed that at least the dinner would end well. Baby kept me chatting throughout the meal, smoothly sliding his credit card to the server to settle the bill.

Rising from the table, he extended his hand to help me from my seat, gently guiding me to the exit, signaling the end to a wonderful first date. As we walked toward the exit, his hand curved under my elbow to gently direct me forward, I reflected on how different from all of my other dates this evening had been and wondered exactly when the evening would take a turn at crazy as so many of my other so called dates had. He walked me outside, giving my ticket to the waiting valet.

Ok, now, I thought. Now he would expect me to invite him back to my place for a little repayment for the wonderful meal. I peeked a look at him to find that he was smiling at me. Waiting?

No, Mikki, not on the first date, not ever, I reprimanded myself, pushing aside the fog created by good food, good wine and good company. I cleared my throat, turning to look at him.

"I've had a really nice time," I tried, surprised at the tremor in my voice. He continued to smile.

"So have I, Mikki." He said simply, his hand still at my elbow. Ok...maybe he hadn't? Maybe he had rethought his decision to meet me. I don't know why that thought bugged me, but it did. We both watched as my SUV came around the corner and stopped in front of us.

The date was over. Tipping the valet, he thanked him and led me around to the driver's side. Settling me inside, he leaned down, smiling at me. I smiled back, the action trembling along my lips. Reaching forward, he wound a long strand of my curly hair around his fingers, watching as the hair slid between his fingertips.

"I know that you have your reservations, Mikki, but I want to see you again." He stated. I opened my mouth prepared to speak, my heart singing "yes, yes!" as common sense tried to interrupt. There were so many reasons why this would never work, he had to know that. But the heart wants what the heart wants, and this heart wanted to see him again too.

He shook his head, seeming to want to head off any objections I may have made.

"I know it's a lot to absorb, but, I know that we could be good together. Don't ask me how I know it, but I do." His hand curved around to cup my cheek and I closed my eyes, exhaling deeply. He groaned aloud, and I looked up into those dark eyes.

"I have a big project that I am working on in Dallas and I will be out of town for nearly a month. I would like very much if I could call you, from time to time. I won't be a pest; I just want to know how you are. Would that be all right?"

I smiled at him.

"That would be just fine." I told him.

Burning In Hell…

"Girl, what is the matter with you?" Sonni exclaimed. What? I looked up at her in alarm. What did I do? I looked around the floor where I sat shuffling through mounds of home decorating materials then back at her, puzzled.

What? What on earth was she talking about? Sonni had text me to come over to her place in a hurry; she was having a redecorating emergency, which could only mean one thing. Man trouble. So I had dragged myself over, in a funk and all, to help her pick out new drapes for the game room that she was remodeling in her condo.

Well, not really a game room, I supposed it was to be more of some kind of entertainment room. "Sonni's Pleasure Palace," she'd said with a wink. For whatever reason, I was just not sure that I wanted to know what this meant exactly, but Sonni, being Sonni, had recently purchased one of the largest televisions that I had ever seen and she'd decided to build her entertainment room around this television.

I had teased her at the time of thinking just like a guy, and Sonni had scowled saying, "Honey, girls like it big too. Besides, I want to experience the entire experience when I watch the new John Legend concert on video." I had laughed at her.

She'd decided to do the entire room in rich shades of wine, gold, greens, and browns. I know that it sounds crazy, like some kind of weird kaleidoscope, but once I saw it all together, I was a believer. Now, she had a dilemma, having to choose between silk or otherwise for her room darkening drapes.

I swear this girl brought home as many swatches as they had available. Now, we sat on the floor of the said "pleasure palace," surrounded by various shades of fabric. I have to admit that after the first ten or so, all of the swatches began to feel the same, maybe I had just rubbed my fingertips numb.

I remember sitting there with a handful in my lap, looking at them one after the other. Then I heard Sonni saying something. I looked at her, I'm sure that I must have looked crazy.

"Girl, what is the matter with you?" she asked with a laugh. I frowned at her, what in the world was she talking about?

"What?" I asked. Sonni began to laugh in earnest then. "Girl, you are a million miles away from here and you're going to rub a hole in that sample! Give me that!" I looked down at the sample that I had been holding and she took it from me, examining the fragile swatch for damage.

"So ..." she prodded.

"So what?" I asked.

"Where were you?" Sonni began to stack the samples in like-colored piles. I watched her idly, wondering where on earth to start.

"Sonni, how young is too young?" I asked, hoping to sound offhand and relaxed.

Sonni, the multitasker, stopped tasking. She looked at me, a slow smile spreading over her face.

"You met someone!" She exclaimed. I held up my hands in protest as she jumped up from the floor, knocking over her little fabric piles.

"You met somebody!" she yelled out loud.

"No, wait, no, no, no ... " I protested again, also jumping to my feet. Sonni wasn't trying to hear any of my denials. She began doing some kind of manic two stepping thing around the room.

"Wait, Sonni, I'm just asking ..." Sonni was not waiting to hear any excuses.

"I cannot believe it!" she did a little jig around the entertainment room; I took this to mean that she was pleased with herself. This matchmaking thing had to be some kind of record for her. She stopped dancing and stood grinning from ear to ear, out of breath from her erratic dancing.

"Ok, tell me everything."

I scratched my head, rolling my eyes at her. "There's really nothing to tell. Just somebody that I met recently."

"Ha!" Sonni exclaimed. "There is absolutely something to tell! You were sitting over there looking as if you were anywhere but here! I called your name three times before you even heard me!"

I turned to look at her. She was exaggerating, she had to be. I felt my face flushing; this was unlike the hot flashes that I had been having lately. "I'm just...I think he's interesting and I wanted to know how young is too young?"

Sonni threw herself back on the buttery soft leather sofa that took up one entire wall, laughing in earnest, my stricken expression doing absolutely nothing to help, causing her to laugh all the more.

"Well, how young is he?" she asked. I did not want to tell her. I could hardly believe it myself.

"Thirty-five." I said and the second I had said the words, I wanted to take them back.

"Damn!" Sonni exclaimed, leaning forward, her arms raised in the air like she had just scored the game-winning touchdown. "Younger is good! This sounds promising! You're a cougar!" She teased.

That word again. I sank onto the sofa beside her, covering my face with my hands, mortified.

"I know, I know. That's crazy! I just want the record to show that I did not pursue this man! I told him that I was not interested. I told him that I was *way* too old for him. I told him that I could be his mother. But he just would not quit."

Sonni hooted, fanning herself with her hand; she obviously loved this and all of the discomfort it was causing me.

"Hm! I like it! So," she turned toward me, pulling my hands away from my face. "Tell me about him. What's he like? Is he cute?" I did more than that, we went to her computer and brought up his profile.

"Damn!" Sonni said again. "Baby is fine!"

Again, I felt sick, just like the first time when I'd met him.

"You're not helping, Sonni!"

Sonni laughed. "No, but I'm sure that he can help you!" she teased me. I felt the strange warm return, the same warmth that had crept over me when I was with Baby at the restaurant.

"Oh God, Sonni! Is that all you can think about?" I was feeling hot again, like my body was a blast furnace.

"Well, it's not all I think about, but I like to think about it!" she quipped, bending over to read Baby's profile.

"He's got it going on," she said. "So, when are you going to meet him in person?" I was speechless then, squeezing my hands together and Sonni turned around to look at me.

"I already did," I said quietly. Sonni whooped and began to do that little jig thing again, taking me by my hands and spinning me around. I was beginning to feel dizzy as well as sick.

"You little hussy! You've been holding out on me!" she accused, laughing at me.

"No, I just…this is…and you know this is really weird!" I stammered.

Sonni frowned. "What's so weird about it?" I threw my hands up, frustrated.

"Sonni! He is way too young!" I exclaimed.

"For what?" Sonni asked.

"Oh my God!" I could not believe that I was even thinking about this. "For me! You know what people are going to think? That I'm some kind of perverted weirdo cradle robber! I'm going to look ridiculous, like one of those old women who have had too many facelifts. People are going to stare at me just like that!"

"Who cares?" Sonni sniffed retrieving her little swatches from the floor. I did… Didn't I? This was getting really strange. I know that I probably should care, but...

"So," she trained those eyes on me. "Tell me about him."

"It was the email that you responded to," I told her, angling a pointed glare at her. I hadn't forgotten, I still owed her a choking for what she'd gotten me into. Sonni whooped loudly again, obviously pleased with herself.

I told Sonni how he had written to me after viewing my online profile, and how at first, I did not write him back. I thought he was joking. After he wrote me a second time, then the third and finally the fourth time. I told her how I had thought that maybe he was cyber stalking me and how I had finally responded if for no other reason than to tell him that our age difference made a chance at getting to know each other unlikely.

And then came Sonni's intervention. She was pleased as punch to learn that when we met we had instant chemistry and that our first date had gone so well.

"I asked if this was some sort of experiment for him," I told her and she shrugged.

"So what? Just enjoy it while it lasts. No one says that he's going to be your happily ever after. It's okay to indulge in a little happiness, Mikki."

This was true, but I was more concerned that more than anything, that he might really be crazy and in need of some therapy to resolve some issues about his own mother. And speaking of mothers, what would Mama Jett think about me seeing a man so much younger than I was?

"Honey," she reassured me. "You already know what I think. And I think that you would probably be surprised how Mama Jett would react. She might surprise you."

Right, I would certainly be surprised. And what about Dereon? What kind of example am I setting for him? Heck, Baby was only seventeen years — oh my God! — seventeen years older than my son!

"Whatever you decide, Mikki, Mama Jett and Dereon will have to respect your choices."

I shrugged trying to appear indifferent. "Well, at any rate, he's given me time to decide if I want to see him again. He's out of town for about a month in Dallas for business. He says that he would like to call me from time to time to check in, but you know how that works, the old "I'll call you" ploy. He's probably forgotten about me already." I shrugged again, feeling the funk that I'd been in for the past few days creep over me again.

Sonni smiled a tight little smile. "Well, that certainly explains the mood," she verbally poked at me, at which I shook my fist a little in her direction.

"Granted, it might be a little early to invite everyone into the relationship." She continued. "Use this time to get to know him better. This time, this newness, this time is just for you."

"It's always possible that he thinks you're just a fling, and he might actually have issues with his mother, or who knows what else. He just may be everything you are looking for. Just not in the "age appropriate" package you were expecting. How does he make you feel?"

At that, I felt myself getting hot again, a warm flush creeping up my neck to stain my cheeks. Sonni smiled knowingly.

"I have to admit, Girl, I like seeing that look on your face. Just go with it for a while. Focus on what kind of person he is and how he makes you feel. He sounds pretty wonderful to me. It's good to see you interested in someone again." Sonni said and I shook my head then, irritated.

"But it's nothing serious. Besides, I haven't heard from him since our date." I told her. It could not be serious...

"Oh no, no. Of course not! Certainly not," Sonni coughed, laughing at me. "And it doesn't have to be right now. Just enjoy it, if it is short-lived, then so be it. It will be good for you while it lasts."

"I think that he is just curious, you know, about the difference between older and younger women. Maybe it's an ego thing, you know, I'm so cool, I can score with an older woman." I reasoned. There was no way on this planet that I was going to admit that beyond sexual satisfaction, men of lesser age could possibly have more to offer.

And did he?" Sonni asked a big grin on her face. I stared at her blankly.

"Did he what?" I asked.

"Score."

My mouth dropped open, this I knew because I began choking on absolutely nothing.

"Sonni! Are you crazy! I just met the guy!"

"Well, we are modern women, Mikki," she teased. "Remember, we're seasoned, sensual, and sexy."

"Argh!" I plunked myself back down onto the couch. "Leave me alone; you're giving me a headache…" I grumbled.

"Well, Mikki, if it's any consolation, this is not a big deal." Sonni said her answer matter of fact.

"Oh, so you're saying you would do this?" Sonni smiled conspiratorially. I turned to look at her, perching on the arm of the sofa. My eyes widened with surprise.

"You already have!" I picked up a swatch and threw it at her. She bat it away, laughing at my shocked expression. "Now who's been holding out on people?" She sniffed, shrugging.

"A few times, actually. Look. Mikki, it's probably more common than you think. Look at Demi and Ashton …"

I shook my head. "No. Mr. Know It All has already told me — extensively — how he knew that Demi and Ashton would never make it."

Sonni snorted. "That man would not know about love and human nature if it drove up into his school's lobby and honked its horn."

I laughed at her, having to agree with her on this one, the man really did not seem to have a clue about anything like that.

Wait a minute! Love, nobody said anything about love...

"Nobody said anything about love ..." I echoed the thought. Sonni laughed at me, shaking her head.

"Mikki, you've got to lighten up! This could be good for you. Who knows, you might even have a little fun if you'd get your panties out of a knot over this."

"Sonni!"

Sonni pecked me on the forehead with her index finger. "Look, girl, I'm going to tell you the hard truth, that's why I'm your best friend. You think too much about all of everything."

I knew that it would not do me any good to protest, Sonni was not about to let up on this one. "I have known you forever, and I know why you're afraid to take chances."

I began to sulk; I hated being told about myself. She shook my shoulder gently.

"Sweetie," she said softly. "He is not Dereon's dad. And you cannot continue to punish yourself and every other man that you meet for what that fool did."

I was not, I wanted to say. That was so long ago, over and done with. But I knew that it was true, and I was still letting my mistrust over that joker interfere with any and every relationship that I had or hoped to have with any man I would ever meet.

"It's ok to relax and have fun, Mikki. It's ok to put it away, whether it is for a minute or a lifetime. You've been wearing this pain like an old coat. You're afraid to get rid of it because you think that you will forget where you came from, like you're afraid that if you put it away, it will happen again. Honey, give yourself more credit than that. You're smarter than that. Mikki. And," she turned to look at me again.

"If it's not serious, there's still time left in the summer dating challenge to find someone else."

I threw a handful of swatches at her head. She was not letting me off the hook yet.

Mrs. Dating Married Man

Day forty...

I could not believe that it was already July and within the next month, Dereon would be on his way to Texas to begin his freshman year of college. Lately we seemed to spend a considerable amount of time — and money — in preparation for the big event, buying things for his dorm room, finalizing school enrollment paperwork, transcripts, grant, scholarship and other financial paperwork. There was even a visit to Dr. DeJovne to make sure that his immunizations were up to date.

Dereon and I seemed to have settled into this pattern: I would come home, pick him up and together we would head out to the stores. It was more than a little unsettling to find that a lot of places were already staging their "back to school" sales, and I felt that familiar sadness as I once again had to face the reality that soon my nest would be empty.

The upside was that by August, Sonni's little dating experiment would be over and I would finally be free to enjoy some well earned downtime — no shopping, no crazy dates, no coffee meets. This fact alone was something to look forward to; maybe after I'd had a chance to decaffeinate from all of my recent coffee dates, my fits of insomnia would disappear. One could hope that they would...

Another bright spot was that Baby, true to his word, checked in often: by phone, email, and text and strangely I found myself looking forward to these moments. Sometimes the calls would last ten minutes, sometimes they would last for an hour or more; Dereon seemed a little peeved that now he would have to share "phone time" with his mother.

Dereon had taken a part-time job to try to help pay for some of the "extras" that he felt that he wanted for his dorm room but I couldn't help but wonder if he'd taken this particular job because Jasmine worked at the same place. I was all set to buy him a thirteen-inch color television with a remote, for his dorm room, but Dereon had decided that he wanted, no he needed, something bigger and since I wasn't budging in this area, he'd decided to try to save up for it himself. I admit my reasons are selfish; something tells me that with such a big television in the dorm not much homework would get done. Maybe we should stick with the thirteen-inch...

While I worried about sheets, curtains, storage containers, toiletries, microwaves and all of the typical things that a mom usually worries about and a teenager takes for granted, Dereon worried about the "more important things," like whether he would get a new VCR for his bigger television. Or whether he could have a new stereo since the one he had purchased a year earlier was so outdated and all. What about an iPod? What about a new CD player? What about a new laptop, the one he used during high school had a few keys that stuck. On, and on, and on. All I could see was dollar signs at this stage, I felt as if I should turn my pockets inside out for effect and say to him, "Hey kid, you are robbing me blind. I haven't anything else to give."

Actually, I was enjoying this; this was quite possibly one of the last times I would be able to take him shopping, one of the last times when we could be Mom and son.

Kids his age were always talking about Public Displays of Affection or PDAs and how they were a big no-no. No hugging, kissing, etc. by the parental unit. I wondered what he and his friends would think about my PDMs or Public Displays of Mothering. No, absolutely none of the aforementioned would be allowed. I probably better keep that at a minimum, or sneak in a hug when he was not looking. We would not want to embarrass the poor child, excuse me, the poor young man.

Needless to say, after a long afternoon of spending money and allowing Dereon to drag me from one store to another at the mall, I was ready to just come home and collapse. Live to shop another day.

I stumbled into the house, my arms full of bags and boxes, where had he disappeared to so quickly? I could hear his voice from somewhere in the house. He was on his cell phone, talking to Jasmine. I shook my head. Who knows how these two will manage to live without each other once Dereon heads off to school.

I chuckled. I could always tell when he is talking to a girl; he would cradle the phone to his ear while jamming his free hand into his pocket and his voice would drop at least a couple of octaves and he resorted to speaking in monosyllable words. Yeah, no. Uh-huh. I guess that was code for my mom is listening.

Don't worry about it kid, I got this. You can get the next truckload. Huffing, I pushed the door open with my backside, swinging around to toss my purse into the chair, my keys on to the hall table. I set the bags and boxes on the floor and began to tug off my shoes; sandals were not my favorite style of shoe, but I figured that my standard three-inch heels would not have been shopping friendly.

I tossed the offenders off to the side and lowered myself into the recliner, closing my eyes for a few brief minutes. Thank God! I loved coming home, peace and quiet, no overhead music chafing my nerves, no children running between the racks and up and down the aisles, no parents chasing runaway toddlers, just blessed quiet...

I must have dozed off for a minute, because somewhere in the back of my mind, a tiny sound poked me out of my slumber. I sat up, looking around. How long had I been asleep? My hand instinctively went up to smooth the hair on the back of my head that stood up like springs.

The tiny pinging sound was coming from my laptop, which I had left plugged up on the kitchen counter to charge my battery. The constant, annoying pinging was the sound that reminded me that I had an email waiting.

I wandered toward the annoying machine, wondering vaguely where Dereon had gone. I will tell you, that kid never stuck around when he thought that there was work to be done, a typical teenager avoidance technique commonly used to avoid having to help with any and all household chores. Dereon seemed to have it down to an art form.

The bags and boxes of goodies, I'd noticed, were gone. Well, at least he put his own stuff away. OK, let's see what we have here, I gingerly thumbed the built in mouse pad to scroll down and click. One new email.

What opened and filled my screen was, well, it certainly was not what I was expecting. The picture that filled my screen was a professional photo of one of the most adorable little girls that I had ever seen in my life; big bright eyes, a single dimple on her chin, a wide smile full of those cute little baby teeth. Two big puffballs of hair, and she was dressed in lace and ribbons from head to toe. This was a girly girl, as precious and as beautiful as they come, her little hands were placed together as if she were praying or saying grace.

I smiled at the picture, scrolling down to read the message below. It was probably one of those chain letters that you get every now and then; you know the kind, save the children. Or "this adorable little girl really needs your help today. She needs a kidney transplant surgery; her parents cannot afford it on their own, what with other children to feed in the household. Could you please find it in the goodness of your heart to send a small donation to help this adorable little baby girl?"

I just could not remember how many of these things I received on any given day. There seemed to be a scam every minute as these scoundrels hid behind a perfect baby smile to weasel money out of whomever they could. Can you help?

What the message read below the perfect little baby's picture made my blood run cold and I felt sick. I pulled up a stool from the breakfast bar to have a seat. And then I began to read.

* * *

She chose this restaurant, not me; I was glad that our meeting was in a public place. These days you just could not be too careful, this was a woman who thought that I was having a cyber affair with her husband after all. She wouldn't kill me in a public place, would she? She'd seemed so calm, her email wasting no time; rather, Mrs. Married Man preferred to get directly to the point:

"Dear Mikki. You don't know me, but you know my husband. My name is Jana. The little girl in the picture is Kayla, our daughter. You are not his first cyber affair."

I had frowned then. Affair? It was just coffee! Coffee standing in the corner of his Bank's lobby to be exact. That certainly did not amount to my having an affair with the man by any measure. Hell, it didn't even qualify as a date as far as I was concerned.

Besides, it was not as if I knew that Dating Married Man was married, he had stated that he had lost his wife. He said nothing of a child. Had I known, there would have been no coffee break, let alone some imaginary cyber affair.

The technicality of his "relationship" with Jana had blossomed into a full blown lie; Dating Married Man shared more than a condo and a name with Jana, he also shared a daughter.

"I know that I probably should not contact you like this," she'd continued in her email. "But I feel that it's only fair to tell my side of his story."

She'd proposed that we meet in person and I'd agreed, if for no other reason than to tell my side of the story and to clear my name.

I walked into the restaurant, not knowing exactly whom I was supposed to meet. I had dressed simply for my meeting with Jana. Not wanting to appear as some femme fatale who was after Jana's husband, I wore a simple chambray shirtdress in light blue and a pair of platform sandals.

I looked around the restaurant, my eyes resting on each female face. What would Jana look like? Short, tall, would she know me when she saw me? She had the advantage as she'd seen my picture from Dating Married Man's entries with the dating site. My eyes came to rest on a small woman seated at a table near the window and somehow, I knew that it was Jana, call it intuition.

Jana was also dressed simply and I had the feeling that although she was dressed neatly, the woman at the table was Jana at her best.

Small and thin, Jana appeared plain with no makeup, not even lipstick. Her dark hair was graying at the temples and she wore it pulled back in a plain ponytail at the back of her head. She wore no jewelry, no adornment.

Although the temperature outside was nearly ninety degrees, give or take a degree, Jana wore a long sleeved burgundy dress with a white Peter Pan collar, the style not suiting her small frame as the dress seemed to swallow her whole.

A hostess walked up to me and I waved her off, telling her that I'd found the party that I was looking for. Smoothing my hands along my dress, I walked to the table, stopping at Jana's elbow.

"Jana?" I asked. The small plain woman looked up at me and smiled, the action seeming tired and I could not help but wonder how many of these meetings she'd had already.

"Mikki?" She asked. I nodded.

"Can I sit?" I asked.

Jana nodded and I sat, noting that she appeared to hide no weapons, but if she reached for the butter knife, I was going to have to take her out.

"Thank you for meeting me," Jana began, her voice wavering and I prayed, dear Lord, please don't let her cry. I really wasn't sure how I would handle the situation if she did.

I inhaled deeply, preferring to jump right in.

"Jana," I began. "First of all, I want to tell you that I would have never agreed to meet your husband had I known he was married. He misrepresented himself online as not married, saying that he had "lost" his wife and was wanting to meet someone, I guess to talk to, to commiserate, I don't know." I gestured helplessly.

"Jana," I began, leaning forward to look into her face. It was important, both for her and for me, that she really hear me. "I didn't discover until our meeting that he was married but you have my word, the minute that I found out, I ended our meeting. I have had no further contact with your husband and will not. That I can promise you."

Jana smiled that tired little smile again, raising one hand to rub it along her brow, the action resigned.

"Unfortunately, you're not the first, Mikki, or the only one," she said, her voice soft, her eyes sad. "I met my husband on the rebound when I was newly single, just months after a very nasty divorce. I had been married for five years to a man who cheated on me almost from day one. But he seemed different. My divorce was a very long, very painful time consuming ordeal. He was so sweet to me, so supportive. I told him that I just was not ready to jump into something new with anyone."

The waiter arrived to take our orders and we ordered coffees to start. Jana just seemed to need someone to talk to and I figured that I could do this for her, now that I knew that she wasn't planning to kill me for having coffee with her husband.

"If you don't mind me asking, what happened? How did it all come to this?" I asked, setting my purse down on the floor next to me. Jana shook her head, her hand trembling as it smoothed over her hair. I followed the motion, stopping at her face, noticing that she could be so pretty if she took care of herself. I remembered how well taken care of Dating Married Man had appeared to be during our coffee break and it became clear to me where all of Jana's time and energy was spent: making sure that Dating Married Man's every need was taken care of while giving little thought to her own needs. She continued.

"The scars were just too numerous; too painful and raw, the ending of my first marriage was still too fresh in my mind. I told him that I needed time. He seemed to understand. He was patient, so different from my ex-husband. But I met him too soon. I was in a vulnerable state. We dated and I got pregnant." She took a sip of her coffee and I did the same.

"I really had no idea what was going on with him initially, he was so quiet, so sweet that I would not have suspected what was coming next. He begged me to marry him; he wanted his baby to have his name. He did not want me to work; he said that he wanted to provide for his wife and child. In the beginning. I thought that this was sweet, again, so unlike my first marriage. I thought this to be noble. Unfortunately, I did not see the bars of my cell until I was locked securely behind them." She laughed wryly.

"I was six months pregnant with Kayla when he said that he had a meeting to go to, something to do with system changes and such at work. He had to be there." She placed the napkin in her lap, her eyes going to stare out the window.

"Little did I know that he was having an affair with a woman who worked in his department. When he refused to leave me for her, the woman decided to try to force his hand."

I shook my head, pausing when the waiter came back, waiting until he'd refilled our cups and retreated before I spoke again.

"What did she do?" I asked. I had to know. Jana shrugged.

"She called our home phone number and told me the details of their affair, what they would do, where they would meet. How that he was feeling trapped because of the baby. That he ran to her because I was neglecting his "needs". How she would be there for "whatever he needed" without question." Jana stirred creamer into her coffee, then set down her spoon.

"The thing that really hurt most was that she claimed that he told her that he did not want the baby, that he was only staying with me out of pity because I had no job, no money of my own and no place to go and no family nearby to help out should he decide to leave me." Jana gave a little laugh then.

"She actually asked me what it would take for me to let him go. He had promised her all kinds of things. Once the baby arrived, things would be different. Once the baby reached a certain age, he would be able to tell me that he wanted to break with me and marry her. He told her everything that she needed to hear to keep the affair going."

I stared at Jana, a slow prickle crawling up my spine as I reflected back to my own history with Dereon's father. Is this how the situation had appeared from the other side? With only the names changed, this could easily be the story from Darren's wife's point of view. Having never met her, all I had was his side of the story and my stomach clenched as I thought of the part that I'd played in that drama. I felt sick. Jana smiled, not noticing my own discomfort, caught up in her own drama. She continued speaking, her voice seeming to come from very far away.

"If she had not called me, I would probably never have known what he was up to. At first, he denied seeing this woman; he denied even knowing her, although she worked in his department and reported to him directly. Then he promised, actually crying, that he would never, ever do it again. He blamed it on him being so lonely now that I was pregnant and not particularly interested in sex with him at that stage."

Great, I thought. Blame the woman… Jana shook her head, anger flashing across her features, disappearing as quickly as it had appeared. Maybe I should keep my eye on that butter knife after all… She shook her head again, sighing deeply.

"Looking back on all of the late after hour "meetings" and "trainings," I became skeptical. All of the numerous excuses. I told him that I could not live like this. He promised, vowed that he loved me and he wanted Kayla and our marriage more than anything. Things got better for a little while; we had a good few years. I figured that either he had stopped cheating, as he had promised that he would, or that he got a lot better at hiding it."

Her eyes fastened on me then, and she shook her head again.

"Recently, the late meetings started up again, and again I was suspicious. Experience is an excellent teacher, sometimes a cruel teacher." She stopped to gaze out the window.

"That's how I found you, Mikki," she stated. I felt my brow rise and wondered if this was when I should take my leave. Jana continued.

"One night while he was sleeping, I checked his computer, the laptop that he carried with him everywhere. I discovered that he was using a different name, different email account; at the same time he was telling me that he loved me. That was where I saw your profile saved on his computer along with a dozen or more profiles of other women he was communicating with from the online dating service. That was when I found your telephone number and other info stored in his telephone and I learned that he was up to his old tricks again. He never stopped seeing other women, he just got better at hiding it."

I tried not to look shocked, but was unsuccessful. A dozen or more profiles? Dating Married Man was a player, a big time player.

"My trust in this man has been completely destroyed," Jana stated. "I cannot honestly say that this is the man that I thought I had married and I cannot say that I still love him, not the way I had. It is only for the sake of our daughter, I have attempted to stay. But I don't think that this will be enough. Not this time."

I shook my head as well. No, it should not be. Dating Married Man is a perpetual cheater, like a child, he has tested the boundaries of his marriage and knows exactly how far to go and how hard to push against the boundaries. In the past, the baby was enough to keep the marriage, such as it was, intact.

"What are you going to do?" I asked. She shrugged, the bulky dress seeming to weigh her down like an anchor.

"He says that he loves Kayla and me. When I confronted him about his meeting with you, he admitted to meeting other women and agreed to go to counseling."
How noble of him! I frowned.

"Now despite his confessing that there are for sure two other women, he still wants me but I have the gut feeling that there are more than the two he is admitted to. I still want to raise my daughter with him, but a part of me will never be able to trust him again."

Holy cow! Two other women? Dating Married Man was busy and it pained me to realize that I had been right, Jana had conducted more than one of this type of meeting. The thought of this made me really sad for her because she seemed really nice.

A storm of emotions tumbled over me, one wave after another, as I was forced to acknowledge that eighteen years ago I was the other woman, I knew this place, all too well. Dereon's father, though I had never told Dereon, was married.

God! How ashamed I was to say it even after all of this time. The words themselves sounded so ugly to me. A married man. Even now, it still shamed me. I had an affair with a married man. He had always said all of the right things. He knew what to say and when, and to the younger Mikki that I was, I had foolishly believed that I would be the one. I believed that I was special. He made me feel loved. Appreciated. He had told me time and time again that his life did not start until the day that he had met me.

And I had believed him. He explained that he had been so lonely, so sad in his marriage. That he had married much too young. That his wife was not well, or that she was too busy or that leaving her would be difficult. Little did I know that all of his lies had been cleverly crafted to do exactly what it did, draw me in.

I believed him when he told me that I gave him a reason to get up every morning. That he hated it when we were apart, that he could not wait until we saw each other again. I found myself postponing plans with friends and family, I put friendships on hold, waiting for his calls, which sometimes came, but most times did not.

At his suggestion, I had even tried to put my friendship with Sonni on hold to be with this man, but she was having none of that. Sonni, God love her, never condemned me for my decision. She allowed me to make my own decisions and my own mistakes. And she was determined to be there for me, come what may.

I shook my head angrily. The man was incapable of choosing anyone but himself. And I was here, in that place once again. Against my wishes this time. In a situation that I had sworn to myself I would never be in again. But this time was different. I had stayed in the situation with Dereon's father knowingly, with the full realization that I was having an affair with a married man.

This time? I did not choose this. I would never have chosen this. Dating Married Man lied. I would have never, ever agreed to meet him had I known that he was married. Been there, done that. Not after everything that I had gone through, that I had put myself through with Dereon's father. I knew firsthand how the lies and dishonesty and half-truths could wreck your life. And the life of your child. I reached across the table, taking Jana's small hands in mine, forcing her to look at me.

"Jana," I began, squeezing her hands gently. "I cannot tell you what to do, I have no idea how this must feel from your side of the table. But I too have a child, a son, and a handsome smart young man. I would be hurt and ashamed if he ever treated a woman in this way. I wish I had some words of wisdom to offer to you but the best I can say is this — be true, both to yourself and to your daughter."

I squeezed her hands again as her eyes began to tear up and she began to cry. I groaned. Lord knows, this woman has probably cried more than her share of tears over this man already and it pained me to cause her more tears.

" You have to be strong for Kayla," I said, looking into her tiny face. "Whether you stay with your husband or not. It's up to you to raise your daughter to expect more for herself, you deserve more for yourself. Teach her to be strong, and courageous. To expect to receive the love she deserves and never, ever settle for less. If she does not, if a man does not treat her the way she deserves to be treated, then she has to be brave enough to let him go. Sometimes, to teach the big lessons to our little ones, we have to lead by example."

I released her then, taking a twenty dollar bill out of my wallet to pay for our coffees. I stood up preparing to leave and Jana looked up at me, her face wet, her eyes shining.

"Thank you, Mikki," she whispered. "You're a good woman."

A good woman… Yes, I do believe that I am. I reached over the table and hugged her , Jana's slight body seeming to crumple as I held her tight.

"And you're stronger than you know, Jana. Be well."

She nodded and I left the restaurant.

Missing You

The cell phone rattled on top of the desk next to my cup of cold coffee, the loud buzzing startling me with its intensity. Frowning, I glanced at my watch and then at the phone. Who now? I had a meeting in ten minutes — now nine minutes — and I still had one report to assemble.

The Temptress had taken pity on me and had printed off and assembled a number of the remaining reports for me before heading off to make sure that the conference room had been evacuated and straightened before the meeting. Lord knows that I hoped that the last meeting had broken up early. The Temptress could be quite intimidating when someone messed up her plans. I picked up the phone, looking at the screen, a tingle spreading through me as I read the message.

"Hi," the screen read and I smiled.

Baby! I looked around feeling giddy and I cradled the phone in my palm. But why was he texting, he'd told me that he would be stuck in one meeting after another and may not be able to contact me until later.

"Hi yourself," I text back. "How are your meetings going?" After a very short pause, his response appeared on my screen.

"Boring, what's going on with you?" I laughed softly, imagining how his expression might look when he was bored.

"On my way to a boring meeting as well." The pause between my message and his response was so long, I figured that he'd had to leave the conversation as quickly as it had began.

"Sorry," he returned. "Had a question from a developer. Any other time this stuff would excite me." His text read. Then half a beat later, "I miss you."

I sat back in my chair, my heart drumming against my ribcage. I could honestly say that I missed him too.

"I miss you too," I wrote back, my admission honest. Another long pause followed then the message appeared on my screen.

"I wish I could see you tonight."

Oh yes, I wanted to see him tonight too. I know it seemed sudden, after all, I barely knew him, but whenever I spoke with him, I felt as if I'd always known him.

"I wish the same," I wrote back, meaning it. His response was quicker this time, the phone vibrating in my hand before I could put it on the desk.

"Soon. I wish I could wrap this process up sooner, the techs seem to be dragging their feet intentionally."

Then I did it, feeling goofy as I engaged in a spontaneous silly moment. I text him an emoticon of a smiling face.

"It will all be worth it in the end. You've worked so hard for this."

He sent a smiling face back. "You're late for your meeting, sweetheart. We'll talk soon."

Sweetheart...I smiled at the endearment, then I realized what he'd just said. Oh goodness! I looked at the clock on my computer. I was late! Silencing the ringer on my phone, I ran down the hall to my meeting.

Oh Baby

Day forty-five… Fifty shades of oh my goodness!

I lay on the couch, my nose practically pressed against the screen of my e-reader, my eyes wide with disbelief as I read. I am certain that my mouth hung open. What in the world was Sonni thinking when she suggested this book? Ugh! I shook my head. Never mind! I pursed my lips as I exhaled deeply. I think that I can figure this one out!

I'd decided that for tonight, I was going to give myself a little break from the whole "click a date" thing and enjoy some much needed alone time. Though she relented just for tonight, Sonni was determined that, since I hadn't "nailed anything down" with Baby or anybody else, I should continue her summer dating challenge, stuffing every free moment of my evenings and weekends with trying to find someone, after all "a deal's a deal," she had quipped in her sing-songy voice. Just for tonight – I couldn't care less about the whole dating thing or Sonni's deal from hell.

Sonni, bless her heart, had a date. And Mama Jett was off somewhere meeting with those wild ladies from her Red Hat Ladies group. Dereon was out with his friends for the evening leaving me all alone — what a shame! The house was still, music streaming through the wireless speakers of my home theatre system from my favorite jazz station, the soft strands of the music filling the dimly lit room, the warm tones and beats wrapping themselves around me like the comfortable throw I was lying under.

Perfect. Good music, good wine. Not an action flick on in the entire place. This evening was going to be just about me. I all but giggled as I sank down into the soft buttery leather of the sofa, kicking off my slippers and snuggling in.

Oh yes, perfect! With my trusty glass of Pinot Grigio at the ready, I engrossed myself in the tawdry tale that everyone seemed to go crazy over.

Sonni had recommended this book, Fifty Shades of Grey, as a means of breaking through my inhibitions about this whole Internet dating thing. I guess that she thought that I could use a little loosening up when it came to throwing myself at virtual strangers. Hey, I am all for relaxing and loosening up, within reason, but this book just had me shaking my head in amazement.

I guess that there had been a lot of hubbub going around about this book; I'd even watched a recorded segment of "The View" on my Tivo where Barbara Walters had been talking about the book. Really? On mainstream television? I don't know, there was just something really weird about watching Barbara Walters, a serious journalist, talking about sex and bondage like it was perfectly normal. I couldn't even bring myself to purchase the book in the store, chickening out at the last moment and purchasing it on my e-reader instead where no one could see it or look at me with shocked surprise at what I was reading.

In the book, the main character, a young virginal type, managed to become ensnared and succumbed to the wicked, wicked ways of her dominant pursuer who likes nothing more than building a relationship on his need to spank and bind her for all types of sexual activity.

Oh, these silly young girls! I chuckled. Some of the, shall I say, techniques explored in the book did not seem very believable — or doable for that matter, especially not for this forty-five year old body.

I am neither young nor virginal and at this stage in the game, the book would have been titled Fifty Stages of Traction. I mean, I can be as adventurous as the next diva but come on! To tie my ankle to my wrist is going to take some maneuvering. And a whole lot of wine. I think it's safe to say that I will not be channeling Miss Anastasia Steele any time soon! But it's a fun read nonetheless.

What I don't get is her supposed to be best friend. She knows about this man's propensity for major kinkiness but makes little to no mention of this to the kinky guy. Even if she were sworn to secrecy under the pain of death, I just cannot see that happening with Sonni. The second she'd gotten wind of some joker wanting to tie me up and hit me, she would have strapped Mr. Fifty Shades to the first train headed out of town, bidding him a fond farewell only after getting in a few "spanks" of her own on his rich obsessed hide.

I'd read somewhere that they were in talks to make the book into a movie though I am hard pressed to figure how they will get a BSDM Romance movie past the censors. Wait, can we honestly say BSDM and Romance in the same breath? What kind of rating would they put on something like that? Hey, stranger things have happened. What's even stranger is that I read an article in a reputable newspaper about the rise in the sales of rope and such since the book was released. Geez…

There is no one I would let tie me up for….wait… now, Baby…don't get me wrong, but even with all of my prudishness — is that even a word? — even with all of my internet virgin-ness, I might consider a spank or two from this man…a little one…

The problem is that I hadn't heard from him in a few days. During the days after our first meeting he'd called me quite regularly just to talk and get to know each other better. We'd communicated by text this week and then nothing. Maybe his meetings had taken a turn for the worse. I know, it is still so early in the getting to know you phase, but I found myself actually looking forward to his calls and texts.

I sat up on the sofa, taking the cell phone from the coffee table where I'd left it. Sipping my wine, I peered at the tiny screen. Damn! Why hadn't I brought my readers from my bedroom?

The phone was fully charged and the signal was fine. I thumbed through the call log. No calls — today or yesterday. Or texts. Was he done with this already? And…I switched over to my email application, nope, no emails either. A lot of other crazy emails though…

Whatever! I tossed the phone back onto the coffee table, frowning. The truth was I had kind of gotten used to his calls. He would call me most days in the afternoon — just to check on me, he says. Then, later, after the workday was done, he would call and we would chat for what seemed like hours. I know, I was acting like a little girl, all giggly and weird whenever I talked to him. But this was not anything serious, right?

"Oh, get a clue, Mikki!" I said aloud to no one in particular. Yes, I liked him. Should I call him? Do modern divas do that kind of thing; call the guy, that is? I rubbed my brow, frustrated. I did not want to seem clingy or needy. That was so not who I was. I hadn't dated in ages; I didn't have a clue what modern divas did in cases like this! Maybe they do nothing. Maybe they just move on to the next contestant.

Baby was very persuasive. When we'd met, there had been instant chemistry and he made me laugh, something the male specimen had not caused me to do in a long time.
Well, another thing, anyway.

I had to admit, I liked talking with him. It had been a long time since I'd actually felt this kind of connection with any man. I checked my phone again, just in case. Maybe he was done. Maybe I had run him off with my ambivalence. Well, he was on the service as I was, maybe he had come across someone else's profile, just as he had come across mine.

I picked up the cell phone again, the glowing blank face of it annoying me. No, nothing's changed since five seconds ago. Smart, sexy, successful, he made me laugh, but the package was, well, don't get me wrong, the package was fine too, but he was certainly not what I was expecting. I was old enough to be his mama. Well, at least his much older sister, this tall lanky cutie was seriously screwing up my mojo!

Fine. I retrieved my e-reader again, and flopped back onto the couch, amusing myself once again with the antics of young girls and Dominants. So engrossed was I with this tale that I nearly jumped out of my skin when the traitorous cell phone rang, startling me out of my BSDM reverie. One look at the number made me want to dance a little jig, but just so that I would not seem so eager, I let it ring a couple more times before answering.

"Hello," I breathed into the receiver, hoping that I sounded sexy instead of weird. I heard his deep chuckle and began to feel weird again. Stop it! You're being goofy!

"What are you doing?" he asked. Smooth as silk…

"Oh, a little of this and that, entertaining one of my many suitors." Liar! "What about you?"

"Have you eaten yet?" he asked.

"No," I said, rising from the sofa and switching off the kitchen light, preparing to head up to my bedroom to continue the call.

The knock on the door caused me to jump with surprise and guiltily; I slipped my e-reader underneath the throw I'd been lying under.

"Then open the door, your dinner is getting cold."

I turned around to look toward the front door. He was here? Outside? I looked down at myself, taking in the plain white sleep shirt I'd put on when I'd thought I would be spending the evening alone. I was so not ready for company and I absolutely did not want him to see me dressed like this!

"Give me five minutes, ok?" I asked. I did not wait for his answer, clicking off the cell phone and running up the stairs. Oh my God! What in the world could I wear? I raced around my bedroom, changing clothes like a mad woman and decided on a baby soft fuchsia colored V-neck top and matching pull on pants. I turned around to look at my reflection from behind in the mirror, liking the way the sumptuous velour clung to my curves, the V-neck of the top accentuating just enough cleavage without screaming, "Let's get it on".

I ripped the ponytail holder from my hair, bending over to fluff my mane, then allowing it to settle around my shoulders in dark waves. Ok, now lip gloss, a spritz of perfume and I was ready. I spared myself one more look in the mirror. Good.

I raced back downstairs, stopping at the bottom of the stairs, my hand pressed against my breasts as I counted as slowly as I dared to three before swinging the door open to let him in.

Maybe I should have counted more slowly… Oh my…I felt my chest squeeze with something I hadn't felt in many, many years. I tried not to stare but it was so very hard to look away. He held up the sack from the bakery/bistro that I'd mentioned was one of my favorites. He remembered…

"I know that it's late and you don't like to eat heavy before you go to bed." He began. Did I say that? Honestly, I could not remember my own name at the moment. "But I didn't want to eat alone."

He extended the bag with a flourish. "Chicken Caesar salad and your Carmel cappuccino, my lady." Cappuccino, even after he'd teased me previously when I'd bragged that I could drink the hot frothy concoction and still sleep all night.

"Mm hmm, you remembered ..." I smiled, surprised. I glanced up into his handsome face. "Come in, Sir."

He brushed past me on his way in and I closed my eyes briefly, drinking in the scent of his cologne. He smelled really good...

"Did you miss me?" he asked, handing me the coffee cup. I was afraid to open my mouth, I had no idea what would come out, but decided to keep the conversation light.

"Had you gone somewhere?" I asked, giving a little laugh. He tugged a lock of my hair, smiling.

"Smarty pants. Come and eat." He instructed.

Chicken Caesar salad for me and a really huge sandwich for himself. While we ate our meal, I learned that he had had decided quite spontaneously to schedule an overnight trip home, much to the astonishment of the techs he'd claimed were dragging their feet and holding up progress. I know, I shouldn't have expected him to tell me every little thing that he was doing, we weren't serious, right? Right! Wait, had he come back just to see me?

Baby finished his sandwich, wiping his mouth as he leaned back into the soft sofa. "So, how was..." he began, then a strange look moved across his face. I knew instantly what had happened.

Oh no...

I felt my face burn with embarrassment as he shifted forward, retrieving the e-reader that he'd sat on. Please floor... please open up and swallow me right now... Briefly he studied the screen, his expression changing ever so slightly as he read the title of the eBook I'd been reading, one speculative brow angling in my direction as I flushed fifty shades of crimson.

Oh   no...now   please...a hurricane...tornado...wildfire...anything will do. I am horrified! Oh my goodness! He must think I'm some sort of sex-crazed old lady! I clenched my hands together in front of me as I willed a natural disaster to present itself.

Blanching, I reached for the e-reader, not daring to look at him. "I'm sorry…I was just…just…" my words faded away on a whisper.

"I'm not really into all of the bondage stuff," he said huskily.

"Oh…" I murmured. Again I flushed, rising from the couch a little too quickly, moving to scoot into the kitchen to throw away the trash from our movable feast. My hands shook violently as I tossed the dinner refuse into the trashcan my stomach churning and I actually felt sick.

"That's good to hear," little Mikki says to me. Yes, I agree. "That's good to hear." I echo her sentiment aloud, if only as assurance for myself.

I thought about hiding out in my own kitchen, at least until the hot flush left my cheeks but this was proving to be impossible as images of being restrained by him flooded over me, causing me to flush all the more. This was crazy!

I was hiding when the only thing I wanted to do was to drag him off to my room and perform some acts of bondage of my own on him. What kind of sense did that make, I mean, I barely knew the guy, right? It made no sense whatsoever; I'd never wanted anyone as badly as I wanted him at that moment and that just didn't make sense.

One kiss, one kiss would be all that it took to erase all the reservations I had and I just could not do that. I'm a mom, right? And a professional. People look up to me, expect me to do the right things at all times, right? I'd never let a man, any man, distract me from my responsibilities, but right now, I found myself willing to chuck it all for a kiss…

"No…" I whispered. Oh goodness, I closed my eyes, pinching the ridge of my nose between my fingertips. I was acting like a lovesick teenager. He likes me, he likes me not. I shook my head, exhaling. I had to keep it together, keep things light, keep things casual… this was going to be harder than I thought, lately just the thought of him had me wondering what it would be like if…

His voice finally penetrated the much too vivid vision and I turned around, blinking at him. When had he come into the kitchen? My heart began to drum crazily and I breathed in deeply, my senses flooding with the musky sandalwood undertones of his cologne.

"At least, I've never been into it before," he murmured, his eyes fastening on my lips. I stood stock still, ensnared by the dark intensity of his eyes as he closed the distance between us. The tell-tale warmth began to spread through my body, tingling along my spine as my heart floundered within my chest. I couldn't read his expression, but the heat that radiated from him seemed to scorch me where I stood, unable to move, unable to breathe and I just could not remember the argument I'd constructed to justify the many reasons why I needed to maintain some sort of distance between us.

He smiled, the slow movement tilting his sensual lips as he studied me, a slow sweep from my toes to my lips. He moved closer and my heart began to race at his proximity and a vision of Baby backing me against the counter and…

He smiled down at me.

"I prefer you to be agreeable and amenable toward my attention, not because I've tied you up or restricted you in any way but because you want it too."

Baby Baby

Slowly, he spanned my waist with his large hands, tugging me toward him, linking his fingers behind my back. He smiled enigmatically, his eyes caressing me, starting at my tousle of dark curls to wander slowly downward, lingering on my lips. I felt myself flush, the rush of heat creeping hotly over my skin.

"Hi," he said softly, his dark eyes fastened on my face.

"Hi yourself" I answered back.

"I've thought about nothing but this since I last saw you..." he whispered. "I've missed you."

"Me too," I admitted. He laughed out loud and I smiled, my hands going to his face, my fingertips tracing the deep grooves of his dimples.

"I love these..." I murmured. He laughed again. "Then get ready to see a lot more of them, Lady..." he teased.

What was happening? How could this man disrupt my whole world with a touch? I released the breath I was holding with a shaky quiver and he knew. He seemed to just know.
"We shouldn't," I whispered, my lips trembling.

"If you're uncomfortable, I'll stop, I swear, just say the word and I'll stop," he promised, pulling me closer, pressing his lips against my forehead. I shut my eyes briefly, enjoying the warmth radiating from his body.

"I need this..." his lips moved across my cheekbone to slowly rubbed against mine. I felt a tremor skip down my spine. Slowly, his large hands stroked me from shoulder to hip, the hands curving around to cup my behind.

"Mmm... just as I imagined," he teased.

My stomach churned, my heart seeming to thud loudly in my own ears as I struggled to keep myself in check. I needed him to stop for my own sanity, but I didn't want him to stop. I swallowed the hard lump that rose in my throat.

He nipped at the sensitive skin beneath my earlobe and I found that my fingers seemed to have a mind of their own, caressing the nape of his neck as I murmured his name aloud. Gently he nipped at the point of my chin, trailing down slowly, slowly down my throat to where my pulse pounded erratically. I gasped as he nipped me there; oh yes, he was very good at showing me that he missed me.

"Hmm…" he purred. 'I think she likes it." I shut my eyes, willing my thoughts to clear long enough to speak coherently.

"She does…" I whispered. He chuckled.

"She wants more…" he teased. I nodded, unable to speak, my lips trembling. His lips wandered past my collarbone to hover over the pulse pounding crazily at my throat.

"Your heart is beating so fast…" he pressed his mouth against the spot, making me catch my breath and he raised his head to look at me, his eyes soft.

"Tell me what you want," he murmured, so close, so very close.

"I … I want to kiss you," I breathed. And he smiled. Leaning nearer, he rubbed his lips gently against my forehead.

"How badly do you want to kiss me?" he teased, his fingertips provocative against the skin at the V-neck of my soft top. Wrapping my fingers around his firm chin, I tugged him forward, moving to curve against him. He gazed at me, his eyes luminous, his look soft, his eyes dark... I feathered my lips against his.

"Kiss me," I whispered against his lips.

"You're not attracted to me at all, are you?" he teased, his breath warm against my face.

"This hasn't happened in a long time," I said, my lips trembling. He continued to rub his lips gently against my skin, teasing the tendrils of hair at my forehead.

Slowly, my hands inched up the hem of his shirt, tugging at the garment to slip underneath, caressing the taut muscles, pleased to feel him shudder against me, delighting in the ripple of the muscles that met my fingertips and I smiled as my palms opened wide to caress him, loving the velvety tautness of his skin.

"You approve?" he asked. I must have made a sound because he laughed. Gently, I pressed a kiss against his chest and was rewarded with a little growl, his laughter ending. My lips followed the path of my fingertips and I felt him tremble. I traced the length of his spine up to the back of his head, my fingers loving the strength of his broad neck. I curved against him and he groaned aloud.

Gently, he took my lips, rubbing, caressing, tasting, his tongue curving along the fullness of my lips to slip inside, instinctively seeking out and finding mine, curling around mine, sucking gently.

Those big hands caressed me from knee to thigh, up to cup my backside, squeezing gently, his other hand curving under my hips as he lifted me to sit on the countertop. His firm lips left mine and he kissed along the line of my throat, the warmth of his open mouth driving me crazy. That was my undoing. My fingers caressed the shape of his head, caressing him, drawing him closer. My leg curved up to hook over his hips, pulling his hard shape close against my warmth and his eyes opened wide, the proximity of our bodies sending a deep flush along his jaw line. Then he took over.

Down my throat to where my pulse pounded crazily. He dipped his tongue there, caressing me and I heard myself groan out loud. He continued to my collarbone, tracing the shape with the tip of his tongue before venturing even lower still.

His hand came up from my backside to the small of my back, fitting us neatly together as his lips returned to mine and my kisses were as hungry as his. I began to tremble, I don't know why, but I shook from head to toe, so badly that he raised his head to look at me.

"Ok?" he asked, his face flushed, his lips swollen. I nodded, my lips trembling. He groaned, parting my thighs so that I sat snuggly against him, the hard shape of him apparent through his blue jeans, rubbing against me as his hand came up to tangle in my hair, the other cupped my rear, pressing me gently, tightly against his throbbing hardness. He held me there, kissing me as he moved against me, the fabric of my thin panties moistening. Sensations ripped through me like a machete as his tongue caressed mine, his body driving me crazy, my thin underwear offering little protection against his hard shape.

"My hands...I have to touch..." he murmured. "God... I have to memorize you, how you feel..." I was speechless, watching as those firm lips pushed aside the fabric to caress my breast, feeling myself begin to shiver involuntarily.

Those wonderful lips moved past my top and bra to close on one sensitive tip and I gasped, my toes seeming to curl. I heard him groan against me then heard nothing else, the pounding of my own heart seeming to deafen me as he took the breast between his lips, suckling deeply. I began to ache deep inside, a slow churning beginning where I was the hottest, spreading throughout my body. Oh goodness, this was so good! I struggled to stay present, struggled to not cry out... then he turned his attention to the other breast, his large hand going underneath my top to cup the first breast.

Oh...I wrapped my arms around him, bringing him, begging him to come closer, an unspoken request he gladly accommodated. My mind kept telling me that I needed to bring a halt to this, that he was a grown man with the needs of a grown man and it would only be a matter of time before we reached the point of no return. Did I really want him to stop? No, but I really needed him to stop. If we didn't stop now, I would not be able to stop him, even if I wanted to. But I didn't want to, not tonight. Tonight, I wanted this more than anything. It was all I could think about ever since I met him.

He chuckled as I groaned his name aloud, my head turning aside, my own fingers clenching into his shoulder as I clung to him, unable to do anything else but feel. Sensation, heat, nothing else mattered until...

Dimly I heard the noise at the front of the house, the door opening, then shutting and then Dereon's tall figure filled the entry to the kitchen. I swear that the earth must have stopped spinning at that moment as I stared mortified at my teenage son, my lips swollen, my clothing in disarray, the warm wonderful buzz from seconds ago replaced with a limb numbing chill as Dereon stopped in mid step, his large hand gripping the doorway as a look of first confusion then horror crossed his features.

Oh...my...God...

Dereon never said a word; looking first at me, then at Baby, the look on his face something I had never seen before. Oh God, could he see...did he see...what he must think, his mother in the kitchen getting busy with a virtual stranger!

Swallowing hard, I wrenched myself away from Baby's embrace, pushing him so that I could slide down off of the countertop. He put out a hand toward me and I pushed it away, shaking my head. This was bad...so bad. I needed to go after Dereon...to explain...explain what exactly? With shaking hands, I tugged my clothing back into place, my face burning.

"No… I need to talk to him," I muttered, moving to go after Dereon. Then I heard the resounding thud as Dereon shut his bedroom door — hard.

Oh no… I could only imagine what must be going through his mind right now. I had to talk to him, explain what was going on. How in the world was I going to explain this? I turned to look at Baby, frustrated. Helpless, I wanted to cry. Baby, bless him, stood where he was. Unmoving.

"Oh my God, what have I done?" I whispered hoarsely. Baby moved as if he were going to reach for me, then his hand fell to his side.

"You were enjoying yourself. Surely your son would want you to…" he said, his voice husky.

I shook my head. "You don't understand." I rubbed my hand across my eyes, groaning as I exhaled, feeling scared and frustrated.

"It's been just Dereon and me for his entire life. And now…" I pinched my trembling lips together. "I feel as if I've betrayed him." I felt sick, my voice breaking. I smiled, the action trembling along my lips and I exhaled, shaking my head. I had no idea how I was going to fix this.

"And I'm scared, I think…" I whispered.

He looked puzzled, his eyebrow quirking upward. "Of me?"

I shook my head, raising my hand to gesture first at him, then at myself. Weakly, the hand dropped back to my side.

"Of this…" I said looking away. I shook my head again. "Of what I'm feeling right now. "

He continued to study me, waiting for me. I exhaled, agitated. "I'm afraid of what I'm feeling right now because I want…" I hesitated. "I want more, but…"

His fingers moved to capture my chin, encouraging me to look at him.

"No regrets?" he asked softly.

I wasn't mad at him, I couldn't be upset, he was doing exactly what I'd wanted him to do. What I'd wanted him to do from the very first time I'd met him. I was angry at myself for not being stronger. When he'd held me that was my undoing. I should have been strong enough to smother the desire that had taken over like a wildfire. And now, I had one hell of a mess in store for me in the guise of one disillusioned and angry teenager. I groaned, rubbing my hand over my eyes again. Slowly, I shook my head.

"No, no regrets." I murmured. "I just don't know what I am going to do now."

He rubbed the back of his neck, clearing his throat, one large hand at his hip as he sighed. "Mikki, I can't let this go."

He reached forward, taking one of my hands in his, tugging me forward until we touched again. I could feel my heart thudding within my chest and I knew that I was beginning to flush again, my body responding instantly the way it did when he was close.

Gently, his hands cupped my head, his long fingers tunneling into my hair, moving slowly down my neck to softly knead at the taut muscles at the base of my neck. Against my will, I groaned, closing my eyes.

"From the first moment you and I met, I knew there was something between us, Mikki," he murmured, his words warm on my face as he stood close, so very close. He was right; I could not deny this, not even when everything that happened this evening had turned my world upside down.

Slowly I shook myself back to reality. "I can't think when you're doing that," I whispered, shivering. He smiled, his thumb tracing lazily along the line of my chin.

'Then don't," he whispered, his lips just barely touching mine. "I know this is a lot to process right now." He straightened to his full height to tower over me and I was forced to look up at him. He smiled down at me, his hands cupping my face as his eyes searched mine.

"I will have you, Miss Robbinson." He promised, smiling. "I want to spend time with you. A lot of time…and when the time is right," his finger toyed with the stray hairs around my face, sweeping a long strand to tuck it behind my ear.

"It will be you and me…" he tilted my face upward. "With nothing between us, no interruptions or second thoughts. We will have all of the time in the world to explore each other." Those firm lips curved into a self-assured smile.

"And we will. Over and over again."

Sweet mercy! I quaked from head to toe, it was still so easy to imagine taking him upstairs to take the rest of the evening to explore him, to experiment and taste… to learn more about the body that strained beneath the fabric of the shirt beneath my fingertips. I shook my head to clear the fog that threatened to settle in. I couldn't force away these feelings, or the memories of how good it had felt to be in his arms just mere minutes ago, my skin seeming to tingle where he'd touched me.

Damn.

He smiled. "I want you." He said simply, the words sending a now familiar heat blasting through me; he was far too close for my peace of mind.

"I don't know if I can do this...with you..." I began. Undeterred, he continued to smile, the dimples deepening.

God help me...

"You will," he stated. I rolled my eyes. Had any other man said those words to me, I would have written him off as too cocky for his own good. But, coming from him it sounded more like a promise than bravado.

It had been a long time since I'd gotten what I wanted; at this moment that was him and I could not let this need take over, especially in light of the situation with Dereon and what he must think about his mother right now.

"I'm willing to wait." Baby said.

I shook my head. "Maybe you shouldn't..." I whispered, not looking at him. The heart wants what the heart wants and right now, it was him. He continued to smile down at me, his hand cupping my face, slowly smoothing my hair away from my cheek. Then he stepped away and I found myself wanting to...cry?

Really?

"When you are ready, I'll be here..." he said simply. Then he was gone. I covered my face with both hands, trying to shake off the heavy feeling of sadness that replaced the heat. What have I done? And why?

Sighing, I went to lock the front door behind him, then leaning against the wall next to the door, I slid to the floor, my head in my hands. What happens now? I'd been able to push these feelings away for most of my life without a second thought;

Dereon always came first, no matter what. Before the job, before the accolades at work, and certainly before any man. Why was I having such a hard time pushing these feelings away this time? How had he managed to slide beneath my radar?

Groaning, I looked heavenward, shaking my head, my lips pulled into a grim smile. This was insane anyway! What would my friends think? They'd look at me crazy, saying, what in the world was Mikki thinking? A couple of years younger, maybe we could have made that work. But an entire 10 years? That was a whole generation! You could fit a whole lot of life in 10 years! But this man - I felt weird even saying it — this man was everything that I was looking for. And more.

And what would I think if Dereon came home and said that he had found Ms. Right, only she was the same age as I was? I would be the first one ready to run that sister out of town! That was just wrong! But herein was my predicament. I was the one who was about to be run out of town! It was true that some of the older men that I had met lately were, umm, laid back, aka boring. But now that I was done raising my son, I was ready to have some fun, not ride off into the sunset. And I wanted to have fun with Baby. Who would have thought?

But there was still that little part of me, that bruised part of me that still ached because of the thing with Dereon's father, and that was the part that kept my walls up. I was scared, terrified that I could not make it work, terrified that this too would end and I could not, I could not withstand it a second time. That was the part that made me keep my distance from any and all forms of intimacy, anything that required that I surrender myself both heart and soul.

I…am…in…so…much…trouble.

And I had no idea how to get myself out of it. I pushed myself up off of the floor, dusting myself off, squaring my shoulders. I would have to think about Baby later, right now I had a big hole to dig myself out of.

With Dereon.

Dereon

"What did he say after he saw what you were reading?" Sonni asked, her voice incredulous. What did he say? What did he do? I hadn't even gotten to the good part yet...

Sonni and I were at the hairdresser as I recounted the story to her about Dereon coming home at that moment, interrupting what had promised to be an evening to remember.

It had probably been for the best; what about the dating site? I knew that I wasn't seeing anyone else, not like that, but was the same true for him? How on earth could I ask him? Wasn't this something that the guy was supposed to bring up? I knew for sure that I did not want to be intimate with him if he was still "playing the field". Awkward, but still I was developing these feelings for him and I did not know if he was feeling the same, so I certainly would not tell him that I was beginning to have real feelings for him.

He treated me better than I'd ever been treated by anyone. He was attentive and caring and he treated me like a queen. He was a hard worker; he owned his own successful business and loved the fact that I was who I was. Everything that Sonni could want for me.

The young hairdresser tried to pretend that she was not listening while she was adding first time ever honey highlights to my virgin never before colored hair. I noticed that as I was reprimanding Sonni, the hairdresser had rinsed my hair and stood frozen on the spot, gaping at me. Sonni soon followed suit.

"What?" I asked, looking at the girl then at Sonni. Oh for goodness sake, really? I grabbed the hand held mirror to see what the commotion was all about and gasped out loud. And then I shrieked, clutching the mirror to my chest, and then looked at my reflection again. My virgin hair, instead of picking up the honey highlights that I craved, had reacted badly to the "organic" hair coloring, turning a dull shade of green. Algae green.

"I can fix it," the girl whispered, backing away from me to run into the back to find another bottle of hair color.

Sonni started to chuckle then she laughed out loud, her eyes tearing up and she dabbed at them with her towel, careful not to muss her makeup.

"What on earth are you laughing at? Look at this!" I exclaimed, and then I put my towel over my hair. On second thought, don't look at it. Where was that hairdresser?

Sonni stopped laughing, if only for a second. "Well, Mr. Know It All said that you needed to be more green." Then she burst out laughing again. I stared at her, wondering if it were too late to disown her.

The hairdresser was able to fix my hair after a lot of work and I feared that I would end the experiment as bald as a coconut. Luckily that did not happen and my naturally dark shade was restored and deeply conditioned. The hairdresser even threw in a manicure for my trouble.

**

I shook my head, laughing softly at Sonni as I struggled with my keys and my bags. Whoever first uttered the phrase "shop till you drop" obviously had Sonni in mind. The woman knows how to shut down a mall. I had dropped hours ago and I think Sonni only noticed within the past hour. Exhausted, both physically and financially, I had followed her around from store to store like a zombie, present but feeling no pain.

A sound from within the house caught my attention and I stopped, my hand in mid air as the door swung open. The alarm had not sounded when I opened the door, I could have sworn that I'd set it when we left. This meant either that either Dereon was home or we had one cagey burglar to contend with.

Obviously Sonni had heard the sound as well; she grasped my elbow, holding me back. The house was totally dark, save the one lone light on the second level at the end of the hallway that extended from Dereon's half open bedroom door.

There, there was the noise again and my skin prickled. Dereon! Was he ok? What if he was hurt? What if something had happened and he couldn't get to the door or to the phone?

All of my mama instincts rushed forward and I snatched away from Sonni and tiptoed into the house, turning on lamps as we moved forward stealthily deeper into the house. Nothing was out of order; everything was in place as it should be.

Sonni and I were practically walking in the same pair of shoes as she hovered next to me, her hand reaching deep into her purse for something. What on earth was she looking for at a time like this?

I felt rather than heard the crackle of the gadget as my hair stood on end. Frightened, I turned to look at her. A Taser? What the hell was she doing with a Taser? Sonni urged me forward, the Taser lowered to point down at the floor. She and I were going to have a serious talk about that later...

We reached Dereon's door and at Sonni's silent countdown, we pushed the door open — and immediately stopped in our tracks. I screamed, falling back into Sonni. Sonni screamed, dropping the Taser to the hardwood floor where it fizzled off.

Dereon, bless him, had the audacity to look stunned and surprised at our intrusion. He couldn't have been more shocked than Sonni and I when we realized what was going on.

"Mom!" Dereon exclaimed, hurriedly reaching down to pull up his pants from where they rested around his ankles and a young girl crouched on her knees in front of him. Hey, I knew her!

What did Dereon say her name was? Janet...no... Jasmine from graduation day. Little Miss Cutie Pie!

"Oh no..." Cutie Pie said, her face flushing bright red as she struggled to her feet and ran from the room. Dereon stood openmouthed; his pants now back in their rightful place.

"Mom!" he said again, then hurried from the room after Cutie Pie. Sonni and I took one look at each other and fell into each other laughing, tears pushing themselves down our cheeks as we struggled to hold it together.

When we reached the kitchen, we could hear Dereon whispering fervently to Cutie Pie and I could only speculate how that conversation was going to end. Sonni stuck her Taser back into her purse, a small smile pasted on her lips.

"I should have used the Taser on her. What the hell..." Sonni erupted into peals of laughter again and I laughed too, covering my mouth as I heard the front door close and Dereon retreat to his room with hurried steps and shut the door. With that, Sonni burst into laughter all over again. Shaking my head, I retrieved two wine glasses and an unopened bottle of Pinot Grigio from the wine fridge.

"So what are you going to do?" Sonni asked, a smirk tilting the curve of her mouth as she watched me. I shook my head, my eyes still damp from laughing.

"Well," I said, removing the cork from the wine with a flourish. "First, I am going to have some wine and then..." I stared pensively in the direction of Dereon's room. "Geez! I have no idea, I just don't know if I am ready to get into this tonight." I shook my head again, rolling my eyes.

Later that evening, I sat on my bed, my nose again buried in my e-reader as I had, having given up on Fifty Shades of Gray, downloaded a number of other less suggestive books. There is only so much masochism that I could take.

I heard Dereon's bedroom door open, then slow steps coming down the hallway. I thought that maybe he's thought that I was asleep and would be going down to the kitchen for something to drink. I looked up as Dereon peered around my doorframe.

"Hey," he said, hesitating outside the door, then coming in to flop his tall frame across the end of my bed, something he'd been doing since he was a little boy.

"Hey yourself," I said, putting the e-reader down next to me, pulling my legs up to make room for him at the end of the bed. He wouldn't look at me and I realized that we had not actually talked — not at any length — since the night that Dereon walked in on Baby and me. And now, this evening, Sonni and I had walked in on him and Cutie Pie. What were the odds?

"I don't know what to say," he muttered, his long fingertips plucking at the fabric of my duvet.

"Well, that makes two of us." I said, moving so that I lay propped up on my elbows at the foot of the bed, looking at him.

"Looks like we are both expanding our horizons," I tried, looking at him out the corner of my eye. "Do I have to give you the sex talk?" I asked, half joking, but totally serious.

"Do I have to give *you* the sex talk?" he asked, reaching out to pull a lock of my hair. I chuckled then in spite of the seriousness of the situation.

"Maybe, you know I've lived the past eighteen years stuck in a cave." I teased and to his credit, he laughed. I thumped his arm, causing him to look at me.

"I know it's difficult to think of your mom as a sexual creature," I said, rolling my eyes as he scowled at me. "Just as it's hard for me to realize that you're growing up into a man. I just want to be sure that you are safe, that you're taking care of things…" I stopped, fearing that I was making a mess out of this.

Dereon turned on his side to look at me. "I need for you to be safe too, Mom," he said and for the first time that I can remember, Dereon looked me squarely in the eye and I truly saw the young man that he was becoming.

All grown up. I nodded my head, my eyes tearing up.

"I am." I whispered. He nodded as well, pulling my hair again before rising from the foot of my bed to head downstairs. Sniffing, I grabbed a tissue from my side table, blowing my nose and wiping my eyes.

All grown up.

Mama's Boy

Day fifty? Oh hell! I don't even remember what day this is! I've been on so many bad dates lately that I think I've just lost count. I mean, with the procession of guys I'd met lately, I couldn't remember who did what and I found myself desperately wishing I'd paid more attention to Sonni's crazy spreadsheet idea.

There was the car salesman who, after determining that we had the same type of phone and answering service, decided that we were made for each other — and should go ahead and get married. When discussing what type of vehicle I was interested in, he suggested that we take the vehicle by my house to see if it would fit in the garage.

What? Turns out that the only thing we had in common was he sold cars and I drove one.

Then there was the man who was looking for a "sugar mama," who was already settled and established. Or Mr. "Too Sexty" who was only interested in a sexting relationship.

Hello? Remember me? Internet Dating Virgin? What this meant only made sense to me after he proceeded to send me pictures of himself and his, as he phrased it "notable assets," that I figured out what was going on — right after I picked my jaw up from the floor.

Oh, and who could forget the date with the man who was using the online service as a means to "vet" his potential love connections...and convert them to his religious beliefs at the same time.

"You seem to be a good woman, Mikki," he told me. "My mama always said that good women could be found in the church. What church do you go to?"

Now, I admit that I'm no saint, but I'd like to think that I behave better than a lot of people out there. I mean, I'm smart. I'm nice, most days. I don't make weird noises in public. I have a good job. I have a brilliant son and I am a fairly decent housekeeper.

I know that it has been many, many moons since I've even seen the inside of my church. Actually, now that I think about it, I have a sneaking suspicion that if I walked into my church on any given Sunday, first my Pastor would probably have a heart attack and then the place would spontaneously catch on fire.

According to Mr. Convert-a-date, there are certain parts of the Bible that he would take quite literally, such as the whole submission thing as well as the woman is "given to man as a help meet", to help him accomplish his goals, to be the quiet force behind whatever it is that he wants to do. Right, I'm all for that, but what exactly was in this arrangement for any woman who took him up on his "gracious" offer to allow her to do these things for him?

My current "date" was just as weird and I found my attention wandering over to the couple in the adjacent booth. I'd watched as they entered the place all lovey dovey, tucking themselves into one side of the booth to share a single dessert.

I smiled as she took little tiny bites while he promptly gobbled down half of the whipped cream confection in what seemed like seconds. I shook my head; she'll probably feel as if she is starving later. Had that been me, I'm probably going to eat the whole thing and Mr. Romantic is going to look like "what happened?"

As they were leaving, Mr. Romantic noticed a friend of his across the café and dragged his girl over to visit with his friend and his girl. I noted that the two men carried on a full five-minute conversation and it was only as they had wrapped up the conversation and were on their way out before Mr. Romantic remembered his manners and introduced the young lady as his "girl". Girl what? Girl friend? Girl Friday? Poor thing!

Mentally, I strip Mr. Romantic of his title. I know, I haven't been at this dating thing long, but I do know that I cannot be satisfied being the quiet force behind the man. Maybe he would remember that I am there and introduce me to everyone else. Maybe not. That's not for me.

I returned my attention to my current crazy date. Yep, lately I've had some crazy dates, but this one? This date had to be the strangest of the strange!

I smiled politely at the woman across the table from me. That's right, a woman. Now, before I even get started, it is not even like that. I mean, if that's the way that you go, then that's your business. You do your thing. Me? Though I've been off of the market and out of action for the past — oh, let's just say forever – I still find that I have a definite affinity for the male persuasion.

No. The woman I am talking about is my coffee date's mother. When I'd initially received his email, I thought, oh how sweet, he's just a little shy. He said all of the right things. Family is important. He loved and respected his mother. He too was in the Marketing field and thought that we should meet since we had so much in common. Why not, it could be fun.

Now, I love Mama Jett and all, but I am not about to take her with me on any potential dates, especially not after the Red Lobster incident. I'm still trying to recover from that one! I smiled at my coffee date's mother and she smiled at me.

"So," she begins. "My son tells me that you work for GBGC. I love them!" My date's mother enthused.

"Yes," Mama's Boy asserts in his whiny voice, edging his way into the conversation as his mother all but bounced up and down in her seat. "Mother has amassed quite of collection of those figurines that GBGC sells, haven't you Mother?"

Mother? Who calls their mother "Mother" during a conversation?

"Well," I smiled, "I don't make them, I just persuade people to buy them, I can't take all of the credit for their popularity." I laughed. Mother laughed. Mama's Boy laughed. Then I had an idea.

"Actually, I can see that you two are close." I continued. "I have a son as well," I stated. "A teenager, he will be going away to college in the fall."

Mother stopped bouncing in her seat, her smile falling to the table. Pow! I mused, my brow rising. I swiftly administered the knockout punch for this date.

"You have a son?" She asked.

"Yes, of course," I smiled genuinely. "I'd be happy to show you his picture", I offered helpfully, a suggestion that practically caused Mother to shudder.

"No...no. That's quite all right." Mother said, pushing herself away in her chair. "Son, I'm not feeling well, would you mind taking me home? My head..." she stated, her chubby little hand pressing to her temple.

Give that lady an Oscar! I chuckled softly.

"Oh," I said, extending my hand to her, "Is there anything I can do?" I asked. I may as well had poked her with a stick the way she'd recoiled from my offer of assistance.

"Oh, no, no dear. I'm just feeling quite ill right now. Son, please..." she said, trying to get as far away from me as possible.

Mother practically leaped from her chair. Ever obedient, Son hopped to his feet, holding Mother's arm as he guided her gingerly to the door, promising to call as soon as he could. I nodded, waving my goodbyes as they left.

I laughed, finishing my coffee — alone — making note that upon my arrival at home this evening, I would cut the cord with Dereon, well, maybe not completely, but I would vow to give him his space.

Rebel Without A Cause

I laughed from the en suite bathroom where I was attempting to tame my riotous tangle of hair into something resembling chic.

"I cannot believe that even against the wishes of his mother, he contacted me again!" I reached for a bobby pin, hoping to ensnare the curls up and away from my neck. I was recounting my story to Sonni as I tried to arrange my hair.

Sonni had text me early this Friday afternoon with four simple words, "Let's go out tonight," and I knew that she was not going to take no for an answer. She never did.

That was fine, I hadn't spoken with her in a couple of days, a rarity for either of us. Mama Jett practically swore that the two of us had been joined at the hip ever since Sonni came to live with us following the death of her mother, teasing that if you looked in the hip pocket of one, you would see the other. So to not speak with her for more than eight hours, well, that just did not happen. And I had so much to tell her!

Mama's boy, the disastrous "date" where his mother attended as part of the "interview" process had decided to go against the wishes of his mother to ask me out on a real date. I chortled as I called from the bathroom at Sonni.

"I asked him what his mother said and he said that it was time for him to start living his own life, that he was no longer going to let his mother tell him what to do and who he should see. I know I turned him down, but I was thinking to myself "Well, go on then, at forty something years old, it's about damn time!"

I laughed at my own clever rebuttal, noticing that Sonni had not commented. I stuck my head out of the bathroom, frowning as Sonni paced the length of my bedroom.

Something was wrong.

"Mikki, I have someone I want you to meet," Sonni said softly. I turned around to look at her, noticing that for the first time since I've known her, Sonni seemed nervous and uncertain.

Oh God! What was this? Was this good? This was good right? I couldn't help it, being the alarmist that I am, my mind immediately zoomed ahead. Something was wrong. She had some news for me. Was this bad news?

I put down the hair ornament that I was studying and looked at her, her tiny brow marred in a frown.

"Meet someone…or *"meet"* someone?" I asked, my eyes fastening on those dark alert eyes of hers.

She shrugged then, her silky blouse crinkling with the motion, then releasing into soft folds around her shoulders.

"*Meet* someone… a man…" she murmured, busying her hands with the bottles on the top of my dresser.

Meet…wait…did Sonni actually say that she wanted me to meet someone? A man? Someone…was she serious about him? She had to be! Sonni, God bless her, seemed to cycle through first dates faster than she could say charge it at the MAC store and to her credit, I can honestly say that she never ever brought anyone around unless she was serious about him.

Come to think of it, I cannot recall Sonni ever bringing anyone around. She, like Niecee and myself, would never have put anyone through the strenuous "Mama Jett Seal of Approval" process unless we were sure that the man was someone that we were even semi-serious about.

Hmmm…now that I think about it, I'd never even once mentioned Dereon's dad to Mama Jett, let alone put him through the process, I think that I knew even then that he would never have passed level one…

"A man..." I echoed. Sonni nodded and I smiled, the action starting slowly then seeming to cover my whole face. Sonni's met somebody...

Sonni's met somebody! I ran out of the bathroom to stop mere inches away from her, in spite of the fact that I presently only wore my underwear.

"You met somebody? How? When?" I grabbed her hands, in my excitement shaking her back and forth. "Spill it woman!"

Sonni laughed nervously, my excitement infectious.

"Ok ok!" She exclaimed, her hands going up to cover her eyes as she laughed. "Any other time, you know I just don't have time for this. But this one..." She shook her head exhaling loudly. "This one was different. He just would not give up, he just wouldn't take no for an answer..." she said, shaking her head again her lips pursed together.

"Hmmm... I know how that feels," I gave her a pointed look. She pointed her finger at me with that "none of your lip Missy" look she gave me so often. I held my hands up in mock surrender.

"So, tell me about him," I queried. Sonni busied herself looking in my closet while I continued to apply my makeup for the evening.

"He's a local business man, he owns a couple of franchises here in the city and an upscale restaurant/nightclub. That's where we're going tonight."

I chuckled from the bathroom, applying lipstick.

"Sounds like a catch, what's he like? How many times have you been out?" I asked.

Silence, then "About four times, tonight will be number five." She said.

Wha -- four times? How was she able to keep this from me? Again I came out of the bathroom.

"Four times? When were you going to tell me?" I asked, a little hurt that she hadn't trusted me with her secret.

"Honey, I wanted to tell you," she said from inside the closet, her voice muffled. "I just needed to be sure that I wanted him to stay around," she finished. She came out of the closet with a red dress.

"What is this?" she asked.

"It's a dress, and don't try to change the subject," I retorted right back. The dress was one that I had purchased on an impulse after reading in a magazine that the Bandage Dress was the dress to have that year. I'd nixed ever wearing the dress after trying it on and deciding that like a bandage, the dress covered and clung to ever single curve, for good or for worse.

"You're wearing this tonight," Sonni said.

Old G

I stood next to the bar, feeling awkward in the bandage dress as the music, courtesy of the nightclub's DJ, thrummed around me like a big bass drum, pounding, throbbing, vibrating until I could feel nothing else but the beat of the music.

I stood because that was all that I could do, the dress was not made for sitting, fitting like a glove and for that I guessed that I could be grateful. The red dress was a modern marvel of carefully constructed straps of wonder fabric that compressed my curvy figure in all of the right places while the back of the dress scooped past my shoulder blades, adding a little allure. The "V" of the front however, did very little to hide my assets as the fabric held "the girls" up and on display for all to see. I could only pray that I made it through the evening without poking my own eyes out with those things.

I looked around the establishment, hanging on to my matching red clutch bag like a lifeline. How in the world did I keep letting Sonni talk me into these kinds of things? I think I knew my fate was sealed once she'd found that "hot little number" in the back of my closet. The second she'd laid her eyes on the red hoochie mama dress that I'd hidden in the back of my closet for good reason, she'd bulldozed me into wearing the contraption, piling my hair high onto my head in a curly knot with curling tendrils whispering around my face and down to my shoulders. She'd jazzed up my safe makeup with deeper more intense shades. As if I needed more drama, I wore the sky high-heeled stilettos I'd fallen in love with during one of our shopping sprees.

So, here I stood, tapping my foot in time to the music as the DJ played an old school set of eighties and nineties club hits, a blast from the past ranging from Prince and the Revolution, Morris Day and the Time, Technotronic, Chaka Khan, Marvin Gaye and more. I stared in awe as the floor filled with well-dressed people all gyrating and shaking their groove things wildly. I hadn't danced in so long and could not say that I would be able to figure it out. I guess that's what happens when you hide in a cave for eighteen years.

A man, a very young man, approached me, his hand extended in a silent request for a dance. I smiled at him, admiring his smooth hands and skin, sparkling eyes and straight white smile — too young — and I leaned in closer to tell him "maybe later." He placed his hand against his chest, feigning a broken heart, his expression turning mournful and I laughed out loud as he took his leave.

Oh you…

Upon entering the establishment, Sonni had gone to the back office to find the proprietor of the nightclub, the man she'd wanted me to meet, leaving me all alone on unfamiliar turf and I couldn't help wonder if this had been part of her plan: to leave me alone in this ridiculous dress in this noisy pulsing meat market. I sighed, shaking my head and then I saw her heading my way.

I watched as Sonni's friendly, open smile as she greeted people along the way, turned downward quickly as first she appeared to be puzzled, then she frowned, a look of anger crossing her features. I frowned as well, wondering what was going on as a tingle of tension worried its way across my skin, cold and icy, and I noticed that Sonni was staring at something behind me, out of my field of vision.

Or someone. I turned slightly to look behind me.

Darren.

I frowned, my throat clinching, my words frozen as I stared at him, motionless. I heard the sound of Sonni's heels as she stopped at my side. I stared at Darren as he came to a stop in front of me, a slow, hesitant smile touching his lips.

"Hello Mikki." He said and I felt my brow quirk upwards. Hello? That was all? I squared my shoulders, my head going back as I stared at him.

"Darren, maybe you should leave..." Sonni began but I held up my hand in her direction.

"No," I told her. "I got this." I said, my eyes never leaving Darren's face. I heard rather that saw Sonni as she stomped away, knowing that she had not gone far. She was furious, this I could tell by the staccato of her high heels. I returned my attention to Darren, my expression unwavering.

Darren watched Sonni leave, his hand going up to smooth along his jaw and down his beard, a gesture that I remembered and used to love.

"Darren." I said simply, my voice flat. He smiled, stepping a little closer to hear me.

"You look great Mikki," he said, his eyes going over me in the dress. "I haven't seen you here before."

I pressed my lips together in an attempt to halt the flow of words that threatened to break from me.

"Thanks. Sonni's friend owns the place." I stated simply. Smiling, Darren mistakenly took my reply as permission to start a conversation. His second mistake. His first mistake was being an ass eighteen years ago.

"So how have you been?" he asked, adjusting the sleeves of the blazer that he wore; sadly, I noted that it was a blazer that I remembered from years ago. How have I been? As if the last conversation we'd had never happened. The night when he'd walked out on me and my baby.

"Are you still married?" I asked, my eyes hard on him, my mouth unwilling to offer him even the ghost of a smile. He seemed surprised by the directness of my question.

"Yes," he said, looking chagrined. And I shook my head at him, disgusted by him and sorry for his wife.

"That's unfortunate," I stated and he looked at me, seeming to expect more. Expecting what exactly? I continued.

"Unfortunate for her, that is," I said, feeling my lips twist, sickened by the audacity of this man. He was still running the same game. This player wanna-be.

"I can't imagine that she knows what you're up to when you leave her alone at nights to carouse at the nightclubs. I feel bad for her. If she knew, she'd probably leave your sorry ass."

Darren ceased his visual appraisal of my form-fitting dress, my words finally making a dent into his reverie as he slowly became aware of the fact that I was not going to cut him any slack, not now, not ever.

"Wh—" he began and I held up my hand again, shushing his response abruptly. I shook my head.

"You probably shouldn't speak right now," I told him and I could see the fury begin to creep across his features, angry because I had the boldness to speak to him this way, the old Mikki would not have dared to be so direct. I laughed a bit and he looked at me, unsure of what was so funny. Old Mikki was gone, I'd kicked her butt to the curb and all she could do was stand with her mouth wide open and watch this new Mikki take over and take control.

About damned time.

"Oh, and in case you were wondering, Dereon turned out just fine." I said, looking him directly in the eyes, noting the question that I could see forming there. Who?

" Oh, that's right" I snapped my fingers in a disingenuous "A Ha!" motion. "You never knew his name, you just ran away like a scared little boy eighteen years ago. Your son, Darren. His name is Dereon, your namesake but nothing like you."

I laughed out loud then, the sharp sound cracking the air that surrounded us. He actually had the nerve to shrug his shoulders, his hands moving upward in a helpless gesture. I rolled my eyes, willing my annoyance caused by his indifference to abate.

"Dereon Robbinson. *My* son." I pulled my shoulders back and smiled, the action dismissing. He'd long ago dismissed himself from playing a role in Dereon's life eighteen years ago; now I was dismissing him from the role he'd played in my life eighteen years since.

"Dereon's going to college this fall, Darren. He grew up to be smart and he has integrity; he's a 4.0 student with a full ride scholarship to a top-notch college. I did that. I taught him that, not you. Dereon was raised by a village of warriors: me, Sonni, my mother and my sister. Strong women who raised a champion to know how to respect a woman. Nothing like you."

Darren tried to break in again and I silenced him with a look that told him he was better off not saying another word.

"This," I gestured toward him with my hand, the action reminiscent of his dismissive action eighteen years ago. "This, whatever it was, is over." I smiled at him then and truly meant it.

It was over. All of the hiding from myself. All of the self deprecation and self neglect. I felt the past rolling off of me like waves, feeling lighter and happier. I felt hopeful for the first time in a long time and willing to give myself a chance at living again. Gone was the contempt that had kept me bound to this man, now I felt nothing but pity for him, the man who represented the sad tired memory of what I had mistakenly accepted as love.

"I offered you the most precious gift that I had to give and you turned it down. That was your loss and I feel nothing but sorry for you now."

I looked at him then, my eyes resting on his tired blazer, his worn shoes and world-weary expression. I no longer remembered what I thought I saw in him at that time, but I knew what I saw standing before me now, a tired, broken shell of a man desperately trying to hold onto delusions from his own past. A past where he was, even if only in his own mind, everything that a naïve young girl thought she needed.

I saw him for what he was, a faded relic from my past, a past that had nothing to do with my future and until now, a past that stood in the way of everything that I could have in my life. A life that could be wonderful, if I could just be brave enough to reach out and step into it.

Yes, I inhaled deeply, closing my eyes briefly, and then opening them again to gaze into his worn out face. And just like that, all of the years of anger and resentment I'd felt toward him lifted from my shoulders, shattering in front of me like broken glass, releasing my heart and falling to my feet in shards.

Someone touched my elbow and I turned, expecting to see Sonni. The young man from earlier in the evening had returned and stood in front of me again, his hand extended, asking me to dance.

I smiled, a real smile. I was free. Finally free.

"Why yes," I told the young man, accepting his hand "Yes I would."

I smiled, walking around the statue of the man that was, for all intents and purposes, my past. And I danced, and danced and danced. Shaking my booty and the past from my shoulders onto the floor where I trampled it to death beneath my stilettos.

***

I cannot say how many dances or drinks I had that evening as I celebrated my emancipation from my past. Hours passed without incident and at last Sonni took me home. I allowed her to tug me, giggling, liberated and very intoxicated into my home.

Dimly, I remember Dereon standing in the hallway staring at me, open-mouthed and I waved at him as Sonni poured me into my bedroom.

I flopped down onto the bed while Sonni went into my bathroom, coming back with a cup of water and two tablets of pain reliever. I tried to push her hand away and Sonni pulled me up to sit upright.

"I'm fine," I pouted, moving to lie back on the bed, stopped only by Sonni's firm hold on my arm. Man, she was strong!

She laughed, pushing the tablets into my hand, giving me the water.

"Right, you're fine now, tomorrow morning," she shook her head. "Not so much. Now let's get you out of that dress, I can't have it cutting off your circulation while you sleep."

Protesting, I did as I was told, allowing Sonni to peel off that dress, then my shoes. Gruffly she tugged my sleep shirt over my head, finally allowing me to lie back on my bed, my hands covering my eyes, the glow of the lamp seeming awfully bright.

She sighed deeply and I could feel her pulling the bottom of the comforter over my legs. I exhaled, my thoughts hazy, the room seeming to spin as I lay there. Oh goodness, was I going to be sick? I felt Sonni touch my hair releasing the rambunctious curls from the hairpins that held them, in place.

"I'm proud of you, Mikki," Sonni said softly as she freed my hair. I smiled, trying to relive the evening, the events misty as the memory retreated quickly into sleep. I lay against the pillow.

"I'm proud of me too," I murmured into the thick softness of the bed coverings. Sonni laughed at me, pulling the comforter up as far as it would go.

"Now go to bed, you lush." She instructed, chuckling quietly. "We'll talk later."

I waved goodnight to her, at least I think I did, and then darkness claimed me.

Huckleberry

Day fifty-four…six days to go, I was just so tired of the whole online dating thing and anymore I just felt as if I were going through the motions. I still checked the profiles as Sonni instructed. I still chatted, winked and whatever else but deep down, I knew this wasn't for me. Besides, none of the others could compare with what I had already found.

Baby! I sniffed, laughing at myself as I felt the familiar tingling begin anew, the flush wafting over me, making me tingle with longing for him. If only Dereon hadn't chosen that moment to come in.

Though I hadn't heard from him since the night in my kitchen, he remained firmly in my mind. His touch, his smell, the way his skin had felt beneath my fingertips, I couldn't shake him no matter what I did, no matter how many dates or coffee meets I scheduled to chase away the memory.

During this sixty-day period, I'd met a lot of candidates and I found myself measuring my meetings with them against my date with Baby, setting the bar so high that none of them could have measured up.

My date tonight was no exception. With only six days left in Sonni's "Summer of Love Challenge," I was ready to call the experiment over but had allowed Sonni to talk me into going on this last date. The very last date. His profile had described him as a "Southern Gentleman looking for a lovely lady to adore. Enjoys music, cooking, wine, dancing, and late nights talking."

"And he's age appropriate," Sonni had ribbed me, her way of poking fun at me over my ambivalence about the age difference between Baby and me. Fine, I would go on this last one. Then, I would call Baby.

Southern Gentleman was certainly saying all of the right things, he was handsome, well groomed, dressed in a white short-sleeved knit shirt that could not help but emphasize the fact that he worked out regularly. Dark hair with just a hint of silver at the temple. A wide smile hinted at a fun, maybe even ornery side. Dark slacks that fit in all of the right places. Soulful eyes and dimples. His smile was disarming, a sort of a sexy, come meet me under the Magnolia Tree kind of smile. And he *was* age appropriate.

Hmmm... Not bad, just not for me. All I could think of was Baby.

"This will be the last one, Mikki," Sonni told me so I agreed to meet Southern Gentleman. One for the road…

It was Friday and I didn't have the interest, energy or the desire to doll myself up to go out to meet one more date. The day had been excruciatingly grueling what with screaming customers, screaming vendors, screaming bosses. There had to be a full moon rising tonight.

The last thing that I wanted to do was go out to some bar only to have to endure the next hour or two trying not to be mauled by guys full of libations and themselves.

"Hey baby, what's your name, where do you work, can I get your number?" The game was always the same; I think that most of the guys I encountered wanted to know where I work before they knew my name. Then there were the ones who repeated pick up lines verbatim that were so tired, well, I cannot even tell you how tired they were, but you know it's a line if you've heard it at least three times in the last hour.

Or the guy who takes you by the hand as you walk past on your way to the restroom. "Can I talk to you for a minute?" attempting his best come home with me look. "Excuse me Miss, can you give me directions to your place?" Please! Does this stuff really work?

Someone once told me that when a man offers you a drink, or offers to open the door for you or just offers anything at all, he is really looking for sex. "Here, let me get that door for you. Do you want to have sex?" I'd thought they were crazy when I'd been told this, but now, I had to consider the validity of this information. I certainly wanted no part of that craziness tonight.

Thankfully, Southern Gentleman had suggested dinner instead of meeting at a bar or club. My feet hurt, my feet hurt if I even looked at them. Standing on them or having them stomped on was not part of the program for tonight.

We had dinner reservations at seven at a nice restaurant and I had dressed appropriately, a nice sheath dress in a soft rose color, high heel sandals and no jewelry. Resolutely, I drove to the restaurant, a well-known seafood and steak restaurant in the Country Club district. Parking my car myself, I headed inside.

Southern Gentleman sat at a table against a far wall, reading a menu, his fingers drumming against the tabletop. I wasn't that late, was I? He stood up when I walked toward the table and I smiled, extending my hand, which he accepted, squeezing it gently.

"Mikki, thanks so much for coming," he said, his voice a deep drawling baritone. I smiled.

"Thanks for the invite," I sat down, looking around as I did so. "This is a great table." I remarked.

He smiled. The waitperson appeared at my elbow to take my drink order and I requested a white wine. I needed to keep my wits about myself tonight; I was already exhausted and too much wine would only exasperate the situation.

Southern Gentleman placed a request for an order of oysters on a half shell for our appetizer and I frowned, guessing that he hadn't really read my profile, as I did not eat oysters or any other seafood.

I smiled tightly, refusing his offer of the appetizer, my fingertips wrapped around the stem of my glass as I watched him slurp down one oyster after another. The waiter took our orders, I'd decided on Parmesan crusted chicken while he'd ordered a seafood mixed grill of filet and shrimp.

"So, tell me about yourself," I prompted after a bit, wanting to move the meeting forward, if only to get it over with. From him, I learned that he had founded and owned his own Corporate Cleaning Service, having secured the contracts to clean the buildings of quite a few well known corporations in downtown Kansas City as well as a few in the outer suburbs. He explained his thoughts on how to grow his business and perhaps even branch his business into a franchise.

I listened patiently, picking through the salad that had been brought out before my meal, listening for an opening during which I could speak a little about myself. An opening that never appeared because Southern Gentleman never asked any questions about me. He never asked about my work, my goals or otherwise.

Strike two. First the oysters, and now disinterest in anything I might have wanted to interject. I think strike three occurred when I noticed that Southern Gentleman's attention appeared to be focused on anyone but me as his attention darted from one woman to another in the restaurant.

"So," I began. "What kind of person are you looking for?" I asked. Evidently, it wasn't me since his attention was on everything and everyone but me. He leaned back in his seat as the food arrived, his surf and turf with three types of shrimp and my chicken.

"Well," Southern Gentleman began in his slow measured drawl and proceeded to launch into his list of the qualifications that a woman *must* have to date him from his ideal dress size to shoe size. From his summation, I learned that I was a little taller and "larger" than most women he dated. And he dated — a lot.

My lips curved downward at that, at five feet seven inches and weighing in at a healthy one hundred forty pounds, I was certainly not on the large side. Frowning, I pushed my plate away. In my mind, the date was over; he certainly did not need to stress himself out by trying to make me fit into any of his neat little specifications. I understood why he was still single; there was no one on this planet that would fit into the description of the perfect woman that he felt that he deserved.

I waved down the waitperson, asking for my check. Surprised, the waitperson looked at Southern Gentleman, then he hurried off to accommodate my request. After receiving my box of leftovers and taking care of my check, I explained to Southern Gentleman that I'd had a long day, thanked him for meeting with me and I left.

I walked back to my car, furious. I wasn't mad at him, not exactly, Southern Gentleman had not pretended to be anything other than what he was, a player who used his "aw-shucks" mannerism to reel women in. With his roving eyes and body, he would never find Ms. Perfect and would never settle down and commit to anyone or any *one* woman because he was much too much to waste with just one woman. Perfection like his should be shared liberally and often. Any woman who wanted to be with him would have to accept that and be happy to just be "one of the crowd".

Not for me. If I can't be first, I'm certainly not going to be second, third or fourth. I just don't play well with others. Southern Gentleman was a hound. I giggled out loud at that. Huckleberry Hound. I'd reached my car when I heard someone calling my name, turning to find Huckleberry Hound within arms reach of me.

"Where are you going?" He asked, his words clipped and dark as he stared down at me, his expression heated, his lips tight. I could tell that he was angry, his hands clenched at his side as he looked at me and little warning bells began to tinkle at the back of my mind.

Careful Mikki, please be careful…

" I thought that we were getting along." He said.

Wordlessly, I pressed the button on the key fob, unlocking my door. I smiled up at him, looking around the parking garage for anyone. There was no one, the garage was dim, dank and empty and unwittingly I had parked my SUV just out of sight of anyone who might walk past the entry.

"We did, it just wasn't the right fit, you know?" I tried, smiling up at him as I stepped away. He did not return the smile, seeming to bristle; my rejection was apparently something that he was not accustomed to. Quickly he closed the distance between us, stopping within inches in front of me.

"Don't walk away from me." He warned, his formerly smiling eyes now dark and hard, the "aw shucks" amiability replaced by something hostile and frightening. The small warning bells graduated into full-blown alarms as I stared at him. I moved to step away from him. Every instinct that I had told me that I was in danger and I had to get away from him. Now.

"I'm leaving now," I told him. "Good night."

Huckleberry's large hand snapped out toward me faster than I could react and he curved his long fingers around my throat, squeezing hard. Terrified, I tried to push away from him as he dragged me closer, his fingers tight around my throat. I began to flail, my fingers clawing at the fingers that clamped on my throat as I attempted to scratch him, pull his fingers away, push him, anything. My restaurant container of leftovers fell from my hands to the ground as he continued to shake me, his face ugly and twisted.

"Never walk away from me." He ground out, enraged, and I began to cough and wheeze as the pressure of his fingers made me struggle for breath. I tried to kick him but could not.

"Nobody leaves me, do you understand?" He demanded, shaking me again. I gasped and sputtered. Then, as suddenly as the assault began, he pulled me against his body, holding me still for a long second.

"It's ok, sweetheart," he crooned and I became aware that someone had entered the garage and was walking in our direction. What?

He hugged me closer, burying my mouth into his chest, his hand coming up to rub my back as if he were consoling me.

"Shhh… it's ok now," he murmured. I could hear a man and a woman speaking to each other as they approached where we stood and Southern Gentleman continued to speak soothingly into my ears. I knew it was for their benefit, not mine.

"It's ok, baby. It's going to be all right." My throat clenched and I felt as if I were going to throw up. This man truly was crazy!

I heard the car start up behind us and knew that I had to do something — anything - right now. I knew with a doubt that once the couple was gone, if I were left alone with this man in this empty dark parking garage he would hurt me. Or worse. I knew that I had to get away now.

With everything that I had in me, with every ounce of strength I had left, I raised my face, biting his chest hard through the fabric of his shirt. Stunned, he shouted, his grasp loosening on me and he released me. I pushed away from him, screaming as loud as I could. Coughing, I held my hand to my throat, sucking in huge gasps of air as I was struggled to stay on my feet.

"You bitch!" he screamed at me. I turned around to get into my car, fumbling with the handle of the car door, my escape prevented when he grabbed a handful of my hair, snapping me back around to face him. Whipping me around, he dragged me upright like a rag doll, my feet in my open toe sandals scraping painfully along the ground. Cursing, he slapped me hard across the face, my head snapping back from the blow, the white hot flash of pain zipping through me, briefly paralyzing me.

Dumbfounded, I raised my hand to my mouth, staring at the blood in the palm of my hand and I could feel my split lip swelling, blood trickling down my chin. He'd struck me. I grew incensed. No one, not even my parents had ever slapped me in the face.

I opened my mouth and began to scream, long and hard and loud, the sound of it deafening. Huckleberry moved forward to grab me again and I ground the high heel of my shoe down onto the top of his foot. Screaming in pain, he swung his fist at me, attempting to punch me in the face and I evaded him, turning to pull at my door handle again, this time successfully jumping inside the car.

He grabbed the door, attempting to drag me back outside of the car and I kicked him, grabbing the handle of the door, slamming it once, then twice against his head. Staggering backwards, he slipped on the remnants of my leftovers that littered the ground, falling back onto the dirty floor of the garage, cursing obscenities at me as I pounded down on the button to lock the car door.

With shaking hands, I started the engine, lurching backwards out of the parking spot then stomping on the gas pedal, roaring out of the parking garage without even a look backward.

***

With shaking hands, I let myself into the condo, nearly crying with relief that Dereon was not there. I could not let him see me like this. Not turning on any of the lights, I quickly went into my bedroom, shutting the door behind me.

Relief, sweet relief, surged through me as I realized that I was safe. I was home. I had driven home like a madwoman, my hands and legs shaking; I was terrified that somehow Huckleberry would have made it to his car and would have followed me home to do God only knows what to me. It was not until I had parked my car in the garage, lowered the garage door and escaped inside did I finally feel safe.

Sitting down on the bed, with trembling hands I pushed my tangle of hair away from my hot face. My scalp hurt where he had seized my hair and my face felt as if I'd been punched by a prizefighter. I looked down at my dress; the soft rose fabric now ruined, covered with streaks of the blood that had collected there from my split lip. I knew I would never wear the dress again, its loveliness had been tainted by tonight's ugly assault. With shaking fingertips, I touched my mouth, grimacing at the pain that followed. Rising on shaking legs, I walked stiffly into the bathroom to examine myself in the mirror.

My lip was split and my cheek was beginning to swell beneath my eye, evidence of the mistreatment I had endured this evening. Gingerly I felt along my cheekbone, wincing at the pain that met my fingertips. I felt dirty and soiled. Stripping off my clothing, I wadded the dress up and threw it into the wastebasket underneath the sink. Turning on the hot water of the shower as hot as I could stand it, I stepped inside, scrubbing myself vigorously in an attempt to wash off the degradation of this evening.

Cleansed from the touch of Huckleberry's hands, I stepped out of the shower, folding myself into my thickest robe, willing my body to stop shaking. I reached for my phone, speed dialing Sonni's number, relieved when she answered on the second ring. From the sounds on the other end of the line, I could tell that Sonni was at a restaurant. Oh no…

"I'm sorry, Sonni" I apologized, my hands beginning to shake badly as the gravity of what had just happened settled over me. I tried to speak, my voice breaking.

"It's ok," I assured her, exhaling deeply, then I sucked in a trembling breath, desperately trying to keep it together. "We'll talk later."

Pushing the button to end the call, I buried my face in my hands and began to cry.

Chivalry is dead…

"What honey?" Sonni asked. I shook my head as I took the ice pack away from my lip and cheek, flinching as the icy cold was replaced by increasingly uncomfortable warmth, the swelling of my lip slowly creeping up to swell along my jaw line toward my eye. I tried to press my lips together and was rewarded with a searing pain as my split lip began to throb anew.

"I said, chivalry is dead…" I muttered through my puffy lip, looking down at the ice pack in my hand while I worked my lower jaw back and forth. Geez! I thought that a gentleman would never strike a lady! Shame on me! That guy really packed a wallop. Lucky for me I could give as good as I got. I sat up straight in my chair, stretching and twisting the slender column of my spine, groaning as I did so. I was certainly going to feel this tomorrow.

Sonni sat back in her seat, her face reddening again. I don't know who was taking this worse, her or me. She'd been crying ever since I called her interrupting her dinner to tell her what had happened. I have to admit, watching Sonni cry is much more terrifying than actually being hit in the face by my date from hell. Sonni, the ever composed, ever sexy, ever confident literally dissolved before my eyes, destroyed at the thought of putting me in danger, her face seeming to crumble in on itself as she sobbed.

"This is my fault," she exhaled loudly, jolting to her feet, taking the ice pack from my fingers, walking into the kitchen to refill the flattening pack. I closed my eyes briefly, touching my fingertips to the bridge of my nose. The headache that had previously flirted around the edges of my temple was now a full force reality kicking me right between the eyes. I squinted, moving my head and neck in a small swivel, lightening seeming to zigzag up my spine to explode at the back of my skull.

"No," I told her, shaking my head, then wishing I hadn't done so. "No, Sonni, this is not your fault. Mama was right; everything that looks good isn't good." I rose stiffly to my feet, my limbs aching from my tussle with Huckleberry. I willed my sore and stubborn limbs to follow Sonni into the kitchen, my fingertips rubbing the small of my back.

"If it's any consolation, you should see the other guy." I joked as best I could manage and actually flinched when Sonni turned around to look at me, her face wet, her makeup smeared. And mad as hell. I smiled stiffly at her my face aching.

"No, you should really see the other guy. I bit him on the chest and smashed his head in the car door twice when he tried to drag me out of the car."

Sonni set the pack down heavily onto the countertop, furious.

"We have to call the police." She was adamant. I gulped. The only thing scarier than Sonni crying was Sonni pissed off. She had been out on a date with Ol' G when I'd called her after my so-called date. I could tell from the restaurant sounds that I had caught her right in the middle of their meal. I told her that she didn't have to come immediately; that I had taken a shower and was going to go to bed. Sonni wasn't about to hear that. I'm not sure what she told him, but Sonni was at my house within fifteen minutes. Sorry Ol' G.

Now Sonni paced back and forth in the kitchen, her stiletto heels beating a steady cadence against my hardwood floor as she stormed around the room, ready to call out the National Guard to find Mr. Southern Gentleman so that she could beat him within an inch of his life. God help him if she ever found him.

"We have to call the police." She said again as if I had not heard her the first time. I may have been smacked around a bit, but my hearing was just fine. We could not call the police. Period. I shook my head slowly. Sonni stopped in her tracks, staring at me dumbly. I shook my head again, crossing my arms in from of me.

No police, I know, probably not one of my smartest moves, but I had to think about Dereon. He hadn't been wild about my exploring my options through online dating from the beginning. If he were to find out one of these "jokers" as he'd called them had battered me, I had no doubt that he would find this "gentlemen" and hurt him.

I could not risk that happening. I had to get my one and only child off to college safe and sound, and I could not — would not — risk anything coming between him and his goal. Ever.

"Sonni, we can't call the police, they will come here asking all kinds of questions, and I cannot risk Dereon finding out about this. He would go after him, and I cannot risk that. He must never hear about this, Sonni, promise me."

Sonni flushed angrily. "What! No...I know. But Mikki, we cannot let this guy get away with this! What if the next woman is not as fortunate? Who knows how many times he's done this already!"

I shook my head again, my fingertips going up to rub my throbbing temple, my head pounding.

"I know. But I've got to protect Dereon." I was just as adamant.

Sonni huffed aloud, her manicured hands balled into tiny fists. She shook her head, her jaw squared, and her mind working feverishly.

"Fine. But we have to report him to the service. They need to know what they are dealing with. He cannot get away with this!" She fumed.

I nodded, agreeing with her. That seemed to appease her, if only temporarily. I looked at her, my best friend in the world, ready to find Huckleberry and beat the living daylights out of him.

"Sonni, I'm done." I told her, walking over to the fridge, pulling out the half finished bottle of Pinot Grigio, motioning to her with the bottle. She nodded, reaching into the cabinet behind her to retrieve two wine glasses.

"I'm done with this whole 'find Mr. Right Now' experiment. I'm done with the site and the whole clicking for dates thing. It's just not for me, you know?" I didn't look at her; I concentrated instead on pouring the wine with my now shaking hands.

Sonni nodded grimly. "Yes." She picked up her glass, taking a generous sip. She exhaled, her eyes sad.

"You know I only wanted what was best for you, honey, don't you?" she asked, her voice a quiet broken whisper.

"I do," I smiled stiffly, putting my glass down to go over to hug her. "Sonni, you have to understand that none of this is your fault, ok?" I held her away by her shoulders to peer into her face.

"But I'm going to do this my way now, ok?" I asked. She nodded. So, with Sonni by my side, I closed out my online dating profile, glad that at last, this wacky little experiment was over. The procession of singles and not so single candidates had finally come to an end, and I had survived, battered but better. I'd met some real characters and decided that if ever wrote a book, this would be a blockbuster. Wait a minute, how about a screenplay? Maybe somebody really hot could play my character. And Baby...

I had pushed away the one good thing that had come from this whole wacky experiment, I thought glumly. Now...it was probably too late. He said that he would wait for me to call and I never did, instead opting to see this crazy experiment through to the bitter end. I am sure that, without a doubt, he had moved on. I don't know why the thought of Baby with someone else made me feel sick, but it did.

I've moved on as well, I've made some huge strides lately. I've finally put my son's jerk of a father behind me, finally telling him the things I wished I'd been brave enough to say all of those years ago. What a weight that had been, the failure of that relationship, such as it was, had weighed me down like a millstone and now I was free to live — and love — however and whomever I wanted to.

But I really missed Baby.

Perfection

We walked through the terminal, lugging Dereon's last minute items behind us as we trekked through the busy airport trying to locate his departure gate. I scrabbled behind him trying in vain to keep up with Dereon's long strides. The bodiless voice overhead said something over the throb of the crowd that I just couldn't make out and I hoped that we were heading in the right direction. Dereon was boarding a flight that would take him away to Texas to join the ranks of first year Aggies at Texas A & M University. Texas seemed so far away, it may as well have been another country!

While Dereon was flying out ahead of us, Sonni and I were going to show up a few days later with a U-Haul full of the rest of his college stuff. This was it, my baby was leaving the safety of the nest to live a whole separate life without me.

I asked him for probably the twentieth time if he had his identification. His boarding pass. Did he have money for the things he might need once he reached his destination? Did he have his cell phone? How about his phone charger? What about — did he have his health insurance card?

Each time the answer was the same, brief, grumpy, monosyllabic. I guessed that I was being annoying, but really I couldn't help myself. I have this annoying little problem with being annoying when I'm nervous, I guess.

Fine, I would stop being a pest, and I would try to stop treating him like a baby. I said that I would try! But he was my baby, and I did not give a patootie how big he got or how far away he went or how annoying he thought I was being, he would always be my baby.

I was a nervous wreck, fidgeting, looking for something, anything to keep my mind off of the fact that he was leaving. Dereon stopped in front of the long bay of windows, gazing out across the tarmac, his expression one of serious consternation as he hoisted the strap of his carry-on bag higher onto his shoulder. He shoved one long hand into the front pocket of his jeans, turning to look at me.

"Are you going to be okay, Mom?" Dereon asked his eyes solemn. He looked a little sad, his jaw set, his mouth quivering ever so slightly. I reached up, patting his cheek, loving that face. That serious grown up man face.

Of course I will be, Baby. Why do you ask?

"I don't know." He shuffled his feet, staring down moodily at the carpet in front of him. That's Dereon, I mused, always the conversationalist. Dereon placed his carry-on bag on the floor in front of him.

"Well," he began again, hunching himself into himself, six feet six inches seeming to transform back into the little boy of my heart.

"I just don't like the idea of leaving you by yourself. I mean, it has been you and me for a long time now." He made this motion with his hand, almost subconsciously. "I mean, I know that you still have Grandma, Aunt Niecee and Aunt Sonni, and you can still call me and everything. But I worry about you being by yourself."

Me being by myself, my little protector, protecting me to the very end. He worried about me ... I chewed my lower lip between my teeth. I would not do this. I would not cry. Must not scare the child, I thought, I knew that if I started now, I would not be able to stop.

"I'm a big girl, Dereon," I teased him, poking him in the ribs and always ticklish, he shrugged away from the probing finger as he'd always had. He tugged at a lock of my hair, a habit he had picked up once he had grown tall enough to look over the top of my head. Little Shorty, he had taken to calling me. It used to annoy me in the beginning, making me sound like some kind of gangster rapper mom but it grew on me, almost like some warped term of endearment.

"You know what, Mom?" Dereon looked away out the window; his profile was tight, drawn. I frowned, waiting for him to continue. "We've never been apart, not like this. Not you in a different city, away from me."

I smiled at my man-child. "You've spent the night with friends before, you've taken school trips out of town, and you've taken your senior trip, all without me. It's not like I've never been alone before." I teased. Now who was getting sappy?

"But I mean, it's always been you and me. All the way, ever since I could remember. But now you are going to be here, and I won't be." I nodded. I know, that was the part that I was trying so hard to come to grips with.

It had always been Dereon and me. What we were doing, where we were going, always Dereon and me even when there was nobody else. I knew that our little team of two, we would always be together.

"I love you, Mom." Dereon mumbled.

I closed my eyes, all right, here they come. A teenager who wasn't afraid to tell his mom — out loud — that he loved her.

"Baby, you are making this really hard for me." I said that I would not do it; I said that I would not cry, but I just could not hold it back anymore. He poked me in the side, distracting me.

"All of those nights that you came into my room to make sure I was covered up. To turn my stereo off. To turn my fan on. I just want you to know that I noticed. I noticed everything you did for me, Mom. You just thought I did not because I never said anything."

Even though he would get up the next morning, salty with me because he complained that his room got too hot, because I had covered him up during the night for probably the hundredth time. Even though he would whine about my choices of cereal, my preference of Cheerios and cornflakes over his choice of anything sugar covered. Even though he complained that we ate way too much chicken or salad, or when he wanted pizza for the third night in a row and I pulled rank and opted for something a little bit healthier. Or turning up his nose at my insistence of at least one vegetable at dinnertime. And that no, French fries did not count as a vegetable.

"I noticed," he said. "I know that you only wanted the best for me. You always wanted and did what was best for me. I just want you to know that I noticed." He said. I smiled, trying to wipe my tears away, trying in vain to maintain the brave front.

"I'm going to miss picking up your sneakers in the living room," I teased, trying to lighten the mood. He knew that I was going to miss a lot more than that. "Those huge ocean liner sized sneakers taking up entire corners of the room ..."

"And washing your laundry, and listening to your loud obnoxious music. And watching all of those videos that you watch with the little girls shaking their ..."

He held up his hand, laughing "All right! I get it!"

I smiled up at him then, appreciating the truly exceptional young man that stood in front of me. Somehow, I don't know, I think that before today, whenever I would look at him, I would still see the little boy running around and around the backyard. Fascinated by everything, every blade of grass, and every insect. In his place, in my precious little boy's place stood this brilliant young man, even if I had to say so myself.

"I will miss you, Dereon. Who else is going to nag me to lighten up?" I poked him in the ribcage. He poked me back. His mouth twisted into a funny little grimace. I knew he was trying not to cry.

"Well, Aunt Sonni is trying. Her way of trying, I guess. But you gotta promise me something," he stooped to retrieve his bag, turning to look at me, his eyes resting on my hair, then on my eyes. My man child was growing up.

"What?" I asked.

He swung the strap of the carry-on bag over his shoulder, shaking his head wryly. "Don't let Aunt Sonni talk you into hooking up with some broke joker, or some old knucklehead who's not going to treat you right. You deserve better than that."

At that I laughed out loud and people looked at us, curious. Now who was the parent and who was the child? Overhead, I heard the announcer on the PA system say that Dereon's flight was now boarding.

He turned to look at me. It was time.

"I don't want to have to come back to bust somebody up," he tapped me on the top of my head with his boarding pass. "But I will. Nobody messes with Little Shorty."

I smiled, my eyes flooding with tears anew.

"Nobody." I affirmed.

The next few minutes were a flurry of activity, "Call me when you get there, I need to know you made it." Hugs, kisses, I love you. I love you too. Love you Mom. Love you more, Baby.

I waved at him until he disappeared into the small entrance of the plane, my heart seeming to break into a million little pieces, as I refused to look away until he had rounded the corner and disappeared from my sight.

And I watched, hugging my arms around myself as the plane left the terminal, taxiing down the runway to ascend into the bright blue Kansas City sky, taking him away from me. A hot wash of tears burned my cheeks as I pressed my hands against the glass, my eyes fastened on the tiny dot of plane until it disappeared from my sight.

That was it. It was done. This time, it was just me.

* * *

I opened the door to my condominium, juggling my purse, dropping the stuffed to the gills planner to the floor with a dull football thud as I entered the end zone, my keys and a few things that I had picked up on my way home. Food therapy, that is what I needed. Chinese food, that is, and double chocolate ice cream. When I'd purchased the food, I thought I was starving. Now, not so much.

The house was so still and quiet without the sounds of Dereon - the sounds of his music playing in the background, the television on as well, playing some mindless video from the song of the latest overpaid, overhyped hip hop artist.

I sighed; this was the way that my life would be from now on. Quiet, blessed quiet. No more tennis shoes greeting me as I walked through the front door. No more teenagers sprawled over the couch as he watched videos while talking on the telephone while playing his Play Station while eating pizza. No more "What's for dinner?" mere seconds upon my entering the house. No more "Dereon, take your feet off of the table." No more "Dereon is your homework done?"

No more...

No more Mom duties. The place was almost unbearably quiet. Having grown accustomed to having someone there at all times, bending and twisting your whole life around this person until there almost seems to be no "you" left, the silence was unnerving.

"Will you be ok, Mom?" Dereon had asked me before boarding the plane. Of course I would, I'd lied but I just did not know, not right now. I knew that I would eventually, maybe not today, with Dereon's departure so fresh in my mind. But I would be.

So this was what it was all about. I had spent years totally focused on Dereon. He took priority over everything from where to eat, where to go on vacation, and what movies to see. Now, it was my turn. I walked into the living room, staring at the flat screen television that seemed to take up the entire wall. Why on earth had I let Dereon talk me into getting a television that large? As it was, I was hardly home long enough to watch the huge monstrosity.

I looked around, seeing the room through fresh eyes, I'd never been here, at this moment, before. No one was coming to rescue me, to shuttle me through this phase, and no one needed to come. I could handle this, I would get strong and grow and generate my own happiness. I would be there for myself. I realized at that moment that I would be ok, totally fine as I was, even if I never met a great "love" during the summer. I had myself. Dereon was gone, winging his way to a new city, a new life, and my summer of so-called fun was just about over.

Now, it was time to go back to being the "responsible woman" I've always been even without finding Mr. Right Now. Never the same, I was a lot wiser after of this summer of misadventures. I would not be with a man for the sake of being with a man.

No ma'am, no Huckleberries for me. Thanks, but no. I would not allow myself to be degraded or mistreated for the sake of being paired up. Forget it. And, judging from the summer I had just experienced with the dating service, that was fine, compared to some of the men I'd met, I was better than fine.

I was more than capable of being happy on my own. It just was not necessary to be partnered up. I was going to be OK. I was not going to look for a partner to fulfill me in ways that I, in the end would be the only one who could fulfill for myself. And, slowly, I was realizing that going solo was not feeling so lonely, not anymore. Maybe I would not have it all, but I would have what was real for me. I looked around, realization slow in coming, but showing up all the same.

Hands on hips, I looked around the room, almost as if I were seeing it for the very first time. I stared at the television, then at the beige walls, the beige carpet, the beige drapes and a slow smile crept over my lips. No more beige. First order of the new day, Ms. Robbinson, was to redecorate, get some color up in here.

I looked at the beige carpet; my mind going back to the time when I'd suggested to Dereon that maybe one of those zebra striped rugs would look nice in here. Dereon had looked at me as if I'd lost my mind. I chuckled. That settles it. Zebra it is!

I stood on the threshold of the living room, grinning like a fool. I would sing aloud with *my* music without Dereon giving me the look. I could dance like a maniac without poor Dereon cowering in shame. I could eat salad for breakfast and cereal for dinner if that's what I wanted to do. And I didn't have to eat a single vegetable, if I didn't want to.

Freedom, so this is what it felt like ... very nice. It dawned on me, that I, me, Mikki Robbinson, would finally be able to sit on my own couch. I walked into the silent room. Yep, same chocolate brown leather couch. I sat down, the cold leather squeaking underneath me.

Funny, I had never noticed that before. Of course before today, I was content to retreat to my own bedroom to watch my television in peace and quiet. The couch looked a lot larger without the over six foot long body that seemed to always drape over it.

Nice. Really nice. Maybe some nice new pillows and a throw to go with the new rug.

Instinctively, I ran my hand along the cushion looking for ... I looked around, smiling in spite of myself. I sat back into the chocolate brown cushions, snuggling in. And the remote for the television was where? I looked on the coffee table, and then I really started to smile.

I pulled the drawer open to reveal the remotes placed side by side in the drawer, exactly where I had left them, where I had asked Dereon to put them time after time. Not in between the couch cushions, or in the kitchen on the counter or even in his room which is where more times than not one remote or the other would end up. No more battle for the remotes.

Things would actually be where they were supposed to be, I thought, where I put them. I picked up the remote, staring at the myriad of buttons and light, releasing a long breath, Dereon had always programmed the television, the digital cable, the TIVO, the stereo, everything. I was going to have to learn all of these things for myself.

As long as I know where the on button was ... ah...there it is. I switched on the television, switching quickly from MTV to the Lifetime Television channel for women. It was time to settle into my suddenly quiet house. It was not an empty nest, no ma'am! I was still here. You discover who you are when you are all alone. When you're all you have left after the dust settles and you realize that you are in fact still standing.

I would be the greater voice in my life. I slowly began to realize that in all of my activities to be a good mom, a good friend, a good sister, a good daughter. I forgot how to be me.

I slid from the couch, heading upstairs to Dereon's room. Pushing open the door, I looked around. I would not change anything, not yet, he would still be home for Christmas, Thanksgiving, whenever.

Walking into the finally tidy room I marveled that yes, the room did in fact have a floor. Dereon's room had always looked as if it belonged to someone else's home. Where I kept the rest of the house tidy, Dereon's room always looked as if it had tumbled out of a tornado and landed onto the back of my house.

Now the room was clean, tidy while still preserving traces of Dereon. I picked up his pillow, burying my face into the pillow sham, still holding traces of the cologne that he liked to wear. In his closet, there would still be clothing, things that he did not want to take with him right away, rows of tennis shoes that insured that their owner would be back, if not right away, he would be back.

I lay back on the bed, looking up at the ceiling of the room, exhaling deeply. I shut my eyes. This was right. And the tears came and I cried until I was exhausted, dozing off as I lay on Dereon's bed.

Downstairs, the doorbell rang once, then again.

Ms. Robbinson

"All right! Just hold your horses!" I grumbled, trying not to fall down the stairs as I went to answer the door. This had better be good! I stopped at the foot of the stairs, running a quick hand over my hair, rubbing the sleep from my face.

I wasn't expecting anyone, Sonni had some things to take care of at her office, and then later she was having dinner with Ol' G to discuss the "state of their union". I really wished them well, I actually liked Ol' G and he, bless his heart, was smitten with the force that was Sonni. It would take a hell of a man to tame that force.

Again the doorbell rang and I unlocked the door, pulling it open to peer out. Oh...my...goodness! What was he doing...oh my God! What must I look like? I closed my eyes briefly...ok, breathe...I opened my eyes. Yep, still there.

Baby smiled at me, the action causing his dark eyes to crinkle at the corners. A sight for my eyes, he stood before me, dressed in a soft V-neck shirt, his sunglasses hanging from the "v" casually, wearing a relaxed fit pair of jeans, his feet shod in dark brown comfortable looking leather loafers. What was it with this guy? Did he always have to be so well put together...and so easy on the eyes?

"Hi." He said simply.

"Hi yourself." I said, smiling a little, my hand going up to smooth my hair.

He rubbed the back of his neck, an action he made only when he was really tired, or really worked up. He cleared his throat, one large hand at his hip as he gestured toward me, his palm upward.

"I know that I said I would give you some time, that I would wait until you were ready to come to me but" He closed the distance between us, his fingertips stroking the wisps of hair away from my face behind my ears. Oh... ok...I closed my eyes, allowing myself to enjoy the feel of his hand against my cheek. I looked up at him and he smiled as I stared at him.

"I missed you," he murmured, his tone teasing, his eyes soft and dark. "Let's start over," he said, his voice husky. He extended his large hand, a sensuous smile playing along his lips...those lips.

"My name is Jackson Charles Cavanaugh, my friends call me Jacks. And you are?"

Ok, I'll play...I placed my hand in his own, a tiny smile creeping along my lips.

"Ms. Robbinson. But you can call me Mikki," I said. He laughed softly, gently pulling me forward.

"I think I will, Mikki." Slowly, very slowly he ran one long finger across my cheek and down to the point of my chin, tilting my face up to gaze down at me.

"Why don't you come in, Jacks?" I asked, stepping aside to invite him into my newly emptied nest. His eyes fastened on my face as he moved past me, brushing against me ever so slightly and I closed my eyes, the scent of his cologne wafting over me, engulfing me as I inhaled deeply, tiny bells chiming and my skin began to tingle. I released a shaky breath. Trouble. He walked into the living room and I studied him, my eyes fastening on his broad back as he entered the room. He turned to look at me, his brow tilting quizzically, his unspoken question clear.

Yes, sir we're all alone. It's just you and me. I followed him into the room, taking his arm as he moved to sit on the sofa, shaking my head "no" with a smile.

"I don't want to talk anymore," I told him. He grinned then, dimples on full display. I motioned him upstairs. To my bedroom.

"Finally!" he breathed, his smile seeming to split his handsome face in two. Quickly he cleared the stairs, dragging me behind him, making his way to my bedroom, not bothering to shut the door. I chuckled softly, allowing him to pull me along.

"What took you so long?" I teased. He grinned, even white teeth bright in his flushed face. With a tight smile pasted onto his handsome lips, he stopped directly in front of me, his huge hands closing around my waist, tugging me forward.

"I want you...now." He stated. Instinctively I stiffened, not sure what...how... I sobered at the thought of what I was about to do. It had been so long, so very long — not since Dereon's dad. Not that I'm counting but that would be eighteen years — talk about the longest dry spell in history! And now this man, this very capable man was determined to end the drought once and for all.

It had been many days since we'd first met and he'd been nothing but gentlemanly towards me. But now that he'd finally made his move, I was terrified. What would happen next? Would I be ok? Would he hurt me? Could I do this? I was scared to death! He tugged my hair, pulling my head back to look into my face.

"Hey," he tilted my face upward, his dark eyes hot on my face. "Are you ok with this?" I smiled a little, my lips trembling.

"Don't hurt me..." I whispered. He sank down onto the edge of the bed, my hands wrapped in his, pulling me forward to stand between his legs. My face burned hot as I avoided his gaze.

"What makes you think that I would hurt you, lady?" he was puzzled and I shrugged. His fingers tugged at my blouse, pulling it from the waistband of my skirt, sliding underneath the silky fabric to caress the sensitive skin of my back.

"Not intentionally," I shrugged again, my skin tingling everywhere his fingers touched. I shivered. "It's just," I chewed my lower lip, watching his eyes darken as he followed the movement. I nodded my head, shivering beneath his searching fingers, his touch scalding and soothing at the same time. "It's been a really long time for me." I finished quietly.

He continued to smile, leaning forward, his hand trailing downward over my legs, stopping at the strappy sandals that I wore. "As much as I like these on you..." his fingers traced the curve of my calf gently. "I think our first time should be without them, hmmm?"

I trembled. Our first time...his words bounced around my mind. Skillfully he removed my shoes, his hands traveling up my legs to cup my behind.

"We can take this as slowly as you need, honey. I'm all yours..." he said, squeezing me gently. Honey... I stared down into his eyes, blinking quickly as he took my hands, placing them against his chest.

"Take it off," he murmured. "Undress me."

Whoa! What? Oh no...I pulled my hands back, feeling suddenly shy. He chuckled again.

"Ok, I'll help." Deftly he removed his shirt and my mouth went dry. I knew that he was fit with his clothes on, but with his shirt off — oh...my...goodness! The muscles of his chest rippled with every move that he made, the skin tight, the muscles defined. And the tattoo — that was unexpected, I'd never noticed it before, a beautifully intricate tribal tattoo that covered one entire shoulder.

Tentatively I ran my fingertips over the tattoo...all mine. He closed his eyes, breathing in deeply.

"Touch me. Get used to me." He said, his voice deepening. Gently, very gently he unbuttoned my blouse, slipping it away from my shoulders and onto the floor.

"Beautiful…" he whispered, leaning forward to press a kiss to the curve of my breast. I closed my eyes, the sensation zooming through my body, exploding at my center. Oh yes, and just like that he had my full attention.

He pulled me forward until we touched, his hand pulling my face down to his as he captured my lips, his tongue caressing past my lips into my mouth to wrap around my own.

I exhaled, my hands going up to caress his face as I returned the fervor of his kiss as it dimly registered that my skirt was being unzipped, the fabric sliding to the floor to join the heap at my now bare feet.

"I don't want to talk anymore either," he stated, his voice a husky growl.

Cupping my backside he rose to his full height, wrapping my legs around his waist, his mouth never leaving mine as with one hand, he ripped the covers of the bed back and settled me among the linens, following me down into the softness that smelled of detergent, fabric softener and him — a heady combination. I gasped as the hard shape of him pressed against me through his jeans…oh…I murmured against his mouth.

"As slow as you need it, lady." I hear his words rumble against me. Just say so if you need me to stop…" I trembled at his words, all ability to form any kind of intelligent sentence deserting me; I wouldn't have been able to say anything if I'd wanted to.

Those lips sweep from mine down the point of my chin, lips and tongue caressing his path to my collarbone, dipping briefly inside the hollow he discovers there to continue down my sensitive skin to my breasts as his hands joined his lips. Gently, he covered my breasts with his huge hands, caressing, worshipping, his thumbs teasing the nipples into hard little diamonds.

He stared down at me, his eyes pleading. I surged up against his hands in response, greedy for more, begging for his touch, whimpering as his lips replaced his thumbs as his tongue traced slow wet circles around the tip before taking it into his mouth, sucking hard. I groaned, the tug on my breast tugging at the center of my body as I felt myself dampening…there…oh my…I guess perimenopause hadn't killed it after all…

My hands caressed the back of his head, his shoulders, and his back as he turned his attention to the other breast, his fingers skimming past my stomach to my every increasingly damp panties, gently, very gently stroking me there through the thin fabric as with a jolt I surged up against him. I heard him chuckle against my breast as his lips continued down my ribcage to the lace of my panties…oh no… down to rub his nose against the moistness.

"You smell good…" he murmured and I felt his words against my heat. I began to tremble in earnest as his hands came down to hold my hips still with one hand, drawing my panties down, past my legs and off, his eyes staring up at me.

"Say the word," he whispered, giving me an out. I said nothing. He grinned. Standing up, he quickly shed his jeans and I found myself wondering when he'd removed my bra as I lay naked watching as this Adonis rejoined me on the bed. He lay face to face with me, kissing me tenderly.

"I'll take care of you lady, I'll be gentle…" he whispered, his hand traveling down my body, his fingers claiming me, one long finger caressing me gently then pushing into my wetness as I groaned, moving against him, his mouth capturing my gasp as he moved first one finger, then a second in and out of me. I think I must have stopped breathing as he pushed his fingers deeper, his lips reclaiming my breast, sucking deeply as his fingers continued in time. I was all motion, all sensation as I moved against him, unable to keep still as he took what he wanted and gave back in spades.

I gasped his name out loud as his lips replaced his fingers, stroking then sucking, his teeth gently grazing me there while his hands tried to hold me still. I curled my fingers into the linens, not trusting myself not to claw him to shreds if I'd put them anywhere near him as he continued his sweet, sweet torture.

I felt myself spinning out of control, faster and faster as he loved me with his mouth and I exploded, calling his name loudly.

"Wait, baby…wait for me…" he whispered, sheathing himself quickly with a condom. Rejoining me on the bed, he grasped my hands, smiling as I stared hazily up at him.

"I'll be as gentle as I can…" he whispered.

"Just take me…" I groaned, lost. He smiled.

"Yes, ma'am." He grinned. I shuddered as he sank slowly into me, my breath escaping as a moan when he pulled out, then moved back into me, filling me up…oh…my…he surged into me then, hitting my sweet spot and I called his name out loud, the sound of my own voice cracking, ragged as he rose up on his knees to thunder against me, releasing my hands to cup my face with one hand while his other arm went underneath me to grasp my hips, holding me tightly as I moved with him, matching him thrust for thrust, his eyes closing as his lips curled into a tight smile, a bead of sweat dripping from his brow onto me.

My fingers wrapped around his shoulder, stroking then digging into him as the pressure ballooned inside of me, taking me higher and higher, alight like a flame, burning, incinerating sensations I hadn't felt in so long, zigzagging through my body as this man lit the flame and doused it with gasoline igniting a wildfire that threatened to consume the both of us. He trembled as he thrust into me over and over again, his eyes screwed shut as he panted my name, his breathing harsh, his body wet and hot as he thundered against me.

I felt myself unraveling for the second time and I tried to fight it, wanting to stay in this moment, enjoying this sensation but I couldn't as this same sensation threatened to take me under.

"Please baby..." he groaned against me. "Please come...I can't hold back much longer...I have to make it good for you..."

That was it as I exploded, clutching him, shouting his name as he slammed into me, collapsing onto me, groaning, his breathing ragged against my ear.

Good grief! I wondered dimly. Is this what I've missed? Oh how I've missed this!

"Mikki..." I heard him whisper against me as I began to drift away, my eyes closing, exhaustion claiming me as I wrapped myself into his body.

***

Slowly, very slowly I came awake, aware of the weight holding me own into the softness of the mattress as well as the stifling heat that covered me, courtesy of one mean hot flash. He lay against me, his huge legs entwined with mine, his cheek resting against my breast as his fingers traced small circles along the curve of my hip.

I moved slightly, goodness he was heavy and I was stiff, I think that I used muscles I'd long forgotten I had. I raised my hand, dabbing at the fine film of perspiration at my brow. He raised his head then to look at me, his eyes dark, and his lips full as he stared down at me, his eyes moving to fasten on my lips, swollen from his kiss. Gently, he stroked my lower lip with his thumb and I drew in a shaky breath...surely he was not ready to go again...

"You, Miss Robbinson, are one surprise after another. You're hot..." he murmured, studying my mouth. I shrugged, smiling sheepishly.

"Sorry – hot flash..." I whispered, embarrassed.

He smiled then, moving up to prop his head in the palm of his hand. "That's not what I meant..." he chuckled, grinning at my faint blush. "You're one heck of a woman, Miss Robbinson." He stated.

"Oh." I stared up at him, still blushing. "You don't have to flatter me now. I've already slept with you." I replied, my fingers reaching down to seek out the sheets rumpled at the bottom of the bed.

Geez! Lights on, covers off? What was next? In the backyard? In the car? A bus terminal? He stopped me, bringing my hand back up to kiss my fingertips, shaking his head "no".

"Not a chance, I want to see you." He murmured, his tongue coming out to trace the shape of my fingertip. Involuntarily, I shivered.

"So..." I whispered.

What would happen now? Would this be it? Now that we'd...done it...would this be it? Would he lose interest and move on? I think about all of the horror stories that I've heard with most ending exactly like that. Thank you ma'am but I must go now... would that be me? Would I turn out to be one of those psycho chicks that refused to let go long after the man has "sampled the cookie" and moved on to the next victim? No, I doubt if I could go that route, but that would affirm all of the reasons I'd given myself for refusing to jump back into the whole messy dating thing. If I didn't date I couldn't get hurt, right?

"So… we do it again…" he murmured. Again? Wait… he sat up in the bed, pulling me to straddle his lap. What… no…

"No…" I whispered, suddenly self-conscious, my hands coming up to wrap around myself. I was in good shape, but let's face it, as this age, gravity worked in my favor best when I am lying down. He shook his head, taking both of my hands, holding them down at my sides.

"No, lady, I'm going to relish every single second of this…" One hand stroked down the line of my spine to cup my behind, squeezing gently.

"You have a beautiful body," he whispered, his lips nibbling along the line of my chin while his fingers traced the curve of my behind, down to stroke me gently where I was the hottest. I couldn't help it, I surged against him, surprised and excited… Are you kidding me? He chuckled, his lips trailing hot kisses against my throat, his tongue tracing tiny wet circles against my hot skin.

Oh no… slowly his fingers traced around me, massaging me as I closed my eyes tightly, my lips parting in a small "O" as I gasped out loud.

"Look at me, lady" he instructed and hazily I stared down into his darkening eyes. "I want to see what I do to you…" he groaned, slipping his fingers inside, deep inside as I began to tremble.

"Your eyes…" he whispered, stroking deep, his lips curving into a sensuous smile as he loved me with those fingers. I was shaking badly, my hands coming up to grasp his shoulders. I whimpered as he took his fingers away, missing them already.

"No, lady, not yet…" he lifted me from his lap, taking a condom from the night table, rolling it onto his length.

"Now…" he grinned up at me, his hands closing around my waist, pulling me onto his lap as he sank into me and I groaned as he buried himself deep inside. He lifted me up, then slid back into me, his eyes bright, his lips parted.

"So good, baby…" he groaned. I swallowed hard, then lost all ability to think as he began to move, his hands setting the rhythm as he took control, thrusting hard into me as I panted against him, hanging on for dear life as I gasped and trembled against him, meeting his thrusts over and over again with my own, my senses spinning drunkenly as I called his name…oh goodness! Was that me? What would my neighbors think? Could they hear us?

None of that matter as his next thrust that seemed to blow me apart and he hit my sweet spot once, then again, then over and over again as his arms came down to fasten me to him as he pounded against me, calling my name over and over again, my fingertips clinging onto him as I struggled me maintain some sort of decorum, trying not to scream like a mad woman.

He wasn't trying to have that as he rammed against me, his mouth opening to close on one breast, tugging on one swollen nipple as he took me, the twin sensations zipping through me like a lightning bolt as I came around him noisily. He laughed out loud exploding against me, his forehead buried against my breasts as he rolled over, dragging me down to lie on top of him.

Snuggling closer, he groaned against my damp hair and exhausted, I slept.

Epilogue

And on this fine day, I was feeling especially fine as I stood at the altar, waiting, the bright June sun beaming down on top of my up do and I feared that I would sweat out of the silk strapless gown that I wore. People murmured from their seats, admiring the shades of silver and ivory that met their impressed gazes. Only the best would do for Sonni.

I looked out over the attendees, my searching gaze stopping to rest on Jacks and he smiled, winking at me, even white teeth flashing as he grinned that grin that seemed to turn me inside out.

"I love you," he mouthed, and I flushed, the sweet familiar heat spreading through me and I consciously made the effort to tear my gaze away from him.

Dear Lord! I breathed. Please let this go without a hitch! I've never been a maid of honor before, and I was a nervous wreck. Not as nervous as Sonni though. Miss "I'm-so-self-confident" had been on the verge of a nervous breakdown. On her wedding day.

"You've got to keep me together, Mikki," she made me pinky sister swear. I chuckled. Sonni would be fine. She always was. The Huntress had finally been captured.

When Sonni told us about Ol' G's proposal, I don't know who cried more, Mama Jett or me. Well, I believe Mama Jett's exact words were "Thank the Lord! My wild child has finally been tamed!"

I smiled, shaking my head. As if! Tamed or not, I think that Ol' G probably wore Sonni down simply because he outlasted her and outmatched her stubbornness. Today, he would make her his bride.

It was so good to see Sonni happy, my girl, my best friend. And, true to form, she had nearly arrived late to the hall. Late for her own wedding day! Typical Sonni, as I've said before, they only thing Sonni wouldn't be late for is her own funeral, and that's only because she wouldn't have to dress herself!

I'd arrived at her condo to find her in the middle of a virtual tsunami of silk, taffeta and tears. After drying her tears and calming her down, I eventually succeeded in getting her to the chapel on time.

And after the "I dos" were said, the rings were exchanged, and the doves — yes doves — were released, I found Jacks in the crowd, walking into his open arms. He dropped a kiss on my forehead as he hugged me close then we walked hand in hand into the reception where the band was getting things cranked up.

And after her first dance with her new groom, Sonni shared her next dance with me as we whirled around and shook our bodies all over the dance floor while our guys laughed and covered their eyes.

Yes, this will be just fine. I didn't have all of the answers, and I absolutely had no idea what came next. But I knew that right now, this was perfect.

You only live once, but what a ride when you get it right the second time around.

--The End—

Thank you!

We hope you've enjoyed "When Crazy's Coming...The Midlife Misadventures of a Midlife Diva". A Midlife Diva's story is never over! Don't miss the remaining books in the Midlife Divas series!

Come back for Book Two, Most Likely, Jacks' Story, set for release early Summer, 2014. Join us for what comes next in the unfolding saga for Mikki and Jacks, Sonni and Geoff and Niecee and Drake!

We want to hear from you! Visit our site for more information about future title releases!

www.brainybpublishinghouse.com